# COTTONWOOD

# COTTONWOOD

## RAYMOND STROTHER

A DUTTON BOOK

DUTTON
Published by the Penguin Group
Penguin Books USA Inc., 375 Hudson Street,
New York, New York 10014, U.S.A.
Penguin Books Ltd, 27 Wrights Lane,
London W8 5TZ, England
Penguin Books Australia Ltd, Ringwood,
Victoria, Australia
Penguin Books Canada Ltd, 2801 John Street,
Markham, Ontario, Canada L3R 1B4
Penguin Books (N.Z.) Ltd, 182-190 Wairau Road,
Auckland 10, New Zealand

Penguin Books Ltd, Registered Offices:
Harmondsworth, Middlesex, England

First published by Dutton, an imprint of New American Library, a division of
Penguin Books USA Inc.
Distributed in Canada by McClelland & Stewart Inc.

First Printing, February, 1991
10 9 8 7 6 5 4 3 2 1

 REGISTERED TRADEMARK—MARCA REGISTRADA

**Library of Congress Cataloging-in-Publication Data**

Strother, Raymond.
  Cottonwood / Raymond Strother.
     p.     cm.
  ''A Dutton book.''
  I.  Title.
PS3569.T7265C68     1991
813'.54—dc20                                                      90-7908
                                                                     CIP

Printed in the United States of America
Set in Times Roman
Designed by Leonard Telesca

PUBLISHER'S NOTE
This is a work of fiction. Names, characters, places, and incidents either are the
products of the author's imagination or are used fictitiously, and any
resemblance to actual persons, living or dead, events, or locales is entirely
coincidental.

Cottonwood is dedicated to my wife, Sandy Peck. She was kind enough to allow me summers in Scotland and weeks in Montana to reflect on the humor and depravity of politics.

But others also lent a hand. Marsha Dubrow taught me about economy of words.

Gary Hart encouraged me to start again when I had given up on ever finding a publisher. He was an intellectual companion and a friend.

Donald Cleary, my long-suffering agent, dusted off this book several times before he finally found the dazzling intellect of immense judgment who agreed to publish it.

# COTTONWOOD

# PROLOGUE

The southern cottonwood tree has an ignoble sadness. It is never planted intentionally for fuel, building materials, or shade because it fails in all categories. The cottonwood sneaks out of the ground between cracks in pavement or in unattended, unmown pastures.

Roots fan out for yards, soaking up ground water to feed the tree's pulpy heart. If it can escape attention for only a few months, the heavy, sodden tree grows large enough for small children to play in its branches. It leaps from the earth because its only chance for survival is to grow too large for casual destruction.

Saucer-sized leaves hang limply from long stems. They spend part of the year covered with webs of small worms. In the heat of the summer the leaves dry, so even the slightest Gulf breeze whips them against each other, making a roaring that masks out sound, a sort of moaning.

Insects find a home in broken places in its skin and leave infections that scab into lumps and bulges. After healing, the tree often looks like it is covered with gaping, seeping wounds.

In the fall, the male tree cries a clear, varnishlike liquid that is difficult to remove from glass or metal. The female sheds cotton fluff that clogs vents and covers the ground like dirty snow.

The cottonwood is cursed and no Save the Tree groups rush to its defense when it is removed. It is truly the derelict of trees. But of all trees, perhaps only the cottonwood has a soul. Perhaps.

*"You come down from that tree or I'm gonna whup you."*
*The ten-year-old boy clung even more tightly to the trunk and pressed his face into the rough bark. The cottonwood swayed and moaned, but seemed to cradle him even more firmly in its limbs. Far below he could see the fat woman with the switch. She walked around the tree to get a better view.*
*"Look, Sonny. I won't whup you. You come down right now and I'll buy you some new shoes. You'd like some new shoes, wouldn't you? You come on down and eat a peanut butter sandwich and I won't switch you. Wouldn't you like a nice sandwich and some new shoes?"*
*"My daddy said he'd buy me some new shoes."*
*"Your daddy ain't coming home."*
*"He said when he got paid he'd buy me some shoes."*
*"Your daddy ain't coming home no more. Me and your Uncle Reily gonna take care of you now."*
*A thin man in jeans and a western plaid shirt stepped onto the weathered back porch and the screen door slammed behind him. A Lucky Strike hung from his lips. He was bald and had a fringe of red hair like a fallen halo.*
*"No luck?"*
*"Naw. He's been up there all day."*
*"Then leave him up there. Funeral ain't till tomorrow."*
*"He can't go to no funeral barefoot."*
*"If he ain't down by tomorrow, I'll cut down the damned tree. You got the goddamnedest kin."*
*"I owe it to my dead sister to take him in."*
*Reily spat. "I don't need another mouth. 'Sides that, the kid ain't right. He hung around that old man too many years. Ain't got a lick of common sense. Keeps his head in a book. Might be queer fer all we know. And if he ain't queer, that*

*old man's made him into another communist. And you wanta take him in with our kids." Reily flipped his cigarette into the neglected yard. "That other Red sonbitch, Calab Something or Other, said he'd move in here and take care of 'em."*

*"Reily, I don't know. That old man is strange."*

*"You think that kid up the tree ain't strange? I'm warning you. I'll just put up with so much. I'm about up to here with your family and that kid."*

*"He just ain't had the right upbringing. Kate died when he was six. Sam wern't no communist. He was just a CIO man."*

*"Same thing."*

*"My daddy's no communist." Tears fell into the cottonwood leaves and the tree moaned.*

*Reily cupped his hand around his mouth and yelled to the top of the tree. "Your daddy's dead. He ain't coming back. The Texas Rangers kilt him with a club at the picket line. You come down here or I'm gonna climb up there and whup your ass."*

*Years later Sonny, now called Christian, could still hear the screen door slamming. It closed behind Uncle Reily and Aunt Betty after they backed again and again through the door with their arms loaded with his mother's dishes, lace doilies, and quilts with the star of Texas in bright colors. Two dishes had fallen from the stack and they tiptoed around the broken crockery. From the treetop it looked like a dance.*

*Aunt Betty looked up. "You'd better take off them new shoes. You gonna scuff 'em up in that tree and only Jesus knows when you'll get a new pair." She turned back toward the house for another load. The door slammed behind Reily. He did this little crockery dance and began loading Christian's father's deer rifle and shotgun into the backseat. Two stiff new shoes bounced off the top of the old Ford, leaving sizable dents.*

*"Betty! Betty! Come out here and see what this little bas-*

*tard done to the Ford. I've goddamned well had enough. I'm gonna jerk him outta that damned tree." The thin man pulled himself onto the lower limbs and began to climb toward the boy, the Lucky Strike dangling from his lips. The boy climbed higher until the branches bent under his frail body. The boy wasn't crying anymore. The thin limbs forced Reily to stop a few feet below.*

*Aunt Betty was sobbing in fear and frustration. "Reily, if you'll come down, I'll call Mr. Calab and tell him he can have the boy." Reily climbed down and went into the house with Aunt Betty. The boy could smell bacon. But he wasn't hungry.*

*When they came back out, Reily had on a dirty western hat. He got into the Ford and started the motor.*

*Aunt Betty stood on the porch and shouted to the boy. "Mr. Calab will be here in a few days. I left you a jar of peanut butter, some Cheerios and milk, and two dollars for bread. You tell him we took some things that belonged to my sister. Reily took the guns 'cause they're dangerous. Mr. Calab gets drunk and we don't want to leave no guns around. We're taking 'em to protect you." They also took the new shoes.*

*The cottonwood held him until the crickets began to make music. He climbed down. The house was empty.*

*The tree grew ten new rings beneath its ragged bark and cried through ten more falls. Infection cut off circulation from one of its largest limbs, which fell during a thunderstorm nurtured to ferocity by moisture from Lake Sabine. The same family of mockingbirds built nests and a thousand generations of worms made lace of its green leaves.*

*Calab Hudson sat in an old metal lawn chair under the cottonwood. He drank coffee from a chipped white cup. The earth in front of the chair was worn bare of grass. A stiff breeze from the Gulf lashed at the August-parched leaves. His left foot rested on his right knee. Over and over he sang*

*under his breath a first verse of the old Wobblie song about
the leader who was executed in 1912.*

> *"I dreamed I saw Joe Hill last night,*
> *Alive as you or me. . . ."*

*The screen door slammed.*

*The boy, thin but grown, walked across the yard to the
chair. He had an olive-drab military duffel across his shoulder.*

*The old man stopped singing and looked up from his cup.
"You going somewhere?"*

*"I'm going to college."*

*"I'm glad. That's good to go to college. Where you go-
ing?"*

*"LSU."*

*"Where's that?"*

*"Baton Rouge, Louisiana."*

*"Oh, I been there. We tried to organize Standard Oil in
1937. There was a bar across the street called the Grizzly
Bar. You might look it up. It's where the union boys hang out.
I can give you some names."*

*"That was thirty years ago."*

*"Well, you never know."*

*The boy stood looking up into the old cottonwood. The
leaves trembled and then frantically lashed at their stems and
then grew quiet again.*

*"We never had that talk, did we?"*

*"No." Christian continued to look up.*

*"I always felt bad. All of them kids dressed better than
you. They had cars. You didn't even go to the senior prom or
your graduation, did you?"*

*"I didn't want to go."*

*"I wanted to go to your track meets and buy you stuff but
it just never happened. We had to organize that paper mill in
Oakdale. Then I was in jail for a spell. When I was home,*

*you was working in that all-night grocery store. Time sorta runs out on us. Life just don't last long enough."*

*"It seemed long to me. If you like, when I get settled I'll write you a letter and tell you where I am."*

*"Don't go to no trouble. I can't read very good. My eyes is bad. But I want to thank you for letting me live in your house. It's been nice to have a roof."*

*The cottonwood braced itself against a stronger wind and moaned.*

*"What you gonna do with the house? Maybe I can rent it from you."*

*"You can have the house. It's about to fall down. Termites have eaten the back porch. The roof leaks in two places. It hasn't been painted since before my daddy died." They looked at the tiny frame house. It was slumping wearily into the ground. "I don't want anything from this godforsaken place. Just out."*

*Calab studied Christian as though he was seeing him for the first time. "I've never knowed a necktie before. I always knowed working people with dirty hands. You gonna get to be a necktie, ain't you?"*

*"Yeah, I'm gonna be a necktie. I'm going to make money and light up the sky. When I come to Port Arthur, my name will be in the newspaper, I won't be delivering it."*

*"You got your daddy's meanness and determination. He stood his ground. He was willing to fight for what's right."*

*"My daddy stood his ground and the Texas Rangers knocked him off it."*

*"Well, they don't use 'em for strike breakers no more. Maybe your daddy's death had a purpose."*

*"My daddy died like he lived, in misery. You can't eat ideals. You can't use them to patch the roof or buy a shirt."*

*The muscles in Calab's neck bulged and his lip quivered. "Well, Mr. Necktie, now that we had our little talk, I'm glad we didn't have it years ago. You forgot where you came from. It's always khakis against neckties. Your daddy was khaki.*

*You're just a little piece of shit. I won't live in this house. I'll burn it down like we burned down that paper mill. It stinks." The gray old man threw the dregs of his coffee across Christian's face.*

*A great steel bridge spans the Intracoastal Canal outside Port Arthur. It stands as the tallest structure in two hundred miles of pancake-flat marsh and gumbo mud, built during the Depression to accommodate the largest ship in the world as an expression of Texas optimism. Christian walked the three miles to the bridge and then to its top, where he paused to look over his shoulder one last time. He couldn't see the house but he could see the smoke. He didn't cry. He didn't give a shit. He turned toward Louisiana.*

*The leaves and the birds' nests on the western side of the cottonwood burned. But in the spring small green stems began to grow out of the charred bark and soon they were filled with tinder leaves without worms or wear.*

*The cottonwood tree is eternal.*

# 1

Darleen lied to save her husband. And that won her points in their war of marriage. Advantage, Darleen.

It wasn't easy for her husband, Christian, to convince her to open the door the length of the burglar chain and talk to the chubby man outside, who was pressed flat trying to stay out of the rain.

"I think he wants to kill me. Just tell him I'm not here until I can get it sorted out," Christian whispered.

The knocking at the front door echoed through the almost empty house while Darleen negotiated. A machine-gun rain pelted the roof. In the background a baby whimpered uneasily in sleep.

"Just a minute," Darleen shouted through the door and then turned to face Christian.

"Do you swear on the lives of your children that this isn't about some girl you've screwed?" Christian looked at the door and calculated how much of his wife's question had soaked through the wood to the assassin.

"I'm not sure what it is, but I think it may be about a story I wrote when I worked for the AP," Christian whispered through hands cupped against Darleen's ear.

Taking Christian's cue, she lowered her voice to a hiss. "If it's some girl's boyfriend or father, I'm going to usher him in and help kill you." She was still young enough to think of her rivals as girls instead of women and their lovers as boy-friends instead of husbands. Experience would prove she should have been more concerned about husbands.

Christian's lips were so close to Darleen's ear a wisp of her hair tickled his nose. A musky perfume seeped from the black silk nightgown and wound its way into the sexual lobes of Christian's brain. "Since when did I become Casanova? Once you accused me of being a virgin."

"Everybody's a virgin sometime, Christian, even you. You've just worked full-time to make up for a late start."

"Can we fight about this later?" Christian put his hands together as though in prayer. Darleen smiled. She was scoring big.

*Bang. Bang. Bang.*

The long black car with smoke trailing from a slit in the driver's window had crept silently up and down the street six times. A searchlight swept like a prison beacon through the rain from one house number to the next. Nervous neighbors peeked through blinds. Under the corner streetlight the vehicle looked like a sinister machine of death, a spaceship, with its blackened windows and belching exhaust. The stretched car seemed to sag slightly in the middle. Considering its cargo, maybe it did.

An editor from the Baton Rouge *Morning Advocate* had phoned a week before and reported that inquiries had been made.

"Christian, I don't know if it really means anything, but a short, fat guy came to the office today to ask about you. The reason I'm calling is I could swear I saw a pistol in his belt. Of course, I could be wrong, it could have been his wallet." A friend reported Christian's file had been requested from the LSU Journalism School by a woman who looked like a hooker.

\* \* \*

"Ma'am. Would you tell him when he gets home that Big Jim wants to talk to him?" The safety chain bit into the door. Darleen pressed her face into the narrow opening. "What does he want to talk to my husband about?"

When the little pig-faced man looked down at his feet, he poured the pool of water collecting on his turned-up hat brim through the crack and onto Darleen's thin gown. His eyes then darted from the wet and clinging silk back to his feet so many times they seemed to spin in his head like the cherries in a slot machine. His face turned red. "Ma'am, I don't think I can say. It's about a story your husband wrote. Sorry about getting you wet." In a grand gesture he jerked the hat from his head and the rain plastered his hair to his skull. He had just remembered that one always removes one's hat when talking to a lady. And this babe was some lady.

Christian watched through a bent blind as the bowling-ball-shaped man waddled back to the car, climbed in, and drove away.

"What did you do this time?" She knew her young husband was guilty of something. She jerked the wet gown over her head. Her nipples were hard. Danger was sexy to Darleen. Life was sexy to Christian. They reached for each other.

An hour later Darleen closed her eyes, rolled over, and coiled into a fetal ball. A shear pink nightgown was bunched around her neck like a Christmas scarf. Christian, still gasping and wet with sweat, climbed from bed and peered through the curtains to find that the car had returned and was sitting at the end of the block under the streetlight. About midnight it left again.

Twice more that week the rotund man with the bulging, close-set eyes, returned to the house, hat in hand, looking for Christian. He was so polite one had trouble imagining menace. Each time, almost as formally and almost as courteously, Darleen met him at the chain-fastened door and protected her man.

Things seemed to be improving in the Simmons household. But that only helped cushion the fact that much was to fear in the black car that prowled through the perimeters of Christian's life.

"Honey bun, why don't you just talk to him?" Darleen posed in an exaggerated southern drawl. "Is big, tough, mysterious, detached, boy-wonder Christian afraid to talk through the mail slot to the itty-bitty man? Or would he rather just hide behind frail, weak, and helpless little ol' Darleen's skirt for the rest of his life?"

"I've heard this man is a killer."

"He looked sweet."

"I'm not sure you're qualified to make that judgment, Darleen."

"You may be right, sweet dumpling. Out of all of the men at the university I picked you. That shows something about my judgment. I said to myself, 'Darleen, grab yourself that young editor because he's going to be rich and famous. Why, I bet he may even one day be the assistant editor, advertising manager, and janitor at the Denham Springs *Enterprise*.' And lordy, just look at us now. You've made it to the top. My shining knight. Come to think of it, Christian, my judgment is so bad that if I think the little gentleman is harmless, he may just poke a stick through my eye when I talk to him through the door."

It wasn't that Christian was a coward. He had scars to prove that he wasn't. And he wasn't brave. He was just detached. A body blow was just a body blow. An instant before it landed it was only a swinging fist. An instant later it was unexpected pain. The swinging fist and the pain never seemed related. Christian lived only in the present.

But the visitor at the door was known as a killer and Christian respected death. It visited his youth and left him without a father and without hope. And the violence that crushed the skull of his last of kin left a scar that was scabbed over but still filled with corruption. He had children he cared for and a marriage that was not yet a lost cause. When he thought of death, he thought of a kid sitting in the branches of a cottonwood tree with a rumbling stomach. No, Christian wasn't a coward. But it wasn't time to die. He had much to do. His life was a mathematical equation that still ended at the equal sign. He was driven to fill in the blank.

Some people go to church in crisis. Christian went to the daily newspaper, the Baton Rouge *Morning Advocate*. The assistant city editor had his feet on his desk and was knocking cigar ashes into a battered antique Underwood manual.

"You plan to use that typewriter?"

"Naw, I just use it for an ashtray like I always did. Get your ass canned around here now if you don't use a computer. Runs up production costs. Listen." The editor bent forward and cupped his ear. Christian heard nothing but the clicking of computer keyboards. "Used to be lots of noise in here. Old Jim McCain would throw his typewriter in the garbage can when it ran out of ribbon in the middle of a deadline story. Now we got computers and smoking sections. It's time to die or go teach somewhere."

"What can you tell me about T. Boy, Big Jim's driver?"

"You mean the guy looking for you?" The ancient editor smiled and blew smoke at the ceiling. It seemed a joke to everyone but Christian.

"Well, he's a killer, but he don't mean no harm." The editor was affecting his best ol'-boy charm. "Big Jim got the pardon board to spring him from prison in some sort of whiskey, pussy, and money payoff. T. Boy, a sweet little guy from Bayou Teche, shot a Texas A&M fan after a football game."

"Takes his football seriously."

"Yeah, after the game it seems T. Boy nudged this Texan's car in the rear and the guy, a former A&M linebacker, jumped out and kicked a dent in the door of T. Boy's new Ford. Now that was the first new car that Cajun boy ever had, so he pulled out his pistol and shot the sucker. Got seven years."

"So it was a crime of passion?"

"Sure, and if T. Boy hadn't shot him twice in the back,

he wouldn't been found guilty. The jury had some reason to be pissed off. The two refs from the Southwest Conference had called back two touchdowns and the Tigers lost the game. The jury argued that somebody needed shooting. So I wouldn't worry about T. Boy.''

"That's a relief.''

"Yeah, I'd worry about Big Jim. That's who's looking for you. Big Jim and some bimbo. T. Boy is just taking orders.''

"I only know Big Jim from when I covered the legislature last year.''

"Yeah, I remember the story. He was using some whores to bribe legislators and you blew the whistle. Good job.'' The old editor smiled and dumped some more ashes in his typewriter.

"Tell me about Big Jim.''

"Tell *you* about Big Jim? You gotta be kidding. You wrote the story.''

"Call this a backgrounder. I wrote about the whores. I don't know much about Big Jim.''

"Well now, his story is a funny one. He's the Louisiana legislator who made good and didn't have to go to jail for it. Seems he was a down-and-out state senator living on what he could steal when he got into a card game with another legislator, an ol' boy from Winnfield. Well, these two legislators were flush with new kickback money from a highway reflector contract and were both dealt full houses. The rumor has it that Jim's was tens over jacks and the other hand was eights over tens. You get my drift. That's five tens in one deck.''

"Who cheated?''

"Probably both. Son, we're talking Louisiana legislators! God knows how many eights were still in the deck. But the old boy bet all of his payoff money and Jim did too. So the Winnfield legislator bet what he called 'one hundred acres of fine pine-timber land.' Jim countered with his herd of 'registered Angus cattle.'

"Funny part of the story is that every tree had been cut

off the timberland Jim won.'' The editor lit another Lucky
Strike. ''But he took it in good humor because all his herd
had been condemned that morning with anthrax. 'Bout two
months later, though, Texaco found oil and gas on the scrub-
land. Made Jim filthy rich. He could finally live in the style
to which he'd become accustomed. And without stealing from
the state.'' He used the paper bail on the typewriter to knock
off ashes.

''End of story?''

''No. There's a sidebar. The Winnfield legislator sent a
killer to murder Jim. But the Lord moves in strange and mysterious ways, his mysteries to behold. Jim met the killer in
the Gate, a whorehouse in Opelousas. They were drunk together. Seems that for months they had been brother-in-lawing
a redhead. As you know, the sheriff's deputy takes your gun
and your driver's license when you go in the parlor. Well, the
two men had a chance to talk and Lou, one of the girls, said
that they struck a bargain. Jim doubled the fee and the killer,
he was a Mexican, I believe, took off north to do the dirty
deed on his former employer.''

''Did he kill him?''

''We don't know. The legislator disappeared. There are
some folks who claim he got all tangled up in some chains
and is sitting on the bottom of the Atchafalaya River. Myself,
I don't know. But I wouldn't eat catfish out of that river for
two years.''

''Do I have anything to fear from Big Jim?''

''Kid, if I was you, I'd lay low for about ten years. Other
than that, I think you're safe.'' He laughed. The editor thought
fear made the kid almost human. And it was a story that
would go down good with beer later at Rip's Huddle.

For two weeks after his conversation with the old editor
Christian went to work through the back door, across a gully,
through blackberry vines, ending up behind big garbage cans
behind Safeway. Here he surveyed the area before crossing
the parking lot to the old frame house that served as his news-

paper office. At night the huge black limo drove through his dreams.

In what he considered his last remaining days, Christian got his life together. He composed long messages to his children that would help guide their lives when they were old enough to open the envelopes and read. There was absolutely nothing to inherit, but he wrote a will and signed it with bold strokes. He rolled on the floor with his children. He got up early enough in the mornings to feed the children and take Darleen coffee in bed. During the day Darleen found poems tucked into her lingerie drawer or under her pillow. The big black car sweetened their marriage.

"Darleen, if I should die, would you marry again?"

"I have to think of the children. It would be tough, but if I found a rich man with oversized equipment, I might consider it." Laughing, she rolled away from him in bed. Christian didn't understand why everyone laughed as he clung to life. He peered out the window through a small opening. All was clear. Darleen watched him. T. Boy had definitely sweetened her marriage. " 'Bout time," she said to herself.

It had been a bad two years. Christian had graduated from college filled with Hemingway, wanting to write honestly and live cleanly. He didn't have passage to Spain for the running of the bulls but he read *Death in the Afternoon* several times and concentrated on prizefighting in New Orleans. There were no wars for ambulance drivers and he reasoned that Paris was too full of tourists for a serious artist of his integrity. Besides, he didn't have money for a ticket.

As a student he had been editor of the campus newspaper, the *Daily Reveille,* and president of the Young Democrats. This made him a campus hero and he developed a studied arrogance. People made appointments and his professors asked advice on campus political affairs. They paid attention. It was important to Christian that he matter. As he walked through the campus he would mutter under his breath again and again, "I am. I am. I am."

But he was never sure. Christian was the invisible man, born of a cottonwood, who had taken form and shape in the past four years. But he feared vaporizing. At one time, people had stepped in front of him in lines, pushing him to the rear. He never again wanted to be the person who never reached the ticket office.

In his new life, despite never having been allowed to be part of anything in the old life, Christian didn't join movements. Christian was a movement of hurricane force that bounced through the university and city, a rogue storm looking for targets of opportunity. It was a student reporter named Darleen who discovered his secret. Late at night she would close the door to his office and sit on his desk while he beat angrily at a typewriter.

"What makes Christian run?" she had said.

He looked up. "What?"

"I'm the reporter assigned to find out what makes Christian run."

"Beans and beer."

"No, that and sex is what makes regular, normal students run. You're not normal."

"I don't know what normal is. You tell me what normal is." Christian's eyes were slits and his neck tightened.

"Normal is going to movies and dating girls and hanging out at the Bengal Bar."

"I don't like those things. I like what I do."

"So you like having holes in your shoes. You like eating in the school cafeteria. Come on, Christian. I know something else. I know you've been living on a cot in the attic of the journalism building."

"I go there to rest between classes. I keep late nights because of my job as editor."

"And I know you've never had a girlfriend. Betty Jo Kern did everything but have sex with you on the desk last Wednesday night and you backed away. You were scared."

"She's not my type."

"So who is your type? Am I your type?"

"I have a professional relationship with you that requires some distance. I'm your editor and boss."

"Bullshit, Christian. I've seen you look at me. I've allowed you little peeks. I've led you on. But you don't know how to close the sale. You've never had a girl. Here's my key. I'll be home in an hour."

"I may have to work."

"Look, Christian." Darleen unbuttoned her blouse, bent over the desk, and kissed Christian. She put his hand on her exposed breast. "Here's a sample. Don't be late. I'd be mad as hell to be turned down . . . boss."

Christian knew of such invitations. He read *Penthouse* magazine. He was on time.

They joined in not-so-holy wedlock in the outdoor Greek theater four days before graduation. Darleen had refused an abortion. Her wedding dress bulged. Christian liked the idea that he was not the end of the Simmons line. An English-department poet read an original work and two cellos played Beatles songs.

After graduation Christian started a novel of short punchy sentences about men at war and took a job in AP's capital bureau to tide them over until publication. The morning of his twenty-second birthday was spent at the finance company attempting to borrow fifty dollars and the afternoon in the doctor's office listening to him prescribe a diet of boiled or broiled fish and chicken, and milk every half hour.

"Christian, you are burning up inside because you hate your job and you hate me." Darleen used his health problem as another lever in their daily battle.

"I'm paying dues," Christian said rather proudly. He had read about artists and pain. But the pain felt like a thousand knives when he was fired just before his probationary period ended. He told Darleen he had been fired because of his failing health and the AP needed sturdy men. The truth was slightly different. Christian was too liberal with bylines when he worked alone on weekends. He decorated the top of most weekend stories with his name, even if most of the stories lacked merit. "By Christian A. Simmons" looked great rolling out of the wire machine. Christian imagined the story with his name on top clicking out of machines all across America. It gave him great satisfaction to know he decorated news spikes in important places. "If I write it, it has merit," he said to himself. "I am. I am."

Christian wasn't disturbed by the dismissal. The *Morning Advocate* had an opening. The newspaper, a good one, at that time filled its openings with LSU's brightest.

He straightened his tie, brushed his hand through his hair, and presented himself to the editor.

"You have an opening and I would like to work for you. You've seen my work but I'll be happy to furnish clips."

"Kid, I can't hire you. You're not right for this paper."

"Why? You even said I was the best reporter to ever come out of LSU."

"That's still true. But we hire people who put this paper first. You don't want to work for this paper. You want to own this paper. You're always looking over the next hill. Look, I mean this only as a compliment. You would be the worst employee I've ever had. Go out and start a revolution in some Latin American country or sail around the world alone in a washtub. Sorry, kid, but I got enough problems."

Christian made his first compromise. He decided the *Denham Springs Enterprise* could be a resting place until he could find a suitable assignment with a major news organization.

To complicate his life even more, Darleen lost count of her pills and presented him with a second child, complete with new doctor bills. The washing-machine motor froze, still filled with diapers, the head gasket blew out on the old Ford, and he had lost almost a week's salary playing poker with some reporters from the New Orleans *Times Picayune*. His jacks-over-tens full house, had been beaten by kings over sevens. The finance company had covered the loss, but the young couple's bills had outgrown their income.

Christian's grand adventure of life had turned into wet diapers, sale-priced beer, rental houses with overgrown lawns, and personal columns in a weekly newspaper. And now there was that lurking black car.

Christian was in danger because of a story about whores and corruption that he had written while he was with the Associated Press. He reported that State Senator "Big" Jim DeBleaux had lobbied for changes in the wholesale cost of liquor by anchoring a riverboat loaded with prostitutes in the Mississippi River across from the capitol building. The reporter watched with glasses from the levy while legislators chased naked hookers around the decks of the *Mark Twain*. Motorboats moved constantly from the water's edge to the riverboat, a Dunkirk of whoredom. Christian had claimed that passage on the boat, renamed the *Poontang,* was bought with a vote for higher wholesale-liquor prices.

The hunt for Christian had gone on for seven late afternoons and nights but none of the limo passengers was in a great hurry. They ate awhile and then looked for the reporter. They drank awhile and then looked for the reporter. They broke occasionally for sex or political meetings and then looked for the reporter.

First T. Boy had checked with the Associated Press and found that Christian had been fired. That cheered Big Jim. It meant that the reporter would be more negotiable. The AP said he worked for a suburban newspaper. T. Boy found a list of papers that they began calling while en route from bar to bar, restaurant to restaurant. Big Jim liked to stay on the move.

"You the reporter who wrote a story about whores on the riverboat?" He got a lot of startled responses.

From a hardware store in Denham Springs they learned where the reporter lived, but failed to find him. T. Boy had

said Darleen was lying, but Jim thought he was out somewhere "laying with some woman." They waited a few times
for him to come home but gave it up. "When you young,
you can fuck all night," was how Big Jim reasoned the absent
Christian.

Big Jim was a three-hundred-pound yellow mountain of
rhinestones and pearl buttons. His huge hat made him more
than seven feet tall. When he slipped on his high-heeled western boots, he gained another four inches. A fence-post-sized
Churchill cigar kept his head enveloped in smoke. Visibility
in the huge limo was reduced to less than instrument-landing
conditions. T. Boy smoked the same cigars. Big Jim was
generous. A woman, one of Ida's "party" girls on a one-
month lease to Big Jim, chain-smoked cigarettes. When any
of them rolled down a window to ask directions, the big car
looked ablaze. Huddled in the corner of the partitioned front
seat across from the driver was a small man in a misbuttoned
vest, sipping from a pint of Four Roses bourbon. A cowlick
stood prominently atop his head. He was drunker than he
was sober.

After a week of no success, they gave up on finding Christian at home at night. Reluctantly Big Jim set his alarm so
they could do more daylight business. By noon the expedition
was ready to venture out. Noon was a startlingly new depar-
ture time that adjusted their schedule forward by at least six
hours. They left the ranch with much pomp. Two maids, both
cooks, a yardman, and a leftover hooker from a weekend
party had staggered from bed before ten to stand on the long
drive and wave as they rolled away on their mission. There
was excitement. It was a major event that changed the rhythms
of their household.

The sleepy group finally located Christian bending over a
drawing board at the *Denham Springs Enterprise*. He was
changing the price of pork hams in a Piggly Wiggly super-
market ad, carefully gluing a smiling pig on the top of a black
box. He sold ads for the small paper on a commission basis,

wrote most of the news, edited the church page, and did all of the layout. Both of his shoes had holes.

"You the reporter who wrote the story about the whores on the riverboat?"

Christian, intent on gluing the pig into its proper place while composing a poem in his head, jerked around, launching unglued type into orbit around the drafting table. Blocking the door was Big Jim, a study in corruption. The killer, T. Boy, and a hooker stood behind him. Christian had always envisioned such a scene and the resulting headlines. YOUNG REPORTER IN SERIOUS CONDITION AFTER BATTLE WITH POLITICAL THUGS. This headline was too long but it had a nice feeling, Christian thought. POLITICAL THUGS BEAT REPORTER was more realistic. *Quill* magazine, the publication of Sigma Delta Chi, the society of professional journalists, would make his battered face the cover with a red ribbon slash reading FREEDOM OF THE PRESS ATTACKED IN LOUISIANA. Editors in New York and Washington would read the headlines and tell an assistant, "Find the kid in Louisiana, that's the kind of guts we need in this newsroom."

James Cagney would have stood, lit a cigarette, shown them two shoulder shrugs, and blown smoke in their faces. However, Christian got his foot tangled in the bottom rung of the high stool and sprawled at their feet. T. Boy helped him up and brushed off his tie. The woman giggled. Big Jim reached into his wallet and pulled out a tattered story with a picture of a riverboat on top. "You write this story?"

Christian backed up against the drafting table and began to glance around for an X-acto knife. He was determined to fight with his last breath. But then he saw the gun stuck in T. Boy's belt. Christian nodded yes and forgot the knife.

"They tell me you the smartest son of a bitch to ever graduate from LSU. Have a cigar." Big Jim thrust one of the huge Churchills at his victim, who flinched, expecting to be hit instead of offered a gift Cuban smoke. As a reflex action he accepted and flinched again when Big Jim pulled out a long spring-loaded knife.

"Let me cut the end off that for you, son."

Christian, who at that time did not smoke, allowed his cigar to be lit by the dark-haired woman who ducked in under Big Jim's arm. She wore a shiny green dress, cut low enough to invite a second look, which, despite his fear, Christian gave. Big Jim watched with approval. Susie was a hell of a woman. She knew how to hold the wooden match just the right distance from the cigar after allowing it to first burn off the bad sulfur smell. She had promise. T. Boy, dressed in an electric-blue silk suit with matching shirt and tie and a Bogart style hat, had wedged himself into the small room and was relighting his cigar. He was a rhapsody in blue. Soon the room was as smoky as the limo.

With his meaty index finger, Big Jim pounded Christian's chest. "You taught me something. That was some fine story. I never understood the power of the press until you came along. You hit it dead center. You was accurate and told it so that all of them dumb-assed legislators could even understand. After you wrote that story, they lined up for trips to the riverboat. Before, I had to sort of whisper it. You went right out there and did it for me. I don't know if that bill would have passed without you."

Big Jim rested his beefy hand affectionately on Christian's shoulder. "That story saved my clients, the liquor industry, half a million dollars. They even added a hundred thousand on top of the million they paid me. I'll never argue about the power of the press again. I think you write like Shakespeare or somebody, and I want to hire you to write a story for me."

Christian liked and agreed with Big Jim's observation about his intelligence and writing skills. He even liked the cigar, which seemed to rush to his head. "My news columns are not for sale, Senator DeBleaux. I will be happy to sell you an ad." He blew a cloud of smoke at Big Jim, who only grinned.

"Shit, man, I'm gonna buy some ads. I'm a candidate for Congress. But I need you to write my endorsement story. I'm a rich son of a bitch but I stopped at the third grade. I need somebody like you to put words down right. I don't got no PR man and I thought I'd hire you to write a story."

Christian took another puff of his new cigar. Big Jim was going to be a paying customer. And Christian made fifteen-percent commission on all ads he sold. One full page would fix the Ford. A half page would repair the washing machine. In split seconds he changed from crusading reporter to advertising salesman and began calculating fifteen-percents. He wouldn't sell his news values, but a paying customer often got little services like a picture of his kid or a few free copies of the paper. The reporter in him said no, but the advertising manager in him spoke another language.

"I'll write your story and, if it has news value, will run it in my paper. However, I will accept no payment. I'll also write and lay out your ad free. That's part of the service of the advertising department of this newspaper."

Big Jim looked around. The newspaper was three rooms in an old frame house. The only other staff member he could see was an old woman typing with two fingers in the next room. The "department" was an old drawing board, a bottle of rubber cement and some page-sized paper with faint blue lines. The advertising manager and reporter was a kid with holes in both of his shoes and a holey sock. He was wearing a vest and a carefully knotted tie but there were blackberry vines dangling from his left cuff. The blimp politician surged with optimism.

"You write the story for free or anything else you want, and we'll go to lunch and talk about the advertising. You get to go to lunch with customers, don't you?" Jim didn't wait for a reply. He was pushing Christian out of the door. "You got to come out to the car to write the story. We got us an important person sitting in the car, but he's too drunk to come in here." He waved his cigar in the direction of the killer. "T. Boy, go wake up Governor Conklin and tell him he's about to be interviewed."

A few local people had gathered in awe around the car, staring at its multiple telephone, radio, and television antennae and double smoked windows. Christian hesitated a moment to relight his cigar and give the locals time to reevaluate his status and perhaps even invent scenarios about the brilliant editor and the huge car sent to fetch him.

Big Jim and Christian sat in the back and interviewed Hugh Conklin in the front seat after T. Boy lowered the glass partition between the two areas. The engine was running to keep the air-conditioning going on the hot, humid, Louisiana winter day. Like all fat men, Big Jim was always sweating.

"Hugh Conklin here is president, secretary, treasurer, and sole membership of the First Democratic Party Participants Association," Jim explained. "He's a registered political organization with the secretary of state." He turned back to the dried-up man who was leaning over the front seat. "Tell College Boy here what you gonna do for Big Jim's campaign."

Before responding, the little man slipped a half-pint of bourbon out of his coat pocket and went through a ritual of unscrewing the cap and wiping the neck off with his sleeve. "We gonna endorse Big Jim for Congress." He took a long pull from the bottle and then held it up to the light and looked for a little amber in the bottom and found none. The woman opened the teak bar and extracted another pint, tore the seal off with her teeth, and handed it through the opening.

Hugh went through the long ritual again of wiping the neck on his sleeve and then took another long pull on the bottle. "I'm gonna say that Big Jim's the man his granddaddy was and that Congressman Joe Bob Smith is a fucking thief and queer. And worse than that, I think he's a secret Republican." He took another small swallow from the bottle.

"And you can write the story for me," Big Jim explained.

Christian, making new fifteen-percent calculations after seeing the car, had already repaired the Ford, fixed the washing machine and made a payment on the birth of the last kid. He wanted to tell Big Jim that without proof, he couldn't write that Congressman Smith was a thief or a queer or a Republican. He wanted to explain that no newspaper would run the story with those kind of charges and that most editors would identify the organization as a fake. But he didn't. Because at that moment Big Jim was stuffing a wad of hundred-dollar bills into the dazed young man's frayed coat pocket.

"I will write the story, but I won't run it in my paper. This money will be used as partial payment for advertising." Christian had already decided to take his commission out in cash to avoid taxes. He had never seen one-hundred-dollar bills and they were causing an amphetaminelike response in his head.

"Fuck your newspaper. Nobody reads it anyway. Talk to Hugh and write me a story I can hand out to the other newspapers in the district." He was laughing and winking at the woman who sat across from Christian. She was exposing much lace, much flesh.

Christian wrote the story on a lined yellow pad as they drove to Bob and Jake's Restaurant in Baton Rouge. He continued after they had ordered drinks and steaks. The woman ate with her hands.

> Jim DeBleaux was endorsed today by the First Democratic Participants Association in Baton Rouge. The organization voted unanimously to endorse DeBleaux because of what they called "questionable activities" by Congressman Joe Bob Smith.

The story was three pages, filled with quotes by Conklin, who had once been a legislative assistant in Washington until the bourbon soaked into his brain. Big Jim made changes in the story while stuffing himself with side orders of sausage and barbecued chicken. Like his companions, Christian ordered two steaks, the first good meat he had had in months.

He ate the first one and had the second wrapped to take home to Darleen. The scotch made a warm protective covering for his brain. He felt he was losing something important but there was no pain. Something was slipping from his grasp, but his only response was another drink. An ache began to develop, not in his head but in a tiny recess behind his heart. He was in a public restaurant with a whore, a symbol of political corruption, a neon-blue thug who carried a gun and constantly hummed Cajun tunes, and a drunk derelict who had sunk so low even the lowest clerks of court and justices of the peace had someone to spit on and laugh at. Any of the four would have created a public spectacle. Four of them together almost emptied one of the rooms in the crowded restaurant. It was not Christian Ahab Simmons' proudest hour. But the one-hundred-dollar bills still peeked from his pocket at the edge of his vision when he looked at his lap, which he did constantly.

Hugh Conklin cut steak into bite-size cubes and pushed them across his plate. He was on a liquid diet. Later he moved his plate, put his head on the table, and slept. Christian glanced nervously around to see whether any of the other diners noticed. Of course they all did. He had another defensive drink. To cover, he made loud statements for the benefit of the other diners.

"Senator DeBleaux, when I first met you and your group this morning, I agreed only to this lunch and to no other arrangement." And louder. "I believe that corruption in government must be stamped out and I have devoted a major part of my life to that end." As Christian raised the volume of his drunken pronouncements, the diminutive derelict with the cowlick began to snore lightly. Had Christian known the future, he would have embraced the little man or run screaming from the room. Years later, in reflection, Christian still puzzled over this question. Run or embrace? It could have all come out differently.

A week later Big Jim returned to the "advertising department'' and noticed Christian wore new shoes. He and the reporter/ad manager designed six full-page newspaper ads filled with eagles, stars and stripes, pictures of dead Democrats like Truman and Roosevelt, and, of course, Huey and Earl Long. The cigar-smoking colossus and the anxious young man bent over the drawing board. Occasionally Big Jim strode in circles and dictated headlines. SAVE OUR COUNTRY FROM GODLESS COMMUNISM. EVERY MAN CAN STILL BE A KING. PROTECT SOCIAL SECURITY WITH A VOTE FOR BIG JIM.

Stars were put in all four corners. Every inch of space was filled with circus type or Big Jim's picture. ''College Boy, put that star next to Big Jim's head so when they read it they'll think, 'Big Jim—Star.' And get your scissors and cut off some of Big Jim's chin in that picture on the bottom. That was taken by a bad photographer. Makes me look fat.'' Christian knew that these ads were worthless but didn't yet know why. So he simply rearranged the stars and eagles until Big Jim slapped him on the back in glee at their masterpieces. T. Boy and the woman sat outside in the smoky car with the motor running.

Seduction is a slow, careful process that must have the participation of both parties. Champagne, music, a button, a snap, a feel, a calculated campaign from breast to thigh, from stocking to lace. Polite refusals, promised ''maybe's,'' whispered ''should not's,'' nodded ''yes's,'' next-day questions about how it happened, next-week acceptance, but this time the process is speeded up. This time there is no champagne or music, only the hot, panting acceptance of both parties that valuable time could easily be wasted through ritual. Seduction begins in ritual and ends in resignation and passion.

The ad bill totaled eighteen hundred dollars and Big Jim paid for them from a roll of one-hundred dollar bills that barely fit in his pocket. He counted out the bills on the layout table.

''Fourteen, fifteen, sixteen, seventeen, eighteen.''

"Jim, I think you made an error. You gave me twenty-one."

"Bullshit. I'm not educated, but I can fucking well count."

Christian counted again. ". . . fifteen, sixteen, seventeen, eighteen, nineteen, twenty, twenty-one."

Big Jim snatched the money away. "Fifteen, sixteen, seventeen, eighteen." He palmed the extra bills and slipped them into the bottom of the stack. Considering the size of Big Jim's hands, what he did might have been called "sleight of ham." He looked at Christian. "Right?" Christian realized finally that Big Jim was trying to pay him for composing the ads and the story. He calculated fifteen percent of eighteen hundred dollars and added the extra bills. They amounted to paid-in-full doctor bills and on-time rent. "Right." He nodded. The pain in the recess behind his heart eased. The greenbacks masked the hurt for several months.

T. Boy moved Christian's hockshop Underwood into the limo the next week when he joined the campaign as press secretary. He reasoned that one's personal conduct did not have to be influenced by corruption or ignorance. While they rode from newspaper to newspaper, rally to rally, he beat out stories on the old portable cradled in his lap.

Big Jim turned out to be less of a bad man than Christian thought. Jim would order T. Boy to stop on deserted roads and feed stray dogs from the car's vast stores of junk food. He would slip five-dollar bills into the pockets of small black children. He was always polite to older people and gave them extra attention. He never raised his voice to women who rode with them. Though they all were similar in height, coloring, and build, he would change them twice a month, all except Susie. Christian's pockets stayed filled with one-hundred-dollar bills. At night in one of the endless succession of Holiday Inns, Jim would be concerned about Christian's comfort and offer him a woman.

"I'm kind of tired tonight with this campaigning and all.

Why don't you take the woman. There's no charge. She's paid up for a month.''

Christian wanted to obey Darleen's rules of marriage and always refused until the final days of the campaign when the dark Cajun girls were traded for a blonde who carried a Bible. Big Jim called him one night. ''College Boy, come take this woman off my hands. She won't let you drink.''

''Jim, you paid the going rate, didn't you?''

''Hell no. I paid twice the going rate. You should see her.''

''When you pay, don't they have to play by your rules?''

''Well, sure, College Boy, but I just can't be rude to a lady.''

''A lady?''

''Most of 'em is ladies. They's just in a tough business. That's why I paid so much for this one. She's just getting started and needs a little help.''

Other than Darleen, Windy Dawn was the most beautiful woman he had ever met. And she was most happy when her client was happy—if the client didn't drink. As he helped undress this beautiful creature he had no idea that their lives were to be intertwined for good and noble causes in another time. In passion she unintentionally told him a secret that he would use to change hundreds of lives. Without uncoupling, she turned around on him, drew her hair over his feet, and said breathlessly, ''Brother Tracy loves me to do this.''

At home things changed for Christian. There were no bills, and no sick kids, no broken washing machines, no finance-company notes, and no sputtering car engines. Money changes things. It insulates you and brings you luck. Things don't break when you have money to repair them. One-hundred-dollar bills can also buy new draperies, make your wife sexy, and improve your posture.

Christian loved one-hundred-dollar bills. He laid them in a row and then in a stack and then in a checkerboard and then in little tents that seemed to go on forever. And he found mystery in them. They are cleaner than smaller bills, and many of them have numbers scrawled in the corner, as though someone had so many that a reference was necessary to keep count. He had twenty of them with numbers and sixty-seven of them without.

The first thing he bought with those beautiful bills was Darleen. He crumpled five of them and threw them back after ducking a shoe. Nothing is a better antidote for a temper fit than one-hundred-dollar bills that appear mysteriously out of pockets that had previously gathered only lint. And things purchased don't require emotional involvement or even personal reflection. When a woman with holes in her stockings and babies with tight shoes and overdue doctor bills picks money from the floor, even hundreds, something is surrendered. Darleen made a brief but conditional separate peace in an effort to mend her family and heal her marriage. The bills were hot in her hands and she turned to the wall to hide her tears. Smiles from her husband and laughter from her children were growing more important than victories in the brushfire wars she had grown expert in helping to flame. Darleen felt something slipping away.

"I'm sorry I threw the money."

"It's all right, Christian. I appreciate your consideration. Sometimes I don't deserve it," she said to a wall that was marked by tiny handprints.

"Will you use some of the money to buy silk lingerie?"

"Sure, Christian," she almost sobbed. "You won't be disappointed."

Big Jim lost the election, but Christian's life had been changed forever. The ache in his chest slowly turned into only a burning sensation. Based on an inflated ego and his recent experience with Big Jim, he opened a small office for the "limited practice of political consulting." Some say it was only a slight tremor, but the earth shook that day. The gods were amused that a curious spectacle had begun to unfold. With the money stacked on the table before him, he clasped his hands as though in prayer, closed his eyes, and rocked gently in cottonwood rhythms. He imagined he could hear the rustling of the dried leaves and feel the cradle of the limbs. He was twenty-four.

**2** He ran until his chest felt it would explode. And sometimes Christian ran until he vomited. There was no choice. He had only moderate ability and running was work, difficult work. He did his sprints before dark and endured the coach's insults and the isolation from his teammates. He had to hang on to the track scholarship. They all knew, the coaches and his teammates, that he ran only hard enough to hang on. They hated him for it. He didn't laugh on the team bus or gang around the screen to see reruns of the last meet. But they needed him . . . barely. In a large meet he would come in fourth with a 4:05 mile time and then in a dual meet come in fourth with a 4:17 mile. He only hurt enough to survive.

He was offered a paying job on the college newspaper the day of the Southeastern Conference cross-country meet. He ran a pace just a breath short of pain and crossed the finish line somewhere in the middle of the pack with the nonscholarship runners, who, amazingly to Christian, ran for the hell of it. When he crossed the finish line, he continued over the next hill, through the entrance of the golf course, down the road to the college dairy farm, and to the campus lake, where he angrily dunked his running shoes and lay in the cool, dead grass.

Between pants Christian screamed at the sky and pounded the earth with his fists. ''Fuck . . . ah . . . coaches and . . .

ah . . . whistles. Christian Ahab . . . ah . . . Simmons . . . ah . . . will . . . will . . . light . . . ah . . . up the sky. You got that . . . ah . . . God?'' He took several deep breaths and put his head between his knees. "When I stand up, it will be different. The world starts today, God. Fuck Adam and Eve.'' Then he slept.

With this oath, Christian set upon a new life to escape the pain of the last, moving forward, looking for new targets of opportunity.

Now, though, four years later, six months after the campaign with Big Jim, Christian was discovering other pains. The pain of rejection and the pain of failed ambitions. He gave a party and nobody came. He had sandwiches and white wine and a new box of cigars. Brass letters on the office door said "Southern Political Consulting.'' The sandwiches grew stale and in a couple of days grew a curious green mold that formed geometric patterns. The ice melted in the ice chest and the labels came off the bottles and floated to the surface. The bruised consultant sat for days watching the mold grow and smoking his new cigars. It was his first, honest-to-God, full, brand-new, cellophane-wrapped, sealed-with-a-nail, wooden box of Cuban cigars. He had displayed them proudly next to the old Underwood with a new cigar cutter and a fake crystal ashtray and a box of matches from Antoine's restaurant. The matches had left scars. They were souvenirs from his foray into a big-name restaurant that had turned out as badly as the party for his new business.

As a reporter he had studied the life-style of people who traveled without typewriters in their laps, people who knew when to laugh and when not to laugh. They had good complexions, always had the beautiful women on their arms, and never had to stand in line. Their coats fit well. (Later Christian would find that no coat would ever fit him well. Even after he could afford his own tailor, he would look disheveled walking out of the tailor shop.) He studied where these people ate. And in New Orleans, they ate at Antoine's and Brennan's.

Christian had always wanted to know when to make noises and when to shut up. He wanted to know when to stand and when to sit. Once at a trial he covered for the AP, he noticed that the Boston attorney never let the flame touch his cigar. That was one of the impressive tricks known by Big Jim's whore Susie. The attorney simply held a wooden match several inches below the cigar, and it mysteriously lit without absorbing any of the sulfur smells. The reporter was sure that attorney ate at Antoine's.

So, with his pockets stuffed with hundreds from Big Jim, he made reservations two weeks in advance at the old restaurant on St. Louis Street. It was his reward for holding on to most of his virtue while traveling with Big Jim. He wanted to share this night of reward and discovery with his wife, Darleen, but the day before they were to go, his wife found a shirt collar stained with something that looked like red lipstick. The reporter knew that his last female companion had been weeks before when Windy Dawn had shown up at his room with her Bible and astonishing talents. Even with his wife throwing things and children crying, he was stirred thinking about Windy.

The shirt was stained with red grease pencil used to lay out advertising pages. If one holds a ruler and draws a line with a grease pencil, the red goo builds up on the edge. If that ruler is then used to scratch one's neck while bending over the drawing board, it would leave red on the shirt collar. That is truly what happened. He had spent the night on his office couch considering the strange justice. He had lain with the whore without problem but had been caught because of an aggressive grease pencil. Windy Dawn had been a lot more fun. He wondered briefly what had happened to the almost transparent blonde with the multiple orgasms. He had never considered a prostitute who enjoyed her work.

The old Ford had been traded for a slightly worn and half-as-dependable MG convertible. He put down the top, put a newspaper-wrapped bottle of champagne on the floor, and set out for Antoine's. He made the drive alone. His wife had vanished with ten of the hundreds and the children. They could be retrieved from her mother's house, but the reporter had to decide if it was worth the effort. Ah, but the children looked astonishingly like him. They were worth the effort. He deferred judgment. First he would become an Antoine's person and then view the world through those eyes.

The wifeless young man stood in line and smoked two cigars, lighting them so that the flame never touched them and blowing smoke away from the ladies in the line. When it came his turn to push through the two glass doors into the new life, the captain stopped him and checked a computer-typed list for his name. And it was there. He took a thoughtful puff on his cigar and stuck out his chest just slightly. He was on a list of Antoine's people. He knew at that moment, or so he thought, that he had the tickets to everything in the world inside his right front pocket in his newest and cleanest one-hundred-dollar bills.

Then, however, he began finding out the things that Antoine's was not. First, it was not pretty or romantic. There was a wooden counter supporting the elbows of several waiters against the back wall next to a door to the kitchen. The floor was small white tiles, the walls were white, cracked plaster partially covered by a ribbon of mirror that stretched around the room at shoulder height. Then, after a waiter with that curious, Brooklyn, New Orleans, Lower Ninth Ward accent in a frayed tux took his order, he found out something else Antoine's was not—they were not glad to see him. Oh, they weren't sad. They simply didn't give a shit. Another thing they were not was full. The line outside was one hundred people long, but there were four or five empty tables in the overly lighted room. And when he left (or retreated) that night, there were still four or five tables, though the line had gone away when the doors were locked at 9:29.

The menu was in French, but he was competent enough from college classes. He remembered that in *Across the River and into the Trees* the colonel had ordered cauliflower braised with butter, so he did. The colonel ordered beef, so he did. And he ordered a bottle of iced Valpolicella. The newly proclaimed political consultant did also, but the waiter frowned at the cheapness of the wine order and the fact that he was drinking a red wine cold. The truth was that fifteen percent of a bottle of Valpolicella is not a good tip. But the colonel's waiter had made small inside jokes, and the young man's ignored him.

Another thing Antoine's didn't have was music, so he could hear the sound coming from the other room. Through the door was another room filled with people. They were *real* Antoine's people, laughing and having a good time and making small inside jokes with waiters. The walls were filled with pictures of famous people who had eaten there. He discovered this on one of his three trips to the men's room. He didn't need to answer nature's call. He just wanted to peer beyond the swinging doors.

"Sir, can I hep you?" The captain of the restaurant had the rough voice of a public-school kid in New Orleans who had never left Orleans Parish and never intended to. He positioned himself between Christian and the dining room. "Sir, there are at least two gentlemen and their companions who are uncomfortable with you watching 'em."

"I was just looking at the restaurant." Christian retreated to his table. He had violated some unwritten rule.

His crisp new one-hundred-dollar bills had let him in, but they had not let him in all the way. He was still a door away. Later he found that he was actually an alley away, and that the alley was more than just a few steps down the sidewalk from the outside lines of people. It was years away. Because those people confirmed his suspicions. They had not stood in line. They had come in through a hidden passageway and used a secret red telephone. These diners had been met by a small-talking waiter and ushered to their regular tables, out of sight of those poor unfortunates trying to buy their way into the restaurant with one-hundred-dollar bills after standing in a ridiculous line.

The bruised, would-be consultant left and got drunk with a B-girl on Bourbon Street, who took one of his hundreds, and he ended up sleeping with an ugly girl he had known in college who had bad teeth and thought he was the new political genius on the horizon. He may have told her that.

**3** The day after the day of the girl with the bad teeth and the Antoine experience, Christian retrieved his family from his mother-in-law's, retreated to his small office, and lay on the sofa to heal. He healed for almost six months. The spell had broken. As the hundreds dwindled, things began to break. The MG destroyed three fuel pumps and he was reduced to opening the trunk where the fuel pump is oddly located on an English car, and beating on it with a hammer until he heard its temperamental electric motor begin clicking. Children got sick. Doctor bills falling through the mail slot were explosions to Christian's bill-sensitive ears. Rent was raised on the newer and larger house in Baton Rouge and Darleen began talking to real-estate agents about "a place of their own." And there was so little business the office door hinges rusted, making it both noisy and difficult to open. Things corrode quickly in the Louisiana humidity.

But rusting worst of all was the young political consultant. He found that his only political experience had been in a losing campaign for a man not highly regarded in the better sections of town. The rust began to work on his ego. He switched to factory-made American cigars advertised on television. He read the newspapers about successful Washington consultants and realized that perhaps he did not really know enough to call himself a professional. While they talked about demographic targeting and focus-group testing, his only frame of reference was "how much you got to pay for the nigger vote" and "them cocksuckers vote every time for the sheriff's man."

The only change in his life was that a spring broke in his couch and he had to turn around so his head faced south instead of north. And the battle at home moved to the trenches as the money dried up. Darleen was a lovely girl but she had received her basic training on a mother-dominated battlefield.

Nothing about Christian fit Darleen's definition of marriage as she knew it or husbands as she had been trained to view them. The advice her mother gave her on her wedding day was "Don't put up with anything. A man will take all he can get and leave you with a couple of babies. Stand toe-to-toe until you get the upper hand." If Christian said "good morning," Darleen responded "why?" Darleen was strong-willed enough to think she could change him, and Christian, because he didn't know the rules of combat, absently fueled the conflict. His back was against the wall, but he had the barest idea of a plan to bring him fame and Darleen fortune.

He knew that if he made enough money, she would have to shut up. He had learned in sociology classes that fewer rich people divorced than poor people. The clock was ticking on his future but he could not find the lever to put his plan into effect. He wanted to stay with Darleen, but he could see the time when he might once more have to run across the hill and escape to a life on the other side.

He was facing south, smoking the next-to-last cheap cigar in his box when one small piece of the plan fell into place. Big Jim called.

"College Boy, I got big trouble and need your help. Get your ass down to WBRZ-TV and I'll pay you well."

The door squeaked, bounced against the wall, and Christian ran down the hall. Ten minutes later, still panting, he met Big Jim, all maroon with white stitching, with Mrs. Molly Pierce on the twelfth take of a thirteen-take television commercial. He had always heard her name in Louisiana politics but had only ever seen her on television or in the newspaper. When he arrived in the studio, she was crying, and her vocabulary had degenerated to saying "darn" because of the high temperature under the lights, her makeup running, and the camera angle making her look fat. She was a little fat.

Big Jim had called because they were in their third hour of producing the commercial, and it was to go on the air that night. Jim was sweating more than ever and taking big gulps out of the glass on the speaker's stand. It smelled of bourbon.

For a man who constantly searched for targets of opportunity, Christian suddenly found himself hurdling toward the bull's-eye. With deliberate actions, he calmly and slowly lit his cigar. A drought of twenty-three weeks was going to end. Christian nervously swept the room with his eyes. Opportunity was knocking so loudly he feared it could be heard by others. Molly Pierce was a candidate for state treasurer and Big Jim owned three banks. And at that time, before the reform governor, the state didn't require banks to pay interest on state deposits. The office was worth a bundle and candidates were willing to spend big to win it. "What's been wrong with the other takes?" Christian asked.

Jim whispered as well as he could. "Well, in about seven of 'em she kept hitting the table with that damned charm bracelet, and the echo would drown her out. Her dear, departed husband gave her the bracelet. In the first two, she said we were shooting her from the right side and not the left, and the left was her best side. One time she thought her tits threw too much of a shadow, and one time something under the desk shocked her—damned wire or something. We got about forty-five minutes left, and now she's crying."

"Why don't we just postpone it for a couple of days?" Christian asked.

"We got to announce officially and strongly today, or that son-of-a-bitch Wilton Mackie is going to get in the race and divide all of the governor's people right down the middle. If we announce with a television campaign tonight, I think we can cut him off at the pass.''

Christian thought for a moment, attempting to look terribly wise. What he was really doing was trying to get the lay of the land. He had never been in a television studio. The man in the glass booth was obviously the director.

"What does the director say about all of this?''

"That's the son of a bitch who made her cry. He made her take off the charm bracelet.'' They walked over to Miz Pierce. She had been a beautiful woman who had gone to the chocolate éclairs too often. Her complexion was still perfect, and one could see the foundation of what had once been a striking young woman. Louisiana politicians called them "sweeties.'' But sweeties get old and the curves get padded, the chins multiply, and they have to find a new asset or direction. This one had gone into politics.

"If you can solve this mess in the next thirty minutes, I'll stay in the race. If you can't, I won't turn in my qualification papers tomorrow,'' she said to Susie, T. Boy, Big Jim, and the other concerned citizens.

The target of opportunity. The break. Christian slowed his movements to disguise his eagerness. "I am, I am,'' echoed through his head. Almost in slow motion he began to speak, pronouncing each syllable carefully.

"Miz Molly, get up and go to the ladies' room and repair your makeup, and I will have a conference with the director. When you come back, we will finish this in about ten minutes.''

Big Jim cocked his head and studied Christian but then did as directed and escorted her out of the studio, and the emerging consultant charged the director's booth. Nothing else was slow motion. The director sat with his feet up on the video control panel. His headset was pulled down around his neck. He was young and disgusted. Red, yellow, and green lights from the panel glowed in his round glasses like Christmas lights. He sighed as Christian came through the door.

"Pal, I don't know anything about television. This is the first time I have ever been in a studio, and I am sure that I will screw up every time I open my mouth. I need your help and experience."

They went through the usual introductions and sizing up of each other common to young men with big egos and then got down to business. The consultant searched the inner resources of his wallet and pulled out one of the last of Big Jim's hundreds.

"Here's a little advance payment. Back me up and make me look brilliant, and I will give you another one of these. If I get the campaign, I'll pay you double for every television spot we make, and the money will go directly to you." The consultant hadn't needed a lot of formal training to understand greed.

The creative conference was over when Big Jim and Miz Pierce came back into the studio.

"Miz Pierce, I have looked at the other takes"—he had not—"and have several suggestions to make. The first is that you should only be shot from your left side. You really look beautiful from both sides, but I think you handle the camera better when it is slightly to your left."

She nodded an "I told you so" to the director.

"And let's take you from behind that desk. Sit on that sofa over there and turn to the camera. Let's get something very feminine to put on you. Is that your bracelet on the desk? Put it on and let it make a little noise so that the commercial will seem spontaneous and sincere."

The commercial was finished in one take. Then they gathered around the videotape machine to see the replay.

"This is brilliant," the consultant exclaimed, and hit Big Jim on the shoulder. "She handles a camera better than anybody I have ever worked with—a real pro."

He couldn't stop. "Look how strong you look. Your voice is wonderful. Brilliant. Just brilliant. You are the most talented candidate I have ever directed. Brilliant." Then, seeing approval in her face, he repeated the compliments at least twice. Finally the director walked away in disgust. Soon even Big Jim was making signs to him, but he couldn't stop.

"Brilliant. Look at your eye contact. That sort of thing can't be directed. Brilliant."

The only person who didn't seem to tire of it was Miz Pierce. It was impossible to overdo the praise. It was a rule he would use for many years. It never failed. He learned years later that given a choice between praise of the candidate and skill, praise always won. It became his Rule Number One in How to Survive in Politics.

As they left the studio, Big Jim shoved three of the big beautiful bills into his pocket. But instinct told him that this would weaken his position with Miz Molly.

"No, Jim, I can't take your money." He handed him back the hundreds. She watched with interest. Sweeties have a special relationship with one-hundred-dollar bills.

Big Jim laughed. "College Boy has trouble taking money."

"It's not that, Jim, it was just an honor working with a woman I have admired for years, a living legend." They had stopped in the parking lot. "And with somebody that talented, all I had to do was watch. Pay me one day when you have something difficult to do." For the second time he pushed those crisp tickets to freedom into Jim's pocket.

"I can't tell you how much I appreciate your contribution to my campaign." She patted his arm and then rubbed it in an old and practiced reflex action. The young consultant had taken a three-hundred-dollar gamble. But he had a feeling.

Christian was getting nervous about his gamble when three days later Big Jim appeared at his office door in lime green and without a whore. He sat across from Christian and put his green alligator boots on the desk.

"College Boy, that the best fake-dick deal I've seen in years. All that woman can talk about is that nice young man who wouldn't take money."

Big Jim was looking at the meager furnishings. He took

ten of the beautiful big bills out of his pocket and stuffed them into Christian's coat pocket. This time Christian left them there.

"I want to get that lady elected, but it won't do me a damned bit of good if she gets elected and I lose her." Big Jim lit one of his trademark cigars and then lit the consultant's. The Cuban smoke tasted wonderful after the American imitations. "I can't travel with her. People will say we're fucking and all sorts of things. But you can. I want to hire you to travel with Miz Molly around the state. You could almost be her kid. And you're the only son of a bitch that I can halfway trust."

"I won't let you down, Jim, and I really need the work."

"Let me tell you a few things about the lady, and you can take it from there. For one, she don't drink or smoke. For two, she's a Baptist. Three, she was the sweetie of Governor Dooley Martin, one of the finest gentlemen to ever hold office. He treated her like a queen. If his wife would've met some untimely fate, Miz Molly would have been first lady." Jim paused to let that sink in. Jim admired the fact that women could earn respect, fame, and money by lying on their backs. That, he reasoned, was much better than sweating or stealing.

Jim went on for an hour painting a portrait of virtue. All that protected her from sainthood was the fragile thumping of the heart muscle. She didn't curse or drink or think dirty thoughts. She sang in the choir and never missed Sunday school. A few weeks later the consultant learned that she really didn't smoke.

"Young man, we have to be very careful as we travel this state not to leave any false impressions in anyone's mind."

"Yes, ma'am."

"We have to remember at all times that any little word or gesture could ruin my chances of being elected. Some men find me . . . ah . . . attractive. And if it happens to you, you will have to be careful."

"Yes, ma'am."

"Whatever happens between the two of us must be kept highly confidential." She bent forward and whispered in Christian's ear, "The silence of the tomb, Governor Martin used to say." When she straightened up, she left one hand on Christian's knee. "In World War Two, I remember there was a poster that said, 'Loose lips sink ships.' "

"Yes, ma'am."

"But there is something else. We must be discreet. You may find that I have a little weakness or two. . . . "

"Yes, ma'am, we all do but—"

"And I demand privacy. When you learn something personal or political, you have to go to the grave with it."

"Yes, ma'am, and I—"

"And I demand loyalty."

"Yes, ma'am."

He said, "Yes, ma'am" a lot because it was one of his mother's lessons he could remember. It got to be a habit that most southern children break at about eighteen. Christian did just the opposite. He used the expression more than ever. He "yes ma'am'd" everything female. Whores and young girls loved it. His contemporaries would ask him to stop saying "ma'am" and he would always respond by saying "Yes, ma'am."

Christian usually said "Yes, ma'am" even when he disagreed. He found it was always easier to agree than to disagree. Therefore, when Miz Molly gave her new consultant the little speech, Christian gave her the same response he would have given had she asked something impossible. Christian's feeling was always to agree and work out details later. It made both sides feel good initially and then made the other party feel benevolent when a compromise was reached. But he wished she would move her hand. She was twenty-five years older than him but the warmth from her hand had begun to run up his thigh.

"Big Jim is paying you five hundred dollars per week."

"Yes, ma'am." She moved her hand to her lap. Maybe she was observant, Christian thought.

"That makes you loyal to Big Jim."

"Yes, ma'am."

"And that's proper. You should be loyal to the man who feeds you. So I'm going to pay you a little, too, so that you must also be loyal to me."

"Yes, ma'am."

"The First National Bank is going to send you a thousand dollars a week. You will cash the checks and keep five hundred. The other five hundred you will give to me for expenses. I can't take money from banks, you know. It would put me under some obligation when I took office. And I don't want to owe a living soul."

"Yes, ma'am."

Poor Big Jim, Christian thought. When Big Jim found out about the other five hundred dollars, he suggested that College Boy send him a box of good cigars every week. Christian did. It was good business.

Christian called himself "consultant." He even had some business cards printed to prove his point. But he was also a driver and a press agent and a bodyguard and a source of constant speculation at scores of political cocktail parties and coffees throughout the state. He was met with sly smiles. Christian grew accustomed to glances in his direction and whispers behind cupped hands.

In his travels he discovered the institution of Louisiana sweeties. The best are tough survivors. They endure wives and business setbacks and boredom and religious revivals. A shell grows around their souls and they trade tricks for curves, threats for romance. The best of them are left with a dress shop and a car, a house or a luxury apartment in payment for their youth, enthusiasm, and girlish dreams. Every party was attended by hordes of these women paying homage to their leader, Miz Molly, the queen of sweeties.

At a Tuesday party in New Iberia, Christian escaped to his customary position in the back of the room and fueled fantasies about some of the guests. It was a fine and harmless way to kill time. He was watching a bleached, tanned girl wearing a dress too tight, with a skirt too short and so transparent it exposed the lacework on her little undies, hug and kiss another young girl with pushed-up breasts in a skirt too short, too tight, and so transparent it showed the lace on her little undies when an old sheriff with white hair growing out of his ears moved next to him. The old man and the young consultant stood shoulder touching shoulder, in a pose of intrigue.

"Son, they tell me you dipping your cock in some famous stuff." Christian got two stiff elbows in the ribs and a chuckle in his face that smelled of bad teeth and snuff. "Me and the boys got a bet. I say you skin your elbows on her sheets at night. The mayor says that she wouldn't fuck a little pissant like you."

Christian thought about the question while he watched two strumpets giggle and whisper. "Sheriff, loose lips sink ships." For some reason he wasn't sure which answer would please Miz Molly. He was spared more cross-examination when Miz Molly crossed the room with another woman in tow.

"Mary Sue, I want you to meet this nice young man, Christian Simmons. He's the smartest thing. He writes speeches that make you cry and produces the best television in the country. You saw my spots, didn't you?"

The young man dubbed College Boy, the Reporter, the Driver, and Hey Kid, finally had a name. He winced. He had always preferred the anonymity of labels. Names were confining. He thought Indians had the proper relationship with names. "Man Who Runs Like Deer" was a better name than John Smith. It said something. He had chosen his own name when he graduated from high school.

His parents may have anticipated his feelings about names

or they were simply indifferent because they didn't allow the hospital to intimidate them into putting a name on the birth certificate. Later, they were afraid to give him a name he did not like and called him "son" until he was five. Then people began to call him "Sonny Simmons."

Before he went to college, he collected character traits in other people he liked and adopted them. Then he boldly wrote "Christian Ahab Simmons" on the yellowed certificate.

In Texas where he grew up, most people were born-again Christians. With the name he became one without need of baptism, dedicating his life, or being reborn. He was both reborn and Christian. Ahab he added for a little evil. It struck a nice balance with "Christian." Simmons was all that survived the ashes of boyhood.

Christian began to notice a cooling in Miz Molly's attitude toward him after two months of driving around Louisiana. So he tried even harder to please. He rushed around the car to open the door and every day praised her dress or her hair or her political exploits. "Miz Pierce, I think this campaigning is good for you. I'm sure you've lost ten pounds." "Miz Pierce, that dress really goes with your eyes. Next time we make a television commercial I want you to wear it."

At such lavish praise, she merely grunted and stared forward. One late afternoon outside Abbeville on a bayou road, Christian began to get a hint of their problem. "Christian," she said, "I don't know whether to be flattered or insulted. I forgot to lock the door between our rooms last night and you didn't even notice. Of course it was a mistake, but this morning I began to think about it. Am I that unattractive or do you respect me so much you could not bring yourself to open the door?"

Christian guided the car even more carefully and deliberately as he thought of an answer that would not injure his relationship. "Miz Molly, my hand was on that doorknob last night for ten minutes, but I didn't open it because of the tremendous respect I have for you."

"You may call me Molly."

"Yes, ma'am but—"

"You know, my friends all think that I shouldn't be traveling with a young attractive man. They think it may cause talk. You know there was always talk that I had something going with Governor Martin. Can you imagine an old thing like me having an affair with the governor of the state?"

She had turned to face Christian. When she turned, her skirt pulled to the tops of her thighs. She made no effort to pull it down. Out of the corner of his eye Christian discovered she had good legs, no stockings, and a hint of pink lace under the shadow of her skirt. She was really still beautiful, if a little padded and a little lined.

"Maybe I should think about getting a nice woman to drive me. You know, there is some talk about you traveling with Big Jim and those, ah, women." After Christian had driven ten miles and run off the shoulder of the road twice, she turned forward and pulled down her skirt. He was disappointed. It showed.

That night in a Ramada Inn, Christian heard a knock on the adjoining door and opened it. It was unlocked. She was standing on the other side with an open blouse. "Christian, I'm really embarrassed, but I have a button I can't undo. Will you give me a hand?" She turned her back and Christian slid his hands around her. She backed into his room. Christian put his mouth into the hollow of her neck and bit lightly. She moaned and reached behind her to draw him close. As he kissed her neck he could see the slight scars that were responsible for her firm skin. The skirt fell around her feet, the blouse was tossed into a chair. His hands explored the rigging of garter belt and stockings. She had come to him equipped for erotic battle. She turned and undressed Christian while he massaged her breasts. When he bent to kiss her nipples, he could see the faint moon-shaped scars of the plastic surgeon. Taking control, she moved Christian to the bed, pushed him to his back, and mounted. She was hungry and Christian was blessed with youth.

Christian held her hips and smashed into her until his stomach muscles began to cramp. She reached down and began massaging herself, and Christian felt the familiar contractions. His and hers.

After she snored lightly, Christian lay watching a lighted Burger King sign across the road. A small, plump king sat on a huge hamburger. Once again he told himself to think of the Plan, the old house in Port Arthur, the cot in the attic. But even with these images pumping in reserve strength, there was that nagging pain behind his heart that was becoming more of a memory than a reality.

"Christian, was it good for you?" Miz Molly opened her eyes and stretched. She still wore her garters and stockings.

"It was great. It was the best I've ever felt." Christian lied only a little. She had been good.

"Now, be honest. An old thing like me? I bet you've had lots of young girls."

"No. I've only had my wife."

"Do you think my breasts are nice? I've been told they're my best feature." She held them in offering to Christian. He bent over her and moved his tongue in circles. No, she wasn't bad.

"Now that we're lovers, do you think you can maintain a professional attitude? Maybe it would be better if you didn't travel with me all the time. If not, we could get together after the meetings and I could get a woman to drive me."

Damn. Damn, Christian said to himself.

"Do you mean you would like to keep me?" He laughed, but there was no laughter behind his eyes.

"I think we could work something out after I get elected. I know some banks who would put you on retainer."

"Yes, ma'am. I'll sure think about that."

Christian watched the comic king on the neon hamburger as he went about his work on the second nipple.

\* \* \*

A few days later at one of the coffee parties he watched Miz Pierce whispering to a friend who kept glancing at Christian and covering her mouth with her hand. He sat silently, but he continued to be the object of giggles and sideways glances during the next weeks. The Plan. The PLAN. "I am. I am."

*"Christian, I want you to take these two red ribbons and tie my wrists to the bedposts."*
*"Yes, ma'am."*
*"That's cute, you saying 'ma'am' when you're in me. Not tight now. Then go down and tie my feet but leave enough room so I can raise my knees."*
*"Yes, ma'am."*

During most of the parties since his seduction (or surrender) Christian sat outside and read political science books. But at the final event of the campaign, Christian made a command appearance. As he stepped into the restored Civil War home draped with red, white and blue which spelled out "Molly Pierce, for Morality in Government," a small event changed his life. It often happens that way. Small rudders turn big ships. The governor's wife was co-hosting the party with Mrs. Reverend D. Tracy, the wife of the minister of the city's largest nondenominational, born-again, spirit-filled, crusading church. The preacher's wife was serving punch and tea cakes. On each cupcake was Molly's name and an American flag. When Christian first saw Mrs. Tracy, she was illuminated by a floodlight recessed in the ceiling and aimed at an object of art behind her. The light gave her a bright edge. She was truly an object of art. Christian stood eating countless cupcakes so he could stand in her glow.

"You must be hungry," she said to Christian. Even her voice sounded like music.

"I'm sorry. Yes, I guess I'm just hungry. I'm the media

consultant for Miz Molly Pierce and we have been too busy to eat.'' Christian lied. They ate constantly. Still, though, he was losing weight. He caught himself almost putting a cupcake in his pocket and shakily returned it back to the table.

"Simmons Christian . . . er, I mean my name is, ah, Christian Simmons.'' He picked up the cupcake and put it down again. He couldn't make his hands be still.

She laughed. "Eat dozens of these cakes. Everybody here is on a diet, or so they say. The truth is that I think it's getting rather unfashionable to eat in public. And I'm Flora Tracy.'' She offered her hand.

"Do you go to many of these political gatherings?'' The fumbling Christian gave up his pride. He would use any line, no matter how worn. Maybe he was even in love. At the least he was in lust.

"No, I stay busy in church activities.''

"Where do you go to church?'' Christian looked at her and seriously considered converting to something. Anything.

"Oh, my husband is pastor at Third Baptist. You'll have to visit us sometime. Please excuse me now, I think there is going to be a prayer.''

The Reverend Tracy himself began the party with a twelve-minute prayer for morality in government, more bombs, and aggressive military action in Central America.

Christian squirmed through the prayer while mentally undressing the preacher's wife and then retreated in frustration to the car. Her eyes were blue. Her dress was white. Her hair was short and blond. Her husband was a preacher. "Shit.''

Love turned to anger. Flora Tracy was another prize out of Christian's reach. As he contemplated his cruel fate, Hugh Conklin, the derelict of smoked-filled limos, and Jim's campaign, staggered by the car. He stank of bourbon and after-shave. The last part of the Plan clicked into place in Christian's mind but he could not resist the great opportunity the drunk presented for revenge on a cruel world.

"Governor,'' Christian called out.

Hugh weaved over to the car and bent down to talk to Christian.

"Governor, I just wanted to remind you that you're late. Those women won't wait much longer."

"I don't think I was invited."

"Then your invitation must have been lost in the mail. You are supposed to speak to those women about, ah, ah, equal rights for midgets." Christian suddenly recalled a wonderful story Big Jim had told him about Hugh's last campaign. Hugh had been persuaded by a cruel group of advisers to take up the cause of midgets. The midget speech had become part of the folklore of Louisiana politics.

Without another word, Hugh straightened his tie and confidently climbed the steps to the house. He understood. This invitation was not unexpected. His speech had won much acclaim. At first he had to shout for attention and stand on an antique chair to be seen. Under Hugh's shoes was a crushed tent card that explained that the frail chair was an objet d'art and must not be used. It splintered as he raised his hands to get attention. His fall began a domino action that felled five sweeties, two strumpets, and the punch bowl.

Christian Ahab Simmons was fired that afternoon but rehired the next morning when he apologized to the governor's wife, Miz Molly, and most of the city of Baton Rouge. But now the pieces were all in place. Hugh Conklin was going to make Christian Ahab Simmons rich and famous. Perhaps.

**4** Jimmy Dodge was angry. He was always angry. Anger was as much a part of him as his hairline or his nose. He was angry that he could not get a job on the *Washington Post*. He was angry that Southern Newspapers, Inc. would not give him the money he deserved. He was angry that he was twice divorced. And tonight he was angry at Bob Woodward. He knew that he was a better and smarter writer than Woodward, but it was Woodward's picture and book in the front window of every bookstore. Woodward had been lucky with Deep Throat. It could have been Jimmy's story. But he was never in the right place at the right time. He was also a little drunk and angry about losing fifty dollars in a poker game. He made a wrong turn off of Rock Creek Parkway, cursed, stopped, and took one last swallow from a flask. It was then he saw two figures standing nude in the tidal basin. Well, they weren't exactly nude. The gentleman wore almost knee-length boxer shorts and the woman still had on black panties. The heavyset man with white hair sat down with a splash in the shallow water, pulling the woman down on top of him. Then he began playing alligator as she danced around to avoid her gator's teeth.

Jimmy Dodge removed his camera from the backseat of his car and slowly made his way across the grass to the tidal basin. He had just discovered Senator Ashton LeBlanc, senior senator from Louisiana, and his rumored girlfriend, Star Brite, the lobbyist and exotic dancer. Jimmy Dodge struggled to focus the camera through scotch-blurred eyes as the alligator and his prey, holding hands, staggered from the water and into perfect focal distance.

Jimmy Dodge was finally in the right place at the right time. He was a little angry, though, that the moon was not brighter so that he could have used color film. The senator was stunned when a voice screamed out, "Senator, will you and the lady go back in the water and come out one more time. I need another angle." Jimmy Dodge was never satisfied.

Ringing telephones made political music across the pine trees and bayous of morning Louisiana. A thousand small-time politicians closed the paper and dialed their most loyal hacks. "Joe D, you and the boys ready to go to Washington?" By night all but a hundred of them had shelved their ambitions because of a lack of money or pending criminal charges. By morning there were only ten still determined to take the LeBlanc seat. For most, the music of opportunity had become a one-handed piano melody in a discordant minor key.

Big Jim chuckled when he saw a carefully edited version of the picture in his morning paper. He studied the photo through the bottom of his glasses. It was the girl that caught his attention. "I think me and Senator LeBlanc have brother-in-lawed that lady. Yes, sir. I think I've screwed me a famous lady. Susie, come let Big Jim show you a picture."

The governor looked at the photo and called his brother-in-law. "Cecil, I think this is your chance. LeBlanc is vulnerable. It goes without saying that you have the support of my organization. I'm a man who will always stand by his family." He hung up the phone, smiled, lit a cigar, and called his chief rival. "Sammy, I know you been thinking about running for governor. I want to make a deal. If you decide to run for the U.S. Senate instead, you can count on my help. You may hear that my brother-in-law is going to run with my support, but if you decide to make the race, I'll get him to pull down. He's a sorry fool, but he's family."

Molly Pierce put down her paper and called Mary Sue Jefferson. "Mary Sue, did you read that awful story about Senator LeBlanc and that terrible woman? . . . Mary Sue. No! No! I had no idea . . . Now don't cry, dear . . . You mean you and the senator had a *personal* relationship? I'm so sorry . . . No, I didn't know. I guess I put my foot in it again . . . Well, you come by here, dear, and we'll have tea. Good friends have to stick together in times like these." She put down the phone and smiled. "Teach that bitch to talk about double chins."

Christian only glanced at the picture. He was interested in the headline. The final piece fell into place for his plan. Not only did he have a candidate, Hugh, he now had an office to target. Fate had finally smiled on him. Free at last. Free at last. He reached for the phone.

"Molly, I think I'm going to have to resign from that bank retainer. I'm going to have a big election to manage."

"Am I too old for you, Christian? Are you tired of me? Tell me the truth."

Christian fumbled for a moment. He didn't like to tell people things they didn't want to hear. "Well. Well, to tell you the truth I've, I've—how do you say this? I've had sort of a religious experience." In his mind he could see the beautiful Flora Tracy with the light shining through her hair. "And I think I'm going to have a big campaign. A big campaign."

"Well, I understand religious conviction. I sing in the choir myself. Did you go to a revival?" Christian could hear relief in her voice. Religious conviction was the one argument that didn't insult her. She had been born again half a dozen times.

"Well, yes, I had sort of a revival, an awakening. I don't know how to describe it."

"We never do. I understand, Christian. I want to stay your special friend, but I'll call the bank and tell them you won't be attending to their business anymore."

"Thank you, Molly."

"And Christian, God bless you."

# 5

Christian Ahab Simmons loved his wife. At least he thought he did. She was his first lover and his guide through the complexities of human relationships. His boyhood with Calab Hudson did not prepare him to live in a world of people with rules. Darleen tried to teach Christian the rules.

She had a sort of Ten Commandments for a husband's conduct and Christian tried to learn them, but the last four or five kept changing according to the argument of the moment. It was perplexing.

1. "If he loves you, he will honor you by being dependable."

2. "If he loves you, he will provide for your every desire."

3. "If he loves you, he will be a kind and loving man who repairs things and does his share of the housework and child rearing."

4. (The most puzzling to Christian.) "If he loves you, he will be absolutely faithful only to you."

He wanted to understand the rules. Often he would try to stand outside his body and understand. It was like jealousy. He wanted to understand that. He had friends who were enraged if you gave their wives a little pat on the behind. He often thought that if he could understand jealousy, he would understand love, because most people seemed to have them so interlocked. Once he watched a friend at a pool party run his hand down the back of Darleen's skimpy bathing suit while kissing her. Her arms were around his neck and the movement of the rest of her body suggested that she wasn't resisting. He watched them intertwined in the dim light behind the pool pump house and retreated to a lounge chair near the crawfish boiler. There, while the huge pots of the red crawfish cooked, he attempted to work up a rage or, if not a rage, resentful indignation.

He knew what the rules said and he wanted to prove that he loved his wife, but she seemed to be enjoying herself. He couldn't understand why being enraged about her having pleasure was a greater expression of love than allowing her the pleasure. He reasoned, though, that if he had been caught behind the pump house with Jimmy D's wife, the reaction would have been swift and physical by both his wife and by Jimmy D, but concluded that perhaps they both knew more about how to love.

But he soon forgot the philosophical question and had another beer and a platter of crawfish. Alabama was playing LSU in the third quarter of a close game. Christian had a bet on Alabama against Big Jim. Big Jim always bet on LSU, even when he had to give fourteen points to get the bet. Christian had talked to one of his former classmates and learned that Shadow Joe Hebert, the LSU quarterback, had a sore arm.

"You don't suck heads?"

Christian looked up from his platter of crawfish to see a former college reporter, Bobby Lofton. He was picking through Christian's pile of discarded crawfish shells to find the heads.

Happy for the attention, Christian began to help his friend pick out the heads. "Look, it took me three years to learn to eat these things. Maybe in three more I'll learn to suck the heads.''

"You fucking Texans. You don't understand anything but barbecue and chicken-fried steak.''

Bobby shoved his index finger into the end of the shell, scrapped out the crawfish fat, and then popped it into his mouth. Cajuns use the fat for flavoring in most of their exotic dishes. An experienced crawfish eater could, in a matter of seconds, pluck off the head, extract the tail meat, and then scoop out the fat. Christian had actually seen Cajuns suck the fat out of the head without using their fingers. The Texan in him still considered that a disgusting sight.

Across the patio a blonde wore a wet T-shirt that said in bold red letters, "I Suck Heads." He and Bobby watched as she giggled across their line of vision.

"Isn't that something?" Christian said in admiration. Out of the corner of his eye he could see that his wife was back in the pool, treading water, and Jimmy D was standing by the keg wolfing down a beer.

"If you think that's something, you should have seen what Jimmy D had behind the pump house. He had the top off of one of the most beautiful women I've seen. I wanted to look but she covered up when she saw me. There she is in the pool." Bobby pointed toward Darleen.

LSU won, but only by seven points, so Christian won the bet on the point spread. He gave two of the crisp new bills from his winnings to his wife as an expression of his love because he had failed so miserably at the pool party. To demonstrate his love, he thought that maybe he should have confronted her about her behavior at the party. But he wasn't sure. He just didn't understand the rules.

Darleen did most of her weeping in private. She was crying in the bathtub when Christian walked in with the money. She was trying to wash the stranger out of her. Two times she had emptied the tub and filled it again with scalding water. Dar-

leen was disgusted with herself. She couldn't decide if she
had been trying to embarrass Christian or to get his attention.
So she cried in frustration. She told herself she had been
drunk. But she knew she had not been that drunk.

There were times when she thought she was breaking
through with Christian. Somehow he had found the down
payment for the house. He had worked for some bank. The
house was to be a home base for her children and her marriage. It was old and solid in a neighborhood of oak-lined
streets. It had the roots that Darleen had dreamed of. Solid.
Solid. Not military bases with a drunk father who volunteered for foreign assignments and left her mother and her in
the shabby frame houses that they had to surrender constantly
to wives with husbands of higher rank. This house was real.
This house was hers. Solid.

Christian bounced around the solar system in his head and
occasionally seemed on the verge of becoming a model father
and husband. It was difficult for her to explain that it was
better to have a house in an old neighborhood than in a new
neighborhood. He only shook his head until she told him
their children would have trees to climb. Contact. "Yes," he
said. Just "yes." But it was a "yes" that seemed to turn on
some switch in his head. There was something in his past she
didn't understand. In fact, she could seldom get him to talk
about his past.

Darleen celebrated to herself the victory of the old house.
It was the same quiet celebration she had when Christian
rolled on the floor with his children. He loved them. The
children were the tap roots of their marriage and their future.
Contact.

"I brought you some money."

"Thank you, Christian." She began to cry again. He bent
to kiss her and she wrapped her arms around his neck and
held him close, wetting his shirt. Contact.

He undressed and joined her in the tub. "I love you," he
said. And he did. Again Darleen celebrated.

They moved from the tub to the floor, where they made frantic, almost violent love. Then, still nude, they held hands and went into the children's room to watch them sleep.

But contact wasn't enough for Darleen. She needed to use hammer and nails to fix Christian to the house and the children and a regular schedule and a regular job and weekend barbecues and PTA meetings. She was impatient. She tried to build a foundation under Christian but he kept shifting away. And something about her didn't like peace, she told herself in a later bout of weeping.

After they dressed, she joined Christian in the living room, where he was having a drink. "Christian, did you apply for that new job in the public-relations department of LSU?"

"No. I don't need a job. I have a plan."

"You don't need a job? This house is empty. Four rooms are empty. Bed sheets cover most of the windows and you don't need a job?" She realized that her voice was on the edge of hysteria and slowed her movements and her speech. Be reasonable, Darleen, she said to herself. He may have a plan. Try, Darleen. Calm, Darleen.

"I'm working on a plan that will make us rich. I think I have a political campaign."

"You think!" (Calm, Darleen.)

"I'm working on a plan."

"Have you found another candidate to chauffeur? That's really all you are. Political consultant." She spat out the term "political consultant" as though it were something awful in her mouth. "You are a chauffeur and a bodyguard. Big pistol under the front seat. You couldn't shoot if a criminal posed for you over your candidate's body."

While Darleen continued listing his faults and mistakes, Christian reflected. Perhaps she was right. Maybe he couldn't shoot. An old sheriff in St. Landry Parish had given him the pistol one afternoon when he was waiting for Miz Molly and made him shoot a box of shells at a stump. Several of the ladies from the party stood outside on the big porch and

watched the instruction and clapped when he made splinters
fly.

"You got to guard the honor and integrity of this fine
woman," was the charge from the sheriff. No, he couldn't
shoot the gun.

It was a mistake, though, to consider Christian a coward.
In high school a two-hundred-pound bully had knocked his
cafeteria tray from his hands, making necessary the ritualistic
afternoon fight. Sonny (this was before he had become Christian) stood quietly before his opponent while the big fleshy
thug took long, defiant drags from his cigarette and flipped
it away. Then he began to roll up his sleeves. He neatly rolled
the right sleeve and had begun working on the left when Sonny
became a whirlwind of fists. The bully toppled but recovered
quickly and broke Sonny's nose. He then cut him above the
eye and knocked him into the dust. Sonny sprang back into
the fight and bloodied the kid's nose, only to be hit in the
head and knocked down again. For more than thirty minutes
the scene was repeated, Sonny being knocked down and coming back with the same energy as before. The bully began
tiring at the persistence of the tiny distance runner. He had
trouble raising his arms and began to swing wildly. Sonny
then pounded him until the bully fell into the dust and began
vomiting. As he heaved, Sonny kicked him again and again
until the big boy passed out. Sonny had become an enraged
machine of destruction. He moved his kicks from the belly
to head and the bully's friends pinned Sonny's arms and pulled
him away. His feet still churned. The bully began heaving
and sobbing. "Get him away, he's crazy. The fucker's crazy."
A week later another of the bully's gang tried Sonny with the
same result. They could beat him but they couldn't outlast
him. As a result he became even more alienated in school.
Sonny Simmons was crazy. He didn't fight by the rules. But
he was never again bumped in the cafeteria line.

"Darleen. I want you to understand. I want to swim upstream. I want to light up the sky. I want to make money and be somebody. And I want you to share in all of it.''

Darleen tried again to calm herself. ''Christian, everybody wants that. That's one reason I married you. You were different. You had ambition. I don't want to take that away from you. What's wrong with working your way to the top? You could be editor of a good paper by the time you're forty. But it takes time. You want to do it all in one year.''

''But I know I can do it. Help me.''

''Help *me,* Christian. Grow up. Get a real job. Get out of that cottonwood tree. That's all over. You have plenty to eat. People respect you. Calm down. A lot of people have bad childhoods, but they aren't consumed by it. They heal. They recover. Maybe we won't be as rich as we thought, but we can live as well as most people. Just defer your ambitions for a few years.'' She ran her fingers through his hair, forcing great control on herself. ''It's as though you came in from some distant planet. You don't understand so many things. You can't become famous just because you want it.''

''I came from a distant planet, Port Arthur.'' Christian could see the old house and the cottonwood swaying above it.

''You could get a job at LSU or the *Morning Advocate.*''

''Darleen, that job would never make the payments on this house.'' He was still too bruised to tell her he had already been rejected by the paper. ''I have to do much better than that.''

''Your problem is your ego. You can't bear the thought of being just another reporter.''

She was right. He wanted to play big games, win big races, have his picture hanging in Antoine's restaurant, be the guest on television talk shows. He had studied the field of Washington political consultants and found little talent. He knew that he could beat them if he ever had a campaign on the same playing field. He had studied motivation, political science, and psychology. He had spent those endless hours reading on the couch. He had prostituted himself for money to buy the house. Why couldn't he make her understand?

But he had also begun to get some insight into her insecurity. Things were a little tight. There were those nude windows and empty rooms, the unexpected doctor bills, the MG's broken fuel pumps. A husband without visible means of support didn't make great talk around the neighborhood dining tables. And those damned naked windows. The whole world knew what they meant.

He sat on the couch with her and rubbed the back of her hand. She moved closer and kissed him on the ear. Soon he was unsnapping, unbuttoning, and holding on tightly.

After they woke and lay nude in the afternoon shafts of light, he felt a bond with Darleen and shame that she was so insecure. The way Christian had learned to avoid her attacks was by keeping silent. She could not hurl failures at his head if she had no ammunition. So they spoke of the lawn, their friends, the children, the MG, the house, and Christian's weaknesses. Actually she spoke of his weaknesses and he did a lot of listening. He thought he might improve if he understood. But they never approached those subjects of ambition or hopes and designs for the future. He was a dreamer and she needed new draperies. He had plans and she had sick children. He wanted to be a better mate. So, as his fingers traced her nipples and ears, thighs, and navel, he slowly and carefully explained his plan to elect Hugh Conklin to the U.S. Senate. He even told her what he called the Plan: "Cottonwood."

"Let me understand," she said sweetly, arresting his hand on her breast. "You are going to elect a derelict to office to make yourself famous."

"Well, it's not that simple, I'm—"

"No, let me finish. You are going to take this wino that everybody in Baton Rouge laughs at, who forgets to zip his fly, who lives in a shack with a paraplegic newspaper vendor, and elect him to some office."

"Let me explain—"

"And to do that you are going to hang around with Big Jim and a killer and a bunch of whores?"

She did have a point.

"While you fuck whores for a living and hang out with white trash, I have sheets hanging over the windows and empty rooms. While you distinguish us by kissing the ass of the most corrupt politician in Louisiana, I can't put the children in private school. Even if we had the money, they wouldn't let us in among decent people."

She began to weep and pound on Christian's chest as he rolled out of bed and attempted to dress. A child in the next room began to cry. He hit the back door milliseconds before a small stool that broke two panes of glass. He could hear both children weeping as his MG rolled into the street. Through one of the empty windows, he could see his wife, completely nude, yelling at him through the glass. He couldn't hear what she said but she looked beautiful. A man cutting grass on a riding lawn mower turned to watch. His mower plowed through a bed of azaleas.

Christian knew the plan would work, but it depended on Big Jim for financing. Big Jim needed to give him enough working capital (new draperies, rooms filled with furniture) to put the plan into effect. But Big Jim had been in a poker game for three days and then had been drunk and slept for three more. Though it threw him off schedule, Christian was encouraged by the poker game. Big Jim's gambling compulsion was necessary to get him involved in the plan.

Christian remembered the editor's story about the cut-over pine land and the oil wells. Big Jim had worked to spend the new wealth only to find himself falling behind the gushing cash flow. Money was made faster than he could spend it. The huge ranch house was filled with expensive objects. There were at least four Remington sculptures. And in the middle of the living room was his full-sized bronze horse with an

Indian slumped over his neck. The Remingtons, however, were used as hat racks for Jim's rainbow collection of hats and the huge bronze horse had a skillfully made pile of plaster horse dung on the floor between its legs. Jim had a sense of humor. In the breakfast nook was a plastic parrot on a perch with newspapers spread under it. Susie, the whore, found this really funny.

With his new wealth, Big Jim bought several banks, tripled the size of his ranch, brought in registered Angus cattle, and changed his style of dress. He was a rich man and he wanted to dress like one. He had a tailor flown in from El Paso to make him a collection of cowboy suits. He and the whore of the moment personally selected all the material. He had yellow suits, pink suits, lavender suits, green suits, red suits, and every other perversion of the rainbow. They were large, tentlike suits with stitched flowers and decorations. Over the coat pocket, stitched in rhinestones, was ''Big Jim.'' Then he had boots and hats dyed to match.

Hanging around the ranch waiting for Big Jim to sober up wasn't bad. Christian had no place to go. Darleen still hung up on him after brief conversations. But that was progress. The first night she didn't even speak. Christian knew that in a day or so she would be loving and calm again and he could return home. But in the meantime the ranch wasn't bad. In fact, Christian had already gained five pounds. Two Cajun cooks heaped food upon the table. There was always pork and beef and chicken cooked in five or six different ways. The drink was huge mugs of beer filled from a keg beside the table. And at Big Jim's table it was not considered ill mannered to eat with your fingers or to burp.

The table was responsible for Jim's constantly changing women. When they had sat at his table for a few weeks, they were too fat for his taste and they would be replaced. A woman with an unnatural metabolism could stay for several months. Big Jim liked tiny women. He called them ''spinners.'' He said that they could mount him in bed and he could spin them around. Christian liked to think about one of the tiny Cajun girls spinning around like a top, dainty articles in orbit around Big Jim's bed.

Christian was sitting at the table with one of the spinners when Big Jim finally returned to life. He was in blue silk pajamas with western stitching. Over his pocket hung a large silver St. Christopher on a safety pin. His face was puffy and his hair standing on end, but he was genuinely glad to see Christian and the whore sitting behind a cornucopia of cholesterol.

Without saying a word, he drew a quart of beer into a huge mug with ''Big Jim'' written in gold and drank it down, wiping his mouth on the sleeve of the blue silk pajamas. Jim burped. He then, still standing by the beer keg, cut a piece of roast beef and rolled it into a tube that he dipped in the gravy and then into the mustard, leaving a yellow and brown trail across the table, across the floor, and across the St. Christopher medal on his chest.

Neither Susie nor Christian said a word. They knew that it took Big Jim a while to awaken. Between being drunk, playing cards, and sleeping, he had not had a solid meal for several days. He burped twice, ate a serving spoon of sausage jambalaya from the big bowl on the table, and drew another quart of beer. Susie jumped up with a napkin and began to dab at the gravy dripping off his chin. Jim took the napkin from her, blew his nose, and sat down to begin his meal. He piled a plate with yams that he covered with pork gravy and then mashed them together with his fork. He opened two biscuits and inserted thick slices of Cajun spiced ham. Three huge spoons of jambalaya were added to his plate along with a turkey leg and a stuffed bell pepper. Two maids kept his beer mug filled. After he had picked the last piece of meat from his turkey leg and made two more stuffed biscuits, this time with roast beef, he straightened up from his plate, mistakenly wiped his mouth on the tablecloth instead of his napkin, which was still next to his plate, and looked across the table at his friend.

"College Boy, when you get here?"

"About three days and five pounds ago, Jim."

He found that amusing and laughed into his beer mug. "You ain't been acting trashy with Susie, have you?"

Susie was indignant. Her code had been violated. "Jim, he didn't lay a hand on me. You are all paid up until next week and you know that I wouldn't do a thing without your permission. College Boy slept in the bunkhouse. I even offered to call Jenny Sue for him and he turned her down."

"Susie, College Boy's in love. Ain't you heard of a man being faithful to his wife?"

"Ida says our girls save more marriages than Father Gillingham. They come to us and don't have to get girlfriends and such. All working girls love faithful men."

Jim looked affectionately at Susie. She was a good woman. A Catholic. And she had not gained a pound. She was as loyal and true as he thought a woman could be. She didn't take money out of his pockets at night and always kept her knees together in company. It stirred Jim to think that she had been with College Boy three days without going to bed with him. Yes, she was indeed quality. She had originally come as a pair with Jenny Sue but Jenny Sue gained ten pounds and began to snore. He had liked having one on each arm at night but he was losing sleep because of the noise. Jenny Sue had been sent back to Ida, the madam, for some conditioning. After she left, Susie became even more attentive and wifelike. It appeared that her best efforts were paying off. She wanted to leave the trade and marry Big Jim. He was everything she had ever wanted in a husband. Of course, being rich helped, but he didn't hit her or make her do things in public that would embarrass her. She had had long dates that demanded she serve drinks topless and even worse. Jim was always a gentleman.

The question to College Boy was a joke because she had

learned that he was one of the only people who Big Jim trusted. She knew that it made him happy when Christian came for a meal or a drink. Once, when one of Christian's children was sick, Jim sent her to secretly pay all of the doctor bills. What neither of them knew was that Christian continued making payments on the bill, and the doctor didn't say a word. The secret had only resulted in the doctor being paid twice. Jim had no children with his three previous wives and Susie thought Christian was becoming unknowing heir to that title.

"College Boy, there's millions of doves back in the west pasture. Let's grab a couple of shotguns and go shoot some doves." He began to shout orders as he rose from the table. "Linda, make me up a couple of flasks of hunting toddy. Sam, fetch my boots." He shouted as loudly as a big man can shout. "President, you and Governor come here. We gonna shoot some birds." The two huge Labs galloped into the room. One was yellow and the other black. As the dogs danced around, Big Jim pulled his boots onto his naked feet and tucked in the legs of the blue pajamas. For once the boots didn't match his dress. They were lime green and clashed with the blue.

It was a familiar pattern to Christian and he collected a couple of the Browning double-barrels from the huge gun cabinet and followed Jim to the jeep. The big dogs were already aboard, barking at the excitement of being asked to do what they were bred for.

Jim often took Christian to the fields when he wanted to talk. It was the only place where two men could talk without looking at each other. Big Jim scanned the sky, the gun in the crook of his arm. "What's on your mind, College Boy? You look like a man with a problem. You know you don't have to be broke all the time. I can get four or five companies to pay you to lobby for 'em in the legislature. All you got to lobby is me." He shot twice and two doves fell. The dogs bounded across the pasture to collect them. Christian fired once and missed another darting dove. The dogs scanned the sky and then looked disgusted when nothing fell. Hunting with Christian was an embarrassment to their sensitivities.

"Jim, I don't want to lobby. I want to be a political consultant." Big Jim dropped another bird. The dogs were much happier.

"Shit, you *are* a political consultant, go read your door." The conversation was interrupted for ten minutes while Jim shot seven more doves and Christian pointed his gun in the air and fired four more times simply to be sociable. Finally, wet with sweat and covered with tiny feathers, Jim sat on a bale of dry hay and took one of the flasks out of the canvas bag. Bright blue against gold of hay, bright green boots against dark greens of grass, framed by white and blue sky. An obscene painting. He took a huge swallow, wiped the lip on the sleeve of his pajamas, and handed it to Christian, who also took a huge swallow of the toddy of bourbon, crushed mint, lemon juice, and simple syrup. It burned down into his stomach and he took another long swallow. It felt even better. Big Jim watched him out of the corner of his eye while he searched for doves. The dogs lay at his feet.

"Jim, I have a plan that will make me a famous consultant and will make you a lot of money." Big Jim belched, took another swallow from the silver flask, and handed it back to Christian.

"I'm going to run Hugh Conklin for the U.S. Senate." Big Jim choked on his toddy and coughed for a full minute. Then he laughed until tears streamed down his cheeks as he walked around the bale of hay, shooting his shotgun wildly into the air with the dogs barking and running hysterically through the field. Jim loved a joke.

Christian was at his best. His marriage and his professional career were hanging in balance. It took a lot of explaining and the remainder of the two flasks to convince Jim.

"Jim, just do some math. Tell me how many votes it could take to come in fourth in a ten-man field."

"Not many."

"Well. What if we used phone banks and organizations outside Baton Rouge where they don't know Hugh and persuaded just enough people for a fourth-place surprise. My plan is to take an impossible candidate in a crowded field and exceed expectations. That's all."

Jim shot a dozen birds and then a smile crept across his face. "Tell me some more."

Christian explained his theories of voter motivation and targeting. Jim liked little stories, so Christian used one of his favorites out of Greek mythology, Marathon. He explained his "Cottonwood Plan" of surprise. Jim liked the idea of the troops watching the superior Persian army from the hillsides and their rush to victory. He almost cried when he learned of the little runner who beat the boats to Athens to warn the home guard. He wanted more of the story and sat in wonder as Christian told him about the light armor and short knives and the Athenian surprise that changed warfare. He liked the final score, 6,400 Persians to 192 Athenians.

"Shit son, that's a better score than the sixty-to-zero LSU win over Tulane." Jim also liked the story because he didn't like Persians. He thought they charged too much for their old rugs and had a suspicion that they were really Arabs and Jim knew that Arabs were competitors for his oil business.

"So you gonna sneak up on a bunch of candidates, finish strong, and surprise the hell out of everybody?"

Christian nodded. "And you are going to make huge bets on the candidate because you will have information no one else has." Jim looked into the sky, thinking about betting a poker hand in the blind, all of the aces hidden. And somehow now it had the flavor of beating some Arabs. He smiled.

Luck is part of the play of the gods. It is the bait that is dangled and caught just often enough to keep their game interesting. On this day Christian was to be favored. Big Jim had won more than $100,000 in the card game with the oilmen. His greatest satisfaction, though, was that the last and largest pot was won with a pair of twos in a bluff against two pairs of tens and sevens. To win with nothing always made Jim happy.

"College Boy, you got a good plan. We could have us some fun. But you can't run that drunk. You gotta get somebody who'll stay sober."

"Jim, Hugh is the perfect fool. Think how easy it will be to place a bet." Yes, Jim agreed, Hugh Conklin seemed the perfect fool. But it took the rest of the night to convince Big Jim to bankroll the first part of the mythical campaign. Christian was over one hurdle. Now he had to sober up Hugh Conklin. Some people in Louisiana that day thought they heard great thunder. In fact, it was a group of amused gods slapping their thighs.

Back in the house, Christian helped Big Jim cook dove sauce picante. He browned the thirty doves after dipping them in a mixture of black and red pepper, garlic powder, and flour. As they were ready he drained them on brown paper bags. In the cooking oil and flour that remained he made a dark gravy. Cajuns call this mixture *roux* and it is the base of most of their food. Seconds before it would have burned, he added seven onions, green peppers, small tobasco peppers, and a full bulb of chopped garlic. He simmered the concoction until the onions were clear and added hot seasoned tomatoes from a can, and large sliced tomatoes. Rice steamed in a pot nearby.

The frying doves had made a scattergun pattern across the pajamas, and the St. Christopher medal wept with dripping grease. Big Jim added the doves to the mixture and simmered them while he counted out fifty thousand dollars to Christian on the kitchen table from a pile of bills that he had thrown on a table in the entranceway the night before. The $107,000 had become $104,000 after the driver helped himself to one thousand, the cook to five hundred, and the maid to as much as would fit in her apron pocket. Susie had been in the money, too, but only to convert small bills into hundreds. Like all whores, she had a fascination with one-hundred-dollar bills.

Jim held a dove and sucked the meat off the wings. "College Boy, I want you to report to me every week. I got a big investment in this project. If you don't sober Hugh up, you agree to go into the lobby business. Right?"

"Right," Christian muttered.

The next morning a small homosexual measured for draperies to cover the nude windows and Darleen forgave Christian for being at Big Jim's so long. It was time to begin "Cottonwood." After a night and morning of carnal pleasure, Christian left his loving wife and set out to find Hugh Conklin. What he found didn't give him any confidence, but he had known it would be tough.

**6** The architect was looking for timber. But Hugh Conklin seemed to have an unlisted life. There was no phone number and no known residence. Christian's best lead had come from the bar at the Capitol House Hotel where the political appointees and hacks hung out for endless hours while accepting public money. "He conducts his business from the cafeteria of the capitol building. Be sure you ask him about equal rights for midgets."

Christian wasn't the only man looking for Hugh Conklin. Hugh Conklin was looking for Hugh Conklin. Hugh looked into the same mirror every morning and shaved, brushed his teeth, combed his hair, and swore off drinking. He wanted to change the man in the mirror. He wanted that man to stop drinking and to manage his hair. He had as much trouble with the hair as the drinking. The cowlick in back never stayed down. For a few seconds, or until Hugh could get away from the mirror, it would stay down if it was completely wet. A few seconds later it would assert itself and stand up, so that Hugh Conklin once again looked like Hugh Conklin.

Today was the day Hugh was to quit drinking. Every day was the day Hugh was to quit drinking. His theory was to taper off by cutting down to a pint and then a half-pint. He reasoned that if he had a large bottle, he would drink that bottle and, therefore, far more. If he had a small bottle, he would drink far less. When he decided this, he called Senator LeBlanc's office and asked the new administrative assistant (he had been there ten years) to change his monthly case to half-pints. When the assistant, who was beginning to show the signs of too much alcohol himself, told Senator LeBlanc about the change, he turned in his swivel chair and looked at the dome of the capitol. It tended to inspire him when he needed to dig a difficult solution from his depths.

"Send his case of half-pints this month and one next month and then quit. It's been ten years. The statute of limitations has run out on most of what Crazy Hugh knows, and besides that, who is going to believe that old sot? He's jumped too far into that bottle." The new assistant winced. He could see himself at the bus station on Friday mornings looking for his case. But he had quit. It had already been three days. He was very proud.

"How much you drink last night?" the senator asked.

"I been dry a month," the new assistant answered.

"Bullshit."

Hugh counted the forty-two empty slots in the box that sat on his kitchen cabinet. He was trying to calculate how many of the bottles per day he had cut down to. If the new shipment was due today, he had done well. If the shipment was due the next Thursday, he had done moderately well, and if the shipment was due in two weeks, he would not have done so well.

But because today was a hard-work day, he put a bottle in each back pocket. He took a third bottle, broke the seal, and poured it down in about four gulps.

The legislature opened today, and business would be brisk. All of his friends would be back in town, and they might have a drink and talk about politics.

A recent election had changed most of the faces. The new ones didn't know about Hugh's position or that he was a member of their society. And he didn't like to be known as the drunk with the cowlick. It was bad for business. He had to lobby them, he decided. Starting today, he was going to pick out the new legislators and lobby them just as he used to do. He was going to sell them on doing business with Hugh Conklin.

He reached into another box on the counter and filled his left pocket with gold plastic donkeys. Into his right pocket, he put a smaller number of gold elephants. He was proud that he didn't handle the elephants himself. He was a Democrat. The elephants were jobbed out to his assistant, Happy, the paraplegic newspaper vendor who always stationed himself just outside the capitol-annex front door.

Happy had been a Republican since he got his own newspaper delivery route. He had two little black kids delivering a neighborhood route while he held down the main office outside the capitol. Hugh was understanding about Happy being a Republican. He knew that when a business became successful, the owner always turned Republican. Hugh resolved, however, that he would not allow any success to spoil his chances of running for office as a Democrat. Hell, he was a leader. He had run for governor once, mayor once, and United States senator once. He was well known. He got sick in the Senate race and dropped out when Senator LeBlanc promised him the case of whiskey every month. When you didn't have to worry about a drink, you could get your life together. That was when Hugh went into the advertising-specialty business.

He returned to the bathroom to survey himself in the mirror one last time and gargle with Listerine. He dashed something on his face out of a blue bottle with Christmas ribbon wrapped around its neck and sprayed under his arms with Right Guard. He was annoyed that he had already put on his shirt but he reasoned that the spray would soak through and do the same good work. He shined his shoes against the back of his pants and tried not to notice that one of his socks was black and the other was brown. He resolved not to cross his legs and to keep his pants pulled down while he was dealing with the public. He carefully cut some dangling threads from his shirt collar and pulled his necktie up tightly so that the missing collar button wouldn't be noticed. Hugh had always been careful about the way he looked and smelled.

When he arrived at the capitol building, he followed a familiar routine. He went directly to the bullet-scarred wall where Huey Long had been shot. The lead from some of the bullets was still lodged in the marble. Other shots had simply gouged holes. Hugh put his head against the cool marble over one of the slugs and closed his eyes in prayer. He reasoned that his head was against a piece of the lead that had gone through Huey's body. It was truly a sacred place and Hugh could feel the vibrations from the huge building and imagine that it was electricity from Huey. "Huey, we ain't through yet. We gonna make every man a king. Talk to God for me, Huey. His servant waits his orders." He then ran his fingers over some of the holes, tears in his eyes, and walked down the steps to the basement.

Hugh stationed himself just inside the cafeteria door in the basement of the capitol. He poured two ounces of bourbon into his coffee and spread his wares out on the table in front of him. He then sifted through the small plastic packages to find the special donkeys that would stay in his pocket.

A fat, gray-haired man waddled over to Hugh's table.

"Good morning, Governor Conklin." They all called him that, he noted with some pride. "You got any of them special donkeys with the red ass?"

"I got some, Senator Bill, but you know they cost two-fifty 'stead of two dollars."

"You old thief. I know all you do is put fingernail polish on their ass."

"But artwork always costs more."

"Gimme two. You ought to go into the public-relations business, Governor. They fuck you over just like that." He pinned one on his coat.

"I've been thinking about it. You know, I know as much

about public relations as anybody around here. You really think I should?''

"Hell no," Bill answered. "You got to run for office—big office—and straighten this mess out. You got to run for U.S. Senator or Congress or president or something."

Everybody told Hugh that. He looked around to see if anyone else had heard the legislator say that. That's why he was drying out. He was going to get straight and run for office. Everybody supported him.

"Mr. Conklin, you through with your coffee?"

Hugh looked up at Billy Jack Carter, the old guard who had been reassigned to the capitol basement cafeteria.

"I got a little left."

"Miz Sara has asked that you leave now because you been here over an hour, and 'sides that, it's against the law to peddle in here." Hugh gathered himself indignantly and straightened in his chair.

"You tell Mizzzz Sara that I got least a dime's worth of coffee still in my cup. Have a special coffee with me, Billy Jack. I just made me some money."

"The Lord Jesus, my precious savior, does not allow me to drink, Mr. Conklin."

"I happen to know that Jesus was a drinking man himself," Conklin said.

"Maybe so, Mr. Conklin, but that was a different time when the drinking water wasn't pure and people had to do a little drinking for the stomach's sake."

"Well, what you think I'm doing? This here is for my throat. The pollution in Baton Rouge makes your throat as raw as hamburger. When I get elected, I'm going to shut down those chemical plants until they clean up the air."

"Mr. Conklin, that sure would be good. I get winded just walking up the capitol steps."

"Does your throat feel raw, Billy Jack?"

Billy Jack's throat did feel raw. His head hurt and his bunions were killing him. Earlier in the day he had dropped his pistol on his toe while demonstrating quick-draw to some schoolchildren on a tour. He was showing them the holes in the wall where Huey Long had been shot and was reenacting part of the scene when he dropped the pistol. Besides the pain, he had to give one of the kids two dollars to get his gun back. Years past, before he found the Lord, he would have taken a drink with Hugh.

"You sure that's not bourbon. I do have a little problem with my throat, but I promised my precious savior that I would never drink again."

"I admit that it comes in a bottle like bourbon, but when you mix it with coffee it's medicine. Also, your intent matters. If you drink to get drunk, to get a buzz, that's different than putting a little medicine on your raw throat. You go to the drugstore and look on the bottles. Most of 'em got alcohol in 'em. But we both know that you ain't drinking if you drink out of a bottle from the drugstore. In fact, Dr. Tichenor's antiseptic will drop you to your knees if you drink enough of it. But you won't find a preacher without a bottle of Dr. Tichenor's in the medicine cabinet. The Lord don't mind if they use it for sweet breath or for mouth sores. In fact, in the Bible it says, 'Physician, heal thyself.' It's intent that matters. You wash your throat out with some of this and the Lord will go right on working on real sinners. Billy Jack won't even get his attention."

Billy Jack looked across the room toward the cash register, where Miz Sara was sorting coins and filling small paper tubes. She counted each penny. Her massive behind seemed to swallow a shaky stool. He coughed and ran his fingers around the base of his throat.

"That pollution burns the paint right off my pickup. It used to be red but now it's kind of a shrimp color." He coughed again.

Hugh poured two inches of bourbon into a water glass. Not only did he not like to drink alone, he was by nature a generous man. He was sure that there was a god who equalized good acts against evil. For every drink he had offered, he had received a drink.

Billy Jack turned his back to Miz Sara, his massive belly extending over Hugh's table, and doctored his sore throat. Then he doctored his sore toe, his bunions, and began to minister to various aches and pains in other parts of his body. As his ailments disappeared he began to feel charity toward his physician. When he used to drink, Hugh would always hand him his bottle, even when it was down to the bottom. He remembered passing out once when he was on guard duty and Hugh hid him in the backseat of the squad car.

"Governor, you've always been a friend. I see these piss-ant legislators come in here and they don't care if I am sick or well. They never even buy me a cup of coffee. You share your, your medicine, and you never say a mean word about nobody, no matter how no-'count they are. You got to run for office so some of your friends can support you. We got to put you in the White House or even the governor's mansion. Hugh Conklin will be a great man like Huey Long."

Hugh poured the rest of the bottle into Billy Jack's glass. Again and again he heard the same thing. People wanted him to run for office. Even the legislators called him "governor."

Dr. Conklin and his patient sent Johnny Mack, the shine boy, for more medicine and moved their clinic to the sunny steps leading up to the capitol, where Billy Jack set up a prayer vigil and Hugh dozed. Tourists from Indiana gathered around the drunk, uniformed policeman and nervously laughed.

"Jesus, we ain't asking for a true miracle. We just need a little push to help Hugh here. Sweet Jesus, send us a sign that you still love Democrats best and make this man governor of Louisiana. And if you can't go that far, make him senator or president. Lord, Lord, Lord, president, president, president." At that point he fell to his knees weeping and began speaking in tongues. The Indiana tourists scattered and Hugh slept on.

"Ombly, sonbip, boosch. Kep touten, kep touten, kep touten. God, God, God, isn, isn."

Soon God sent a uniformed policeman to remove Billy Jack from the steps. The totally healed policeman was sent home, nestled in the arms of a merciful God.

# 7

Hugh lived at campaign headquarters. At least that's what the sign said on the front door of his old house. If one looked closely, under the white paint at the top of the sign, it read faintly "Goldwater for President Campaign Headquarters." Hugh had found the sign and altered it to eliminate any suggestion of anything Republican. He added "Conklin" so that it read "Conklin Campaign Headquarters" and used it to cover a broken window in the front door. Burglars had broken the door glass to gain entry but were obviously so shocked by what they found, they left a nice toaster and a black-and-white television set.

The two-bedroom shack was owned by an old aunt. Hugh would have sold it for whiskey years before, but she held tightly to both her house and her life so that he could not inherit it. If the house had gone on the market, it would have been torn down to make room for a parking lot badly needed by the telephone company down the block. It was worth little, but the location was excellent for a drunk. It was close to a cut-rate liquor store, three bars, and the Salvation Army. All the furniture of any value had been sold, so only a single table with one chair remained in the kitchen. Ten straight-backed folding chairs, remnants of a burned church, sat in the living room with an overstuffed sofa that was undernourished because of the holes in its cushions and arms. There was a Salvation Army cot in the front bedroom and a low bed in the back bedroom that Happy could roll into from his wheelchair.

Years before, Hugh had built a ramp up to his high front porch with boards stolen from a construction site. The ramp had been built so that Hugh could hold a political meeting with Happy and his route boys. Hugh had reasoned that he couldn't afford advertising in the newspaper, but if he controlled the newsboys, he could have them insert fliers into the pages before they delivered the papers.

Happy came to the meeting pushed by three young black boys and stayed to live. Together, Hugh, Happy, and the three boys fashioned the bed after several more trips to the construction site. One of the young black boys was caught stealing a board. He led the policeman and the construction foreman to the house. The large, white boss demanded the return of the number-one-grade redwood. When the policeman rushed the den of thieves and found old Happy, crazy Hugh, and two sweating newsboys building a bed for a cripple, he gave them a five-dollar campaign contribution and left.

The enraged construction man returned with a helper the next day and began to dismantle the ramp. The policeman returned and arrested both of them. They spent several hours in jail, charged with assault.

It was a pleasant life for the two men. In the afternoons they sat on the old front porch drinking. At least Hugh drank. Happy smoked marijuana. He had been introduced to the weed by his black delivery boys. It was perfect. It was cheaper than wine, and he didn't have to compete with Hugh for the bottle. Marijuana didn't tempt Hugh. So Happy sat enveloped in smoke, listening to Hugh talk about politics. Because of his thick, white hair and beard and irregular bathing habits, Happy always smelled like a wet, burned rope. In the mornings, the motorized wheelchair was followed down the sidewalk by a wisp of smoke. In the afternoons, it often ran at will until it dumped Happy against some tree or curb. Blacks in the neighborhood would apprehend the runaway chair and put Happy back in it.

Happy and Hugh had a special place in the neighborhood social order. They were honored white guests in a black neighborhood. No white could walk between North and Twenty-second without being mugged or robbed except for Hugh and Happy. They, in fact, had an armed guard of Black Panthers. It was nice, the blacks thought, to have two whites worse off than they. And beside, Happy was an equal opportunity employer.

Hugh tried Happy's new vice but found it unappealing. It didn't burn the stomach like whiskey, and it made him cough. Hugh had never smoked, and he found it difficult to force the smoke into his lungs. And even when he did, it simply put him to sleep. There was no substitute for whiskey unless it was politics.

And politics was much on Hugh's mind. He and Happy handed the business card back and forth that he found in his pocket early that morning. He vaguely remembered something about Big Jim's college boy talking to him while he was conducting business for the Superior Specialty Company. Happy occasionally held it up to the naked light bulb as though looking for a secret message and he would then reverently hand it back to Hugh, who would put it back into his shirt pocket.

"I think he wanted to handle my campaign," Hugh said for the sixth or seventh time. Happy relit his joint and inhaled deeply. Hugh took a sip from a pint of Four Roses. He had quit drinking but he was tapering off to calm his nerves. The sun was red and smoky behind the oil refinery next to the river. The afternoon was warm and smelled of crepe myrtle and wisteria and marijuana. It was a moist, sticky smell that enveloped the front porch of the shack. A large cottonwood in the front yard shaded the porch. Crickets began to tune up for the night and a boat on the Mississippi signaled two long blasts to indicate to an approaching boat that it was moving to the right of the channel. The two men were quiet, Happy thinking about days with legs and Hugh about holding high office.

Dark came. Hugh looked down at the bottle and found it comfortably half-full. Quitting drinking had been easy. He had simply needed a reason, a plan. When he ran for U.S. senator, he had not even remembered qualifying for the race. Later he learned that some drinking buddies from the Capitol House Hotel had put up the filing fee and had gone with him to qualify. The race had been a series of disasters. Twice he had been thrown into the drunk tank. Another time he had crashed the League of Women Voters' debate and had been arrested. Representative Coon Laurent had told him it would be great publicity and statewide television coverage to crash the debate and had even driven him to New Orleans. He staggered into the Jewish Civic Center and positioned himself between League President Dorothy Mae Clandish and Senator Ashton LeBlanc while reading from a text supplied by a public-relations man who hung out in the Hunt Room at the hotel.

He was arrested as he screamed for equal rights for midgets. It was the only time in his life he had received a standing ovation from a large group. Though he knew that he had had too much to drink when he joined the debate, there was still a warm glow of accomplishment when he remembered the hundreds of people applauding and screaming for more. During the next week his picture had been in all of the newspapers and that part of the debate program shown on all of the news programs. On election day he had received almost fifteen percent of the vote, only two percent less than the Republican. Though he had not heard much comment about the campaign for several years, he still considered it a miracle of strategy that he had received 112,000 votes and had spent less than sixty dollars. The planning had been done by his friends in the Hunt Room. Together they wrote speeches on the backs of cocktail napkins and collected money for bus tickets to send Hugh to the political events around the state. It was a grand feeling to have them drive him to the Greyhound bus station, hand him a return ticket and a couple of bottles of Four Roses.

"Hugh, you got 'em on the run. Give that old thief LeBlanc hell. All I hear everyplace we go is how your campaign is coming on. You gonna ride this bus to glory. One day we'll be sitting in the Hunt Room watching the TV and there you'll be arm in arm with the president of the United States of America, giving him advice on stuff. We'll all say that we played a part in changing America and the Free World. March on, Hugh. March on."

Two years later, the campaign for governor had not gone so well. He had tried the same campaign tactics, but his aunt had convinced Hypolite Landry, the coroner, to lock him in Pineville Sanitorium for three months. He practiced his campaign speeches on the patients there and had honed his skills considerably, but when he was released he got sidetracked at Little Al's in Tangipahoa Parish for a couple of days and the campaign was over before he could find a ride back to Baton Rouge. Still, though, with the bad publicity and all, he had received seventeen thousand votes. He concluded that there was a hard core of Conklin supporters out there that varied between five and fifteen percent.

After the governor's race, he had a long sit-down with himself and reasoned that perhaps he could never be elected to high office in an era that requires so much money. Senator or governor were offices that were growing out of reach. The guys in the Hunt Room were never good for more than a few bucks. Happy was his largest contributor but could only come up with about fifty dollars at one time out of his tip jar. He decided he could dream no higher than legislator. They weren't very smart and Hugh had watched them work for years. They simply voted for the bills that paid the best.

But Hugh didn't want the money. He just wanted people

to be nice to him. He wanted to have conversations on the phone and occasionally give an order. He wanted his own desk in Huey's building with his name sitting on it. His name would be in the papers, and people would want to buy him drinks. . . . No . . . no . . . he would never drink again, but it would be nice to have people offer. And, Hugh said quietly to himself, I'm gonna kick a little ass. Hugh painted mental pictures of himself crushing some people who had once slighted him.

Hugh took several sips from the bottle and felt his pocket again for the card. The corners were getting worn but it still said,

Christian Ahab Simmons
Political Consultant
Southern Campaigns a Specialty

Sometimes wishing for a thing is better than getting it. Life was always a future campaign to be talked about and planned. Every time he walked into the Hunt Room, the boys would ask him about his campaign.

"Governor, I heard just last night a couple of upscales talking about how you ought to run for something. And these weren't no rumdumbs. These was quality people. Drove a Cadillac as long as this block."

Hugh often heard this sort of comment in the Hunt Room. That was one reason he went in—that, and the free drinks the group at the center table always bought.

The fat public-relations man for the highway department nudged the man to his left. "You know what they was talking about, Hugh? They was talking about how midgets don't get the respect they deserve."

The group nodded reflectively. It was always that way. Hugh reasoned, when he could reason, that they perhaps made too important an issue out of midgets. But they said he could easily expand his position on midgets to a position on all short people. Lately, the conversation in the Hunt Room concerned the height limits to qualify as a short person. Wilford Thibodaux offered that the official height had to be one grown into instead of shrunk into. He reasoned that some elderly people had shrunk and should not qualify as a true short person.

When the group at the center table saw Hugh come into the bar, they would launch into a conversation that appeared to have been going on for hours. "Damn it, Wilford, I think we can't go an inch over five feet. Oh, hello, Governor, you got to come over here and hep us. It's your campaign."

Later they would buy him drinks and get him to stand on a table and recite the midget speech from what they now called the "Great Debate."

Hugh took another shallow sip of the Four Roses. The card was tangible. The resulting campaign would be real. He had been trying to stare the question out of the night sky. It lay hidden around the Big Dipper. He didn't want to face the answer to the question that could end his dreams forever. The two men sat quietly staring at a distant celestial puzzle. While Hugh flirted with the question, Happy flirted with the answer. He could see it written across the sky. People who live together begin to have a common thought frequency.

"I got about two thousand dollars in the bank to pay him," Happy answered the unspoken question.

Hugh didn't hear. He snored lightly, the cane-bottomed chair still leaning against the wall, pointing Hugh toward the stars. And that night the stars seemed to shine brightly on campaign headquarters.

Later in the night, Christian drove down the street searching for the house but didn't see the two men screened by darkness and the huge cottonwood. He stopped on the corner and lit a cigar. Two dark figures in sweatsuits leaned menacingly against the corner light pole. They walked over and leaned against the fender. The largest of the two put his foot on the hood. "How you get in that little car?" he asked.

"No," the other one said. "The question be, how you get out that little car?"

"Shit, man, you don't know fuck about little cars. You use a can opener like this." The largest of the black men opened a spring-loaded switchblade knife and walked the length of the car with the knife slicing into the paint. Christian reached under the seat and pulled out the pistol, cocked it with two thumbs, and leveled it at the black man with the knife. In the quiet night, the click of the hammer seemed as loud as a rifle shot and the two would-be felons began backing away. Christian stood and kept the gun pointed at them until they turned and ran down the street. He then sat down and lit his cigar. His hands didn't shake. The Cuban cigar tasted great. From that night on, when the little white car was parked in front of Hugh's house, it was never abused or its driver threatened. They didn't remember the pistol. They remembered the eyes of the man who held it. "He be crazy," they said. They confused crazy with desperate, but is there truly a difference?

**8** Christian finally found Hugh slumped on Massachusetts. Huey Long had built the capitol with forty-eight steps—one for each state. The names were carved into the steps according to the order in which they had come into the Union. So Hugh was sitting near the bottom in the first thirteen. He signaled Christian over with his hand.

"I'm Hugh Conklin, and I want to talk to you about how I can help you while you are in Baton Rouge for the legislative session. Ask around. They all know me here. They'll tell you that I always help my customers."

"Mr. Conklin, I'm Christian A. Simmons. You must have me confused with somebody else."

"You're not a new legislator?"

"No, but we've met. I'm Big Jim's college boy."

"You wrote that story?"

"Yes."

"You ever have the whore?"

"Of course not."

"I tried, but I couldn't get it up."

"I've come to talk politics with you."

"If the boys from the Hunt Room sent you, tell 'em I ain't decided on the height limit yet. I've been praying on it."

Christian was perplexed, but he was also a man with a perverse sense of curiosity. "What do you think?"

"Well, I know you can't be a midget unless you less than four feet tall. That tall, rangy feller who hangs out with Billy Shakes thinks you can be four-feet-six and be a midget."

Christian hid a smile. "Why does it matter if a midget is four feet or four-feet-six?"

"Well, Wilford Thibodaux says that the six inches will raise my constituency by hundreds of thousands."

Christian decided this conversation was worth saving until he was at least half as drunk as Hugh. "We'll talk about midgets later. Right now I want to talk to you about running for office, a big office."

"Everybody wants me to run." Hugh measured the contents of the bottle and took two short ones while Christian watched. He put the bottle gently on the steps.

"I'm not here to talk. I'm here to start a campaign. I want to work for you. We are going to elect you to office."

"For what office?"

"Does it matter?"

Hugh thought for a minute while looking at Huey Long's statue in the park across the parking lot. He had once wanted to be governor, now he was willing to be anything. Huey Long whispered to him that as a man grows older he has to compromise and temper his dreams. Ambitions of being rich change to ambitions of being comfortable. Comfortable changes to secure. New becomes tattered. Young become old. Shoes shined on the back of pants legs still had holes. To ignore the holes was to have cold feet. The realism of cardboard in the shoe was better than the arrogance of pretending the hole didn't exist. Those were the lessons of age. Once being an assistant to a senator wasn't enough for Hugh. Now, being the custodian for the assistant to the senator would be a dream realized. "Dreams change," Huey Long whispered to Hugh. "I died because I wouldn't change my dreams. I was a stone wall and not a twig."

Hugh looked back at the young man and sadly shook his head. "No, it don't matter." But even the old drunk's dreams were still real enough and fragile enough to shatter around Huey's feet. Brittle dreams of being governor traded for a chance to be elected to anything. He repeated, "No, it don't really matter. Just help me, College Boy." The last words were choked.

Now it had started. Christian saw that Hugh was too drunk to speak coherently. And Christian couldn't hear Huey Long. Hugh's pauses seemed distraction. But Christian thought he saw a tear building in the corner of Hugh's eye. A whiskey tear, he told himself, and wrote a note for his new candidate on the back of his business card as a reminder. When he left, Hugh was sitting on Massachusetts with his head between his knees. Christian was pleased with what he had found. The Plan would work only with someone so irredeemable. For the first time in his life, Hugh was almost perfect for something.

The prayers to Huey had worked. That was the break he needed. The other politicians had gone on to be state senators and governors while Hugh sold donkeys with the red ass. He knew it wasn't right but Hugh believed that God evened things out. Huey had talked for him. He knew that when it came his time, he would be elected to something. It had been his only dream. In Sunday school Hugh learned that God was good and rewarded kindness with kindness. Until now, he simply thought he had not done enough to please that god of the ballot box. The college boy changed that.

Oh, Hugh was not alone. There were those who believed in him and campaigned on his behalf year round. There was Happy; Edmund and Matsu, Happy's black newsboys; the almost champion fighter, Sonny Clinton; and Hugh's aunt, who gave him campaign funds occasionally. That was a fair political organization that covered almost the entire political spectrum, Hugh reasoned.

Hugh sat on Massachusetts another hour considering his good fortune and sucking on the last of Billy Jack's medicine.

Tomorrow he had to get sober. He didn't even notice when the legislators passed him. His time had come and he had to make the necessary changes. He had waited until now. The drinking would have to stop. It really wasn't necessary to stop until now, and Hugh had put it off until it was really necessary. Now it was necessary and he knew he could quit.

"Governor," State Senator Bill called, and shook Hugh's shoulder.

"I just had my eyes closed so I could think better."

"Sure, and so you could get an even tan out here in the sun."

"It's getting dark."

"Governor, I need some more of those donkeys with the red ass."

"I'm out of business. I'm fixing to get into your line of work—guvment. Ain't going to sell donkeys or elephants no more. I'm going to write to the Superior Company and resign as their southern representative."

The fat senator stood on Vermont looking down at Hugh. He was only slightly more sober or less drunk than Hugh. But being drunk and being a southern representative for the Superior Specialty Company, and being drunk in the service of the state's people were different. And since Hugh had been anointed by the college boy earlier in the day, he had begun to assume some of the arrogance of the state senator. Hugh Conklin was a man in transition.

"Governor, we are going to be sorry to lose your merchandise. However, I am sure you know that you can count on the support of the Democrats if you get the nomination. Now, if you have any of them donkeys left, I could use them for the good of the party. Ida and her girls want to wear them to the annual legislative shrimp-boil tonight. You figure that each of them girls is going to fuck six or seven legislators tonight. That means your donkeys will be seen by thirty or forty of the more important political figures in the state. That's good for the party. In fact, in the name of the party, I will be happy to make a little donation to your campaign. It's men like you who make us great.''

Hugh reached into his pocket and small plastic donkeys spilled out over Massachusetts and fell down to Virginia. As he reached to scoop them up, he rolled down to Connecticut, where he fortunately fell into a comfortable fetal position and stayed. The state senator stole the remaining donkeys.

Hugh woke in a rain shower and staggered to the back of Huey Long's statue and grave where he relieved himself. Except for that single, powerful beam that shone from the top of the capitol to light Huey and Hugh, the grounds were dark. He looked up at Huey illuminated by the powerful light and made what resembled the sign of the cross. It wasn't exactly right because Hugh was a Baptist but meant the same thing. He was having trouble remembering what the college boy had told him. Was he to run for governor or city council or the legislature or what? He knew he had to remember because their campaign was to begin the next day. In his concentration he forgot to zip his pants. When he stumbled into the legislative shrimp-boil, even Ida's girls were shocked.

Two state policemen, on special assignment to the governor, lifted Hugh by his hands and feet and threw him from the American Legion steps to the lawn five feet below. They were kind men, though, and threw him into an azalea bush that cushioned his fall.

That bush was the site of the start of Hugh's campaign. The next morning he dragged himself out of the bush, broke off one of the purple flowers for his coat, zipped his pants, and went to look for his new start.

**9**
Hugh stayed semisober and in a state of advanced readiness for five days. He wasn't exactly tapering off, because his consumption leveled off at about a fifth of Four Roses each day and a half. Every morning he would wet down the cowlick, carefully button his vest, brush lint from his old suit, and sit on the front porch to wait for Christian Simmons. He kept practicing calling him Christian instead of College Boy. "Hello, Christian, how are you, sir?" He said it several times, always extending his hand. A small child from the neighborhood saw him and ran in panic down the street. "Old Mr. Crazy Hugh was talking to gostes."

He hid his bottle in a paper sack next to the cane-bottomed chair because, as a serious candidate, he didn't want to be seen drinking. Occasionally he would take from his vest pocket a bottle of "No Tell" breath freshener and hide the smell. Actually it made a new and different smell.

On the fifth day Happy could detect despair in his friend. He was on the front porch, vested, tied, and combed, but drunk and sad. The bottle was out of its wrapper and empty. Happy never expected the consultant to appear. The five days had been great but he dreaded the fall. He reasoned that the rise of expectations would make the fall harder and his friend would be doomed to a life without illusion and without hope.

And illusion was the stuff of their lives. Happy maneuvered his chair close to Hugh's and shook his arm.

"Hugh, we got to talk some business."

"Is Big Jim's college boy here?"

"No, but I saw him at the newsstand. He said for us to go ahead without him and he'd get to us as soon as he could."

"He didn't forget?"

"We got to call a meeting of the committee. I'll get my staff together and put out the word for tonight. Be good to start it early before they drunk."

Hugh staggered to his feet and began arranging the living room for the meeting. He put ten chairs in a half circle around the old table that he dragged in from the kitchen. From a box under his bed he pulled out an old hammer that he placed on the table. Next to the hammer he put an old copy of *Robert's Rules of Order* and a glass of water. Then he stood in the doorway and surveyed the scene. He needed some campaign posters to really make it look good. He made a note to take the poster matter up with the committee. Happy sat in his wheelchair at the end of the small table. In front of him was a hand-lettered tent card that said "Chairman." Sonny Clinton, the almost champion fighter, had nominated him. It had been a beautiful experience that had made Happy weep. Sonny's tent card said "Action Chairman." It had already been decided that he would be in charge of protection. He had a nerve condition from one too many blows that made him constantly jerk his head to the side. On occasion he would slap his balled right fist into his open left palm, making a loud sound. Two of Happy's newsboys shared the sign "Co-Chairmen, Colored Community." Happy had made a moonscape of his end of the table, attempting to maintain order with his carpenter's hammer.

"Mr. Chairman." Sonny Clinton raised his hand. "Mr. Chairman," he yelled three times, waving his hand high above his head.

Happy banged his hammer against the table. "Somebody else got the floor right now, Sonny."

"Mr. Chairman, truthfully and respectfully, I don't give a shit. I got something to say." After a threat of violence, the floor was given to Sonny Clinton. He had scar tissue on his ears, over his eyes, and his nose looked like a mistake. His arms were the size of legs and he had a crew cut. He wore a New Orleans championship belt buckle that was almost swallowed by his fleshy stomach. He hooked both of his thumbs into his belt to talk.

"All this meeting has talked about is queers and midgets and niggers. And boys, I don't mean nothing personally by 'niggers,' so don't get you back up. Sure, I think we gotta have a queer on the committee, and a midget too. But I think we missing the important stuff. Me and Happy has been keeping up with what's going on in the world. Every day Happy reads to me from the newspaper. I could read it myself but my eyes ain't so good, so don't none of you cocksuckers get the idea I can't read or I'll beat the shit out of you."

Happy rapped the hammer on the table. "Sonny, you got a point to make, make it. I gotta pee and I ain't gonna sit here all night. We know you can read if you want to."

"Well," Sonny continued, glad to get out of the literacy question, "if you run for one of those Washington jobs, you got to talk about bombs and guns and Russians and shit like that. That cocksucker Nixon got kicked out but we talking about midgets. The Cambodian Japs take one of our U.S. of A. ships and we talking about queers."

"So what's your point, Sonny?" Happy pounded a couple of times for effect.

"Well, Mr. Chairman, we just sitting around here jacking off. We don't even know what Hugh's running for."

"The door." The two newsboys giggled.

The prizefighter shook his fist at the two boys, who winced, and continued, "No, we heard that some college boy—"

"Christian Ahab Simmons, Southern Political Consultant," Hugh corrected.

"Well, some cocksucker we never heard of is gonna come in here and work for us. Mr. Chairman, I respectful ask, where is the cocksucker?"

To relieve the tension at the meeting, Hugh produced two bottles of Thunderbird wine and one bottle of unnamed white port that he passed around the table. Even the two young newsboys took their turn. Happy passed but lit a joint and the two newsboys reached into their socks and lit up joints rolled in blue paper. Clinton staked out the white port for himself after it made one round and put it between his feet on the floor.

Hugh excused himself and went to the kitchen, where he took two long pulls from his Four Roses. He didn't think it proper for the committee to see their candidate drinking. When he returned to the meeting room, Sonny Clinton had resumed command of the floor and was telling the story about his Louisiana title contention.

"So this spick moves to my left and I slip a couple of his blows. I tie him up and move in close. His breath smelled like pepper. I took the laces of my glove and cut the little bastard's left eye like with a saw. When he started bleeding, I stepped back and hit him in the neck. You should of seen that little bastard's eyes. He was covered with blood. The ref stepped in—"

Happy began to pound the table with his hammer. "Sonny, what's this got to do with the campaign?"

"Well, it's got this much to do with it, Mr. Chairman. If that college-boy cocksucker don't show up soon, I'm gonna make him look like that Mexican."

Happy began hammering as the two newsboys sparred with soft and then harder jabs until they were rolling on the floor trying to beat each other's heads into pulp. One of them had started as Sonny and the other as the Mexican, but they had forgotten their original intention and had begun a fight over a quarter tip that had been a point of contention since early afternoon. That was when Christian Ahab Simmons, Southern Political Consultant, finally found the house and stepped through the open front door.

He was staggered. The room was heavy with marijuana smoke. Quart wine bottles were being passed around, an old, white bearded cripple sat at the end of a table with a carpenter's hammer. Two black boys were bashing each other's heads. And a big man who looked like he had been assembled from spare parts staggered over to him and grabbed him by the tie.

"You fuck up one more time and be late on us and I'm gonna make you look like that Mexican." Of course Christian was confused. He had only dropped in for a visit.

"Order, order, order." Happy banged his hammer. Hugh began walking toward Christian but was tripped by the rolling boys and fell heavily at his feet. He didn't bother to stand up. He simply extended his hand. "Hello, Christian, how are you, sir?" Christian disengaged himself from Sonny and sat at the table. The first thing he did was take a long pull out of one of the wine bottles when it was offered. He then held up both hands until the room was silent. Hugh still lay on the floor.

"Gentlemen, I have come here to elect Hugh Conklin to the United States Senate. Will this meeting come to order?"

# 10

Hugh's house squatted under the shade of a cottonwood so old that as a child he had sat in its branches. The
house was like the tree, neglected and unnoticed, waiting for
natural forces to end its life. The thirsty cottonwood sucks
the moisture from the ground around it, causing the earth to
contract. The front porch of Hugh's house sagged into the
depression created by the huge tree. A snaggle-toothed picket
fence had been swallowed by the bark on the street side.

The last of the white paint had flaked off the house years
before. The old house still stood only because it was built of
the almost indestructible, ancient Louisiana cypress, a prim-
itive species that could be pulled strong and whole from
muddy bayou depths after one hundred years underwater. Cut
into lumber, it created a building material perfect for a people
who cared little for details of primer and brush.

The cypress is a noble tree.

Christian sat near the right wheel of Happy's chair and
dangled his feet off the front porch of campaign headquarters.
His face was in his hands. Darleen, her face frozen upward,
leaned against the edge of the wheelchair ramp. Only the
drifting marijuana smoke around her head and an occasional
leaf falling from the cottonwood kept the scene from being
an absurd still life. The approaching darkness had begun to

trigger streetlights, changing the scene to a blue-tinted black-and-white photograph too bizarre even for Diane Arbus.

And there was a man in the tree.

Twenty feet above them, Hugh straddled a limb and hugged the trunk, his cheek pushed against the rough bark. He was weeping.

"College Boy, you got to help me. I can't remember past the part where man is just fucked up." Hugh's plea was punctuated with sobs.

"You been working him too hard," Happy snapped at Christian, who didn't have the energy to look up. "He's been sober a week until you made him learn that speech."

". . . if redemption was not possible, then man would be little more than a drifting leaf on a river of endless . . . endless . . . College Boy, help me, I get all fucked up at the endless part." The leaves hid Hugh enough that it often sounded as if the tree were talking.

Christian was having trouble with reality. It was difficult for him to look up into the tree.

Do you want new shoes.
Your daddy ain't coming back.
I left two dollars for bread. . . .

He understood the comfort of the cradle of high limbs. And he felt for the little man in the tree. He felt. Christian felt. And he was having trouble dealing with it.

Edmund had called to tell him his candidate for the U.S. Senate was stuck up a tree. "Mr. Crazy Hugh is caught like one of them cartoon cats up in a tree. Mr. Sonny and Mr. Happy say for you to come get him down."

Darleen, in yet another revival of effort to save her marriage, volunteered to help. And she was curious also. She had never met Hugh and Happy. Now that she had, she could not take her eyes off the weeping derelict in the tree.

"What's wrong with you, Christian? Do something."

"Give me a minute. I'll be fine. I'll work this out." Christian pulled himself erect and glared at Happy.

"Happy, this is the third time he's been drunk since we started the campaign. I've tried to help him. I took him to AA. I took all of his bottles. You even said you'd help. You're the campaign manager, you should take some responsibility." Christian had an angry bite in his voice.

"He needed to relax a little. He gets up in the morning and starts memorizing your speech and then the boys start drifting in for meetings. Every day's the same. Hugh's just wore out. 'Sides that, Sonny's a trial. Sonny's a terrible temptation. He's always got a bottle and I got to keep my eyes on him. When he's got a couple of bucks, he'll share his wine with anybody. He's a generous man. And Hugh don't like to tell anybody no. You should have my job trying to run my paper business and keep an eye on Hugh and all the committee. Sonny's asleep on the floor in the house. Right now I'm listening to him snore. When he quits snoring, my trouble starts all over again. I can only do so much."

"If redemption was not possible . . . if redemption was not possible . . . if redemption was not possible." Hugh sounded like a broken record on a slow-speed turntable.

"Hugh needed a little relaxation. We had a couple of toasts about the new starts on the paper route. We picked up ten new customers. That means twenty more voters. That means another five bucks a week for the campaign. We was just doing a little celebrating my good luck. 'Sides, he didn't have that much to drink. Sonny had done finished most of it."

"Happy, don't you want Hugh to be successful?"

"We was happy before you came here, College Boy. Hugh had a little biness, we sat here on the front porch in the afternoon. Now all he wants to do is go to Washington. He'll be up north and I'll be back in the shelter."

"How do we get him down out of the tree?"

"We can call the fire department," Happy said, and relit his joint.

"God, this is Hugh. I fucked up again. Your servant got drunk. I guess you know that, though, 'cause you can see me good from there. Put your hand here on my head and heal me of my sin. Take my burden away, God." Hugh slapped himself on the head. It must have hurt. He wobbled on his limb. "Help me this time and I'm going to your house Sunday."

"Who ran the senator up the fucking tree?" Sonny staggered from the house.

"He's always been a climber, Sonny. Remember that time he climbed all the way up Huey Long's statue to kiss his face." Happy brightened at the memory.

"Little cocksucker can climb a greased pole," Sonny added with admiration.

Christian looked up. "Sonny, do you know how to get him down?"

"Last time, I just climbed up there and tied him to the tree till he sobered up. Then he came down by himself. Where's my wine?"

"Hugh drank it," Christian responded.

"Then leave the little cocksucker in the tree. I hope he falls on his fucking head."

"You never gonna get to be boxing commissioner if Hugh gets killed falling out of the tree." Campaign Manager Happy had begun to deal with the situation. Sonny circled the tree, looking for a way to retrieve his future. A man could make real money on the boxing commission. And Sonny didn't know that it wasn't a federal appointment. The distinctions between state and federal office were blurred in his mind.

Darleen finally studied Christian's face. Her spell had been broken. "Could I see you for a moment?" she asked Christian, and walked toward the MG. He followed. She lowered herself into the driver's seat and closed the door. "I am glad I finally got to meet your candidate for the U.S. Senate. I feel much better now about the future of my children." She smiled sweetly, slowly pronouncing each word without using contractions. "U.S. Senate" sounded as though it were in italics.

Christian smiled and shrugged his shoulders. "At least I've got him treed."

There wasn't really much to laugh about. For three weeks he had attempted to keep Hugh dry so that he could put his plan into effect. He was losing the battle. He could see that now.

"Well, Mr. Political Consultant." Darleen spat out the words through her smiling mouth. "I'm glad I came with you. Now I know I'm secure and you really don't need a job. Now I know you're a completely crazy son of a bitch." She still smiled.

"I'll be home for dinner a little later."

"Then you'll eat alone, because I have plans."

"Something come up?"

"You might say something *will* come up." She pressed the words through her lips."

The engine roared and the little car vanished down the street. Only then did Christian realize he was stranded at campaign headquarters without his wallet or transportation. The big prizefighter was climbing out of the tree with Hugh over his shoulder. Happy was cleaning his fingernails with a pen knife, a joint hung from his lips. A wind began to rattle the parched leaves of the cottonwood. The campaign for the future of democracy was soon to be back on solid ground.

# 11

Hugh stood on a chair and gestured with his right hand. When he reached the point in the script where Christian had put a star, he paused, and wiped a tear from his eye, reestablished eye contact with this audience, and continued.

"If it were not possible for man to change, then it would be impossible for man to change things around him. All would be futile, and corruption would be left to breed corruption, mistakes would be left to become reality.

"Today I dedicate my life to making the world a better place. I will start with me. I would like to quote my favorite Scripture. I think it expresses what is in this corrupt heart of mine. It comes from Corinthians. 'When I was a child I spake as a child, I thought as a child: But when I became a man, I put away childish things.' I have put childish things behind me and put my fate in the hands of the Almighty. I need your hep. Please hep me."

Darleen began to applaud. Happy wiped a real tear from his eye and Christian sagged into one of the old chairs. Hugh had been dry for three weeks and Christian was ready to put the plan into effect. Darleen blew her husband a congratulatory kiss. There was silence so profound that the rustling of the cottonwood leaves outside sounded like applause. All eyes were on Christian. No one dared speak. Hugh finally cleared his throat.

"What do you think?" Hugh asked, looking down at his shoes.

"You did a nice job on the conversion speech, Hugh. It's a shame that it took you a month."

"We hoped you would take our campaign back over," Hugh said in a quiet voice. "I fucked up, College Boy. I can't drink. I know it. It's just like there's another person in me who lifts the bottle without my permission. Then he leaves me in the rosebushes with the hangover. I think I have that other person under control and I'm ready to do what's right."

"I swear to god, College Boy, Hugh ain't had a drink since he climbed the tree." Happy was pleading. Tears began to roll down Happy's face. " 'Sides, that was my fault."

"Want me to give the speech again?"

"Do it again, Hugh. Show College Boy how good we did."

"If redemption was not possible, man would be simply a drifting leaf on a river of despair. And if man—"

"Hugh," Christian held up his hand.

Darleen stood. "Christian, may I see you in the other room?" She walked into the kitchen. Christian followed. "How do you think we're doing?" she asked.

"I think I'm back in control. You go in and take their side in the argument. I'll surrender in about ten minutes." He followed her back into the living room.

"I'm sorry Hugh, Happy. I begged him to take your campaign but you can't really blame him. He has me and the children to think about. If you let him down, he would never recover. I want him to do it." Darleen was a wonderful actress. She cried and used long silences to accent her arguments.

Happy began to weep again. "I got two thousand dollars I can give you right now if you'll come back. Them's tips for a whole year."

"We're begging you, College Boy. I'll never drink again. I'll do everything you say."

Darleen's eyes were glazing, so Christian knew that he had made his point. "Happy, you get me the tip money. I'm going to hold it as an insurance policy. If Hugh even smells a cork, I keep the money. If he stays sober until election time, I'll give it back."

The money turned out to be somewhat of a problem. It was quarters, dimes, and nickels in cloth bags that Happy had hidden under his bed platform. The back of the MG sat solidly on its springs after the coins were loaded into its trunk.

But that was the new beginning. There were rehearsals and training for Hugh. The steering committee was given a difficult assignment and all of its members performed better than Christian could have hoped. Darleen began dropping by the shack twice a day to ensure that Hugh was sober and the committee was working. And Christian reported to Big Jim.

"Tell me again about the church, College Boy."

"Well, Jim, the fundamentalists believe in redemption. In one swoop we can clean up Hugh's image and get an organization. He goes forward to accept Christ and confesses some of his sins—"

"You gonna keep those people in church all week."

"—and we make him a model. They need cripples to cure, whores to reform, and Mexicans to leave the Catholic Church. It's sort of like fuel. One Mexican conversion away from the pope fuels them for a month. A drunk of Hugh's reputation will be worth three months."

"Shit, get me to go down that aisle on Sunday and the fuckers could retire. You a fucking genius, College Boy. When you get some free time, come out to the ranch and I'll get some girls for a party. I got a white black girl that you'll love. She ain't even high yeller, she's as white as you. Susie gave her to me for our one-year anniversary. I want to tell you, I'm thinking about tying the knot with Susie. She's one fine woman.'' Jim always had a soft spot in his heart for women of generosity and virtue.

The church was packed. Darleen and Christian quietly put Hugh on the back row after the first hymn. The auditorium seated about a thousand people. Banners hung from the balcony that wrapped around three sides announcing a statewide revival later in the year and reminding people that the Lord demanded a tithe of ten percent of gross before taxes. Banks of television cameras were positioned along the balcony and two were on tripods behind the choir. The hundred-member choir was flanked by a glass piano, an organ, three trumpet players, two electric guitars, and four violins. The preacher, song leader, education director, and assistant pastor all sat on a plush bench that wrapped around the pulpit. A red neon cross shone from the front of the podium. Except for the cross, the business end of the church was a sea of robes, all television blue.

Hugh was clean but tattered. His thirty-eight-inch pants were tucked in four places to accommodate his thirty-two-inch waist. His shirt was starched but the tips of the collar were frayed. His tie was drawn up into a tiny knot that didn't manage to hide his missing button. Both of his shoes had holes. The cowlick was temporarily held in place by oil and spray. That had been an accommodation to Hugh, who complained about the clothing. He looked like a derelict who had been cleaned up for a special occasion. Christian was proud of his work.

By the end of the third hymn, emotion was syrupy thick in the huge hall with hundreds shouting ''Amen'' and most holding their open palms toward heaven and swaying with the music. Eyes closed. Tears flowed. Darleen's face was flushed. Christian tapped his foot. Hugh's eyes grew misty and Christian began to think he might not need to create tears with the small bottle of glycerine in his coat pocket. Hugh could produce the real thing.

But Christian was not moved simply by the music. Seated down his aisle was the beautiful gift from Big Jim, Windy Dawn. She was in white and clutching a red Bible. When she sat, the skirt that buttoned down the front opened enough for Christian to see two inches of downy flesh and a whisper of lace at the top of her stockings. When she stood, she was one smooth, waving line from her throat to her shoes, broken only by the suggestion of hidden lace, snaps, and elastic. Christian sensed he was growing aroused and tried to turn his attention to the audience, the players on his stage.

The Reverend Tracy was a dynamo of energy when he began to speak. His voice would fall to a whisper and then shake the ceiling. His shirt and coat clung to his back. His face was contorted and wet. All that didn't appear affected was his hair. It stood rigidly at attention. And at once Christian's attention was distracted from his voyeurism back to the podium. There was a god and that god was smiling. The topic of the sermon was the "Prodigal Son."

Women wept and men screamed "Amen" when the father accepted his wayward son. Windy's nipples grew hard under the white dress. An older woman fainted and two ushers helped her stagger out of the auditorium. Her swoon induced six or seven more and the auditorium became bedlam. People began to screech in what sounded like Chinese and Arabic. Christian had studied the television shows and knew when the congregation began "speaking in tongues" it was the climactic moment and that soon people would begin running down the aisles to fall to their knees before the preacher and ask to be born again. He had to hit the seam between the crying and the saving. Hugh had to be first because it was customary to be given an opportunity to address the congregation about your divine revelation. The fundamentalists called it "witnessing." Hugh's witnessing was to be his first televised political speech.

The first notes of the invitation hymn began to override the weeping preacher and soon a hundred voices kicked in singing "Almost Persuaded." It took three jabs of the elbow to prompt Hugh to action. The third blow was so violent that the little derelict was breathless for moments before he could jog down the aisle and throw his arms around the preacher's neck. Christian was pleased to note that not only did he win the race to the podium, he froze action in the church. They knew that a historic conversion was about to take place.

"Something important is happening here." The preacher raised his hands. "Sing louder, open your hearts to the Lord. He is in this auditorium. Something remarkable has happened." While Hugh was a sobbing heap at his feet, the preacher raised his Bible to the ceiling and began shouting, "Thank you, Lord. Thank you, Lord. Thank you, Lord." Soon the congregation was shouting in unison, "Thank you, Lord." The building shook. The engineer turned up the power on the amps and the huge choir's voice began to swell.

Reaching behind his back, the preacher directed the choir to sing slower and softer. The audience was captivated by a sort of euphoric calm, punctuated by sobs and a few whispers of strange languages. Soon the preacher and the choir were back in control. He began to whisper, "Thank you, Lord, for this miracle." He turned his face down toward the audience. "The prodigal son has returned. Lying at my feet is a man who was only human garbage minutes ago. Now he is golden." The preacher lowered his voice even more and shoved the mike against his lips. "He was a victim of the devil and now he wants to become a soldier for Jesus. You have seen him drunk on sidewalks. Now you will see him exalted in the Lord's temple. I am going to let the prodigal son speak to you. Join me, Brother Hugh Conklin."

Hugh stepped up to the preacher and took the mike. He spoke to his shoes for the first minutes and then looked boldly at the audience. He was not missing a move.

"This morning I was thrown from my bed. There was a light in the room. A voice told me to clean my body and get ready to change the world. I was told to be at this church and to sit on the back pew. When I tried to turn my feet at the front door, away from here, I was tripped and fell. When I tried to rise, a force was on my neck that became less painful only as I crawled up your front steps. Now I am on my feet. And I want to give the devil back his medicine."

Hugh reached in his coat and extracted a two-thirds-full bottle of Four Roses. Christian studied the bottle from the back of the church. An inch or so seemed to have evaporated since their rehearsal the night before. Hugh sat the bottle on the podium, over the neon cross. The bottle became a red glow. "Praise God," a woman screamed, and fainted. The choir hummed "Almost Persuaded" and Hugh began his confession about a drifting leaf on a river of futility. Darleen put her hand on Christian's. Her eyes were wet. As they left the church, Christian slipped one of his business cards to Windy Dawn. He had plans for her.

Sunday. The Yanks won a spring game against the O's on television, seven thousand pounds of crawfish were captured in roadside ditches, the Mississippi rose three inches because of the thaw in Ohio, Cajun bands played, dancers danced, shrimp fried, hogs were butchered, *boudin* stuffed, hogs-head cheese molded, po-boys were wrapped in brown paper, beer cooled, politicians shook hands, lazy softball and tennis games were played. It seemed like every other Sunday in spring. But it wasn't. It was magic.

Hugh was dry. The members of the steering committee had executed their tasks perfectly and were basking in praise for the first time in their lives. Darleen threw her arms around Christian's neck and told him eleven times she loved him. And Christian spent an hour detailing his plan for the future, allowing her to read from the notebook where it was outlined.

With a grunt, Big Jim fell to one knee and proposed to Susie, who immediately went to a phone and called her madam, Ida, to resign. The preacher watched the replay of the morning's miracle and took only small change, a few hundred, from the day's collection. This Sunday was magic.

**12** Getting an appointment with the preacher had been as difficult as getting in to see Louisiana's governor during a legislative session.

After failing for a week, Christian called the preacher's wife, Flora, the beautiful woman he had met at the political party.

"Mrs. Tracy. This is Christian Simmons. You might remember me from—"

"Of course I remember you. You ate fifteen cupcakes." She laughed and Christian tried to imagine her. There was silence while he assembled what he considered the perfect woman.

"I'm kidding about the cupcakes."

"I need to see your husband, but he is terribly busy. I was wondering if you might ask him. He doesn't know me."

She did.

Two days later Christian was led through the auditorium to offices almost hidden at the back of the church complex. He clutched a brown envelope in his hands and settled into a white leather chair behind the huge oval glass desk.

Inside the envelope were five blowups of the preacher and a blond partner. Christian had remembered Windy Dawn's breathless comment about brother Tracy from the night Big Jim sent her over as a gift. As part of his Cottonwood Plan,

Christian assigned the committee to follow Brother Tracy. It was an assignment they relished. Within hours they had followed the preacher to room 22 of Carl's Motel in Slidell. The second week they followed him there again. The third week found the committee in the bushes with a camera. Through an opening in the curtains on the back window, they shot a roll of film of the preacher and a blonde. Her face did not show but the preacher was captured on 1000 ASA film in various poses of erotic bliss. Christian felt some virtue that the identity of the woman would be a secret. His experience with Windy Dawn had been pleasurable. He considered the pictures a bluff and tried not to think about what he would do if the ploy failed. He would never be able to raise enough money for the campaign without the churches' participation. But he didn't know if an act of vengeance would compensate for dreams lost. He had questions about releasing the pictures if the preacher refused to help.

Christian put his envelope on the desk. Its only other decoration was a pen-and-pencil set, a bloodred Bible that faced the guest chairs, and a sign reading "Preaching the Old Gospel for the Space Age." A small rocket ship was attached by a fine wire and hovered over the sign. The room was all white except for the glass tables that appeared to float over the carpets. A huge red neon cross fit between two windows and clashed with the stained glass.

A toilet flushed and the preacher, zipping his pants, stepped into the room. A local television story had claimed that the bath fixtures were solid sterling and gold.

Brother Tracy didn't look like a preacher. His hair was a little long and he wore suits that were somewhere between conservative and hip. On this day he wore a light blue suit with dark blue stitching. The flap of the coat's top pocket fastened with a mother-of-pearl snap. His sleeves had a sort of cuff that folded over and buttoned with a matching pearl snap. Bell-bottom pants had three-inch cuffs and his shoes were patent leather. That was his background; he had been an aging lead singer in a group called Dick Tracy and the Detectives. Twenty years later, he still dressed like a rock singer. He found Jesus about the same time the bookings and the travel expenses began to match. His congregation called him the "With-It Preacher."

Tracy settled heavily in the desk chair behind the desk and looked over the tops of his glasses at Christian. "What can I do for you, Mr. Simmons? My wife seemed to think it may be important."

"I want to talk to you about Hugh Conklin."

"Oh, yes. A blessed event. Never doubt the power of the Lord."

"Do you think that God did that?"

"Are you one of those doubting reporters who constantly try to undermine the Lord's work? I'll have you know that—"

"No, preacher," Christian interrupted, "I saw it happen. I was sitting in the audience when he went forward."

"Then you believe that Brother Conklin was reborn?"

"Oh, yes, preacher. I truly believe that Hugh has been reborn and is a different man."

"Praise God." The holy man relaxed into his chair.

"Hugh Conklin will be an inspiration to people all over this state and the credit will always go to you."

"Praise God."

"He will become a walking testimonial to your power—"

"God's power," the preacher corrected.

"God's power demonstrated through you and your church."

The preacher nodded.

"I think God has big plans for Hugh Conklin, Brother Tracy, and I think you will play a big part in it."

The preacher leaned forward. His eyes narrowed in distrust, making an ear-to-ear crease across his fat, red-necked, farmer face. Actually, his face seemed to bend in the middle. "And what do you think God's plans for Brother Hugh might be?"

"I think God wants Hugh to run for the U.S. Senate as a representative of morality in government. I think he will become a unifying force for your newly formed 'God in Government' program."

The preacher made a little steeple with his fingers. "I think that would be a little risky, Mr. Simmons. Whiskey is a terrible drug. Many people find Christ and then fall back into its clutches. That kind of representative would destroy our new organization. If we save a Catholic and he falls back under the spell of the pope, few notice. If a college professor finds Christ and then falls away, all he does is pull off his 'Jesus Saves' bumper sticker. But if a drunk is born again and then falls from grace, he becomes a vomiting, staggering testimony to our failure. I've seen Hugh Conklin asleep on the capitol steps. The Holy Spirit is fighting a death battle with the devil at this very moment in Hugh's body, but the fight's not yet over. We'll pray for him but the devil's clever and strong. He was an angel and he knows the tricks of angels. Besides that, there'll be a dozen candidates in that campaign."

"Preacher, I want you to pray on it. If you take this piece of human garbage and put him in even third or fourth place, you will be known as a miracle worker."

"I want to stop you there, sir. God don't make no junk."

Christian paused and took a deep breath. He knew that if God made junk, this preacher would be on the list of inventory.

"If you keep him sober until election time, you will be known as a miracle worker. If you get through the election with him, you'll at least have an army of campaign workers trained by me and ready to do the Lord's work in other campaigns. A man who controls that kind of political organization will control the state. I will leave you in a moment, but I want you to get on your knees about this. I'm also willing to have fifty thousand dollars deposited in your name, payable on election day, if Hugh stays sober and if he places fourth or better in the election.''

"Payable in cash?''

"Yes, in cash.''

Christian clutched the envelope and watched the reaction on Reverend Tracy's face. He was wavering between the danger of trusting his future to a drunk and a smart-ass political consultant, and the glory of a successful political organization and fifty thousand dollars in cash. He put the little steeple over his mouth and looked closely at Christian. He glanced down at the business card in his hand. "My wife says you worked for Miz Molly?''

Christian nodded.

"I will pray on it and talk to you tomorrow.''

Christian was with Big Jim the next day when the call came. "We need to talk again,'' the preacher said. Christian, Jim, and a local banker had eaten lunch and were having drinks. The banker had set up the trust account for the preacher after assuring Big Jim that he would recover the money if Hugh ran worse than fourth place.

"College Boy,'' Big Jim said, "you getting that preacher good. Your rummy runs fourth, it don't cost me anything 'cause we cover it with bets. Your rummy lose and the preacher don't get nothing.'' He looked at Christian with pride. College Boy was everything he would want a son to be. Once again Jim felt he was holding three aces with an extra card up his sleeve.

Life had recently been good to Jim. Susie wore an engagement ring of blinding size and was holding down her weight. A well had just begun producing in a new oil lease Jim had bought from an aging widow. One of the Labs had produced a litter of yellow pups and a federal grand jury had given up on an attempt to charge Jim with bank manipulation. Two of the grand jurors had become partners in Well #37 in the Calcasieu Fault.

Jim had his hand on Christian's shoulder as they walked silently down the brick lane to Christian's car.

"What did that fake-dick preacher say about your pictures?"

"I didn't have to use 'em. He sees the pot at the end of the stained-glass rainbow."

"Hang on to 'em. You'll need 'em down the road," Jim warned.

"You got some fast horses and some pissants in that Senate race," Big Jim observed. "How will Crazy Hugh run, tenth or worse?"

"Crazy Hugh will run fourth."

"Bullshit."

"No bullshit. I've run some sample polls, and I think I can beat eight of the people in the race."

Big Jim laughed. "I'll give you ten to one that don't happen."

Christian had lied about the polls, but he had to keep Big Jim in the game. He had to have his money. "I only have three thousand, but I'll bet that."

"Then you're serious," Big Jim said, rather amazed.

"If I had more, I'd bet more."

"College Boy, let's not take each other's money. If you're sure, I'm ready to find some suckers in Baton Rouge and clean up. I'll bet three hundred thousand if you can keep the odds at least four to one. Then we can split. Shit, man. You might be on your way to being as rich as me."

Christian hoped he would never be so rich that he would wear yellow cowboy boots.

Christian and Brother Dick Tracy met in the marriage-counseling room. It was decorated in powder blue and had a fake fireplace. The room looked like it had been ripped out of the display window of a furniture store.

"Nice room."

"Yes, it is. I was driving down the street and saw this room in the window of Kornmeyer's furniture store. I went in and bought the whole thing right down to the pictures. The only thing I changed was I turned the owl ashtray into an ivy planter. We don't allow smoking in this room.'' The preacher looked around proudly.

Christian was sure that even the ''Do not remove this tag under penalty of law'' tags were still in place. The preacher was dressed in blue pants and a gray tweed jacket with leather shooting patches at the elbows. Christian, amused at himself this morning and a little hung over from his night, imagined that the preacher wore this jacket to shoot down sinners.

''Tell me how you are going to elect Brother Hugh.''

''Reverend Tracy, you have a powerful natural resource in the two hundred churches you control in this state.''

''I am merely president of the Association of Independent Evangelical Churches.''

''Each of these churches was built and survived because of strong leadership. There is at least one natural leader in each of those churches. I propose to make each of those churches an organizational base for the campaign. In other words, we will have two hundred campaign headquarters.

''Church volunteers will call every voter in their geographic area and talk to them about the need to elect Hugh. I'll supply the messages. As the callers get results, we will teach them to key their information into a computer. On election day we will have a list of voters we can deliver to the polls and you have a prospect list for your churches that will enhance contributions and membership.''

The preacher was calculating average membership contributions against hypothetical growth. His eyes shone with hope. He made a small steeple with his hands. ''How many votes will we have to get to place fourth?''

''In an off-year election in Louisiana, only about half of the voters will participate. That's six hundred thousand votes. To place fourth in a ten-man field will require only about seventy thousand votes, about three hundred and fifty votes per church.''

"We have almost that many members.''

"Exactly!''

"What about the contributions the phoners raise?''

"We will need that money for television and campaign expenses.''

"No, I'll need half for our expenses.''

"Will the churches pay for the telephones and the mail?''

"Yes, if the mail can also contain fundraising and membership information.''

Christian reached across to the preacher. "Deal.''

"Deal.''

Christian made a tube of the envelope of pictures and slipped it into his coat pocket.

"But I still have a problem about Brother Hugh's drinking. To cover my investment I want him watched around the clock.'' The preacher was ahead of Christian by about a millisecond. That was the next item on the agenda.

"Brother Tracy,'' he began, "Hugh Conklin is a good man, a restored man, a man who will do much good for his country . . . but Hugh is a lonely man.''

The preacher leaned back and crossed his hands over his chest and nodded. He would have nodded at that moment if Christian had said the world was flat. Christian searched for a way to tell the preacher that Hugh needed a female companion for the campaign as well as for his now-sober sex life. The preacher was still nodding like a mechanical doll, wound tight by dollars.

"I think a female companion would be good for Hugh. He needs somebody to attend church with and have an occasional dinner. He needs a good Christian lady who will show him some attention and respect him.''

"And keep him away from the bottle?''

"Ah, exactly. Keep him away from the bottle.''

The preacher placed his palms together in a prayerful pose.

"The Lord may have already answered your prayers. We have a young lady in this church who found the Lord only a few months before Brother Hugh. She was lost. She was—how can I say it—a Mary Magdalene."

"A hooker," Christian guessed.

"Yes, maybe this sister was a prostitute but she was under the influence of some of the strongest drugs. Now she works in one of our missions downtown trying to help other lost girls."

"Hugh is running for public office, preacher. Don't you have any widowed ladies who might like an occasional companion?"

"This woman is restored. She has all of the Christian enthusiasm of Brother Hugh and is also lonely."

"Who is she, preacher?"

"Her name is Windy Dawn."

*"Windy Dawn!"*

"Yes, I'll have a talk with her. She'll do it for the Lord."

The deal was made. Hugh was going to accompany Sister Windy Dawn to prayer meeting Wednesday night. The gods had indeed played his hand. And the gods seemed to have a great sense of humor.

**13** Windy Dawn was really named Windy Dawn. Her father had been Dr. Charles Dawn of London, who had practiced in Atlanta for forty years. At a late age, he married his young nurse and they had one child. The nurse, whose mother had once been an exotic dancer who disrobed by having her veils blown off by an electric fan, insisted on naming the offspring after her mother, Windy. Dr. Dawn, a psychiatrist, discovered by looking at the blood type of the infant that it was not of his blood and killed his wife and himself. The newspaper headlines called it the "Type B-Negative" murder. Windy attended Swiss schools and returned to the country of her birth in time to become a counterculture flower child and give her inheritance to a series of gurus and terrorist groups.

During seventy-eight days of flying on any hallucinogenic that she could buy or beg, she ended up with an Italian boy in Chicago who put her in a room and brought a series of men by to call. She performed her tricks well and with an enthusiasm that brought repeat business. Windy Dawn liked sex. It didn't matter that Joseph was outside the door collecting. If she had had the money, she would have paid him to bring the men by. She only required that Joseph keep her in a nice room. She liked the sheets to be changed twice a day and usually took a shower after each customer. She took great pleasure in giving pleasure.

She and Joseph were arrested after about five weeks. She demonstrated her tricks in closed chambers and was released while Joseph got thirty days. She woke in jail in Baton Rouge without any knowledge of how she got there or with whom. The only memories she had of that trip were a series of nightmares or hallucinations in which she constantly gave birth to small hairy creatures that would slide down from her womb and begin eating her legs and breasts. The first face she saw other than the little hairy monsters was Brother Dick Tracy asking her to join him in prayer. She would have joined him in anything to have avoided her vampire offspring.

For two years since meeting Brother Tracy, she had not taken drugs. Reading the Bible and obeying all of Brother Tracy's rules had kept the monsters away. And, as insurance, she had developed a few rituals of her own that seemed to help. For one, she would never turn her back on the opened Bible. She backed around her small apartment to go to the bathroom or answer the telephone. She would also bow before opening the Bible. She found that those things worked. She bought a larger Bible and put it on a stand in the middle of the room. All of the furniture was then arranged in a circle around it. For the first time in her life, life was safe. She wasn't religious, she was cautious.

Windy worked at the Hopkins Vegetable Juice Bar and Health-Food Store. When she was hired as a waitress, the store, run by a bead-and-sandal-wearing couple who carried their baby on their backs and rode bicycles, was days away from bankruptcy. But as word of Windy's looks spread through the shopping mall, there was standing room only and people who drank only scotch raved about carrot juice. The owners put her in a brief French maid's uniform with net stockings and an extremely low top. Soon the owners were driving a Volkswagen and pushing the kid in a stroller.

And, if her looks were an asset to the health-food bar, her

quick mind and encyclopedic knowledge of the Bible made her even more valuable at the mission. She was popular with the ladies' group whose project was the Wayward Girls' Mission. She was most effective, though, in talking to young girls about narcotics. Her hatred of everything from speed to aspirin helped convince some children that they might try getting high on life. They could understand when she explained that an orgasm was as good as dope for a high. But she was careful never to discuss sex with the church ladies. She had learned early that they would have been more able to accept dope than sex.

Windy didn't look like a fallen woman. She had long blond hair that she wore piled high or in pigtails. Her skirts were an inch longer than fashionable, and she wore almost no makeup. She was a beautiful woman who walked gracefully like a ballet dancer and talked in almost a whisper.

Her natural beauty, though, was not her greatest gift. Windy Dawn had a photographic memory. She could remember endless addresses, telephone numbers, names, and faces. She could quote statistics about drugs that only a computer could have recalled. The only problem Windy had was turning all of her recall into useful information. Windy's mind was to practical application as a dictionary is to literature. The dictionary had most of Shakespeare's words, but it remained for him to take them out, sort them and write *Hamlet*.

At the mission, she used her memory instead of a directory or Rolodex to call every girl she had counseled. These follow-up calls had been suggested by Brother Tracy and were reaping several converts a month for the church. He had discovered her gift and, being a bright man, had written a series of messages that she memorized and recalled on cue.

Christian sought out Windy after his meeting with Reverend Tracy. He had to check her before allowing her to tamper with Hugh. There was too much at stake.

They crossed the street to a coffee shop to talk. Windy wouldn't have coffee because of the caffeine. That was a drug.

She ordered a glass of milk. Christian and the transparent blonde sat in silence a few moments, with Windy looking blankly at Christian and Christian trying to remember the nooks and crannies of her body from the night in Slidell. He was content for the moment to silently fuel his memory and imagination.

Christian attempted to open the conversation. "The drug center seems like a great project."

She nodded.

"How many people do you work with?" he asked, trying another tactic.

"I counsel seventy-three girls."

She sat without saying another word. This was going to be a difficult conversation.

"Are there a lot of girls involved in narcotics in this city?"

"The official estimates are that seven thousand girls under sixteen years of age are experimenting with drugs in this city." Silence again.

Christian asked several more questions but got the impression that he was talking to an adding machine. She quoted statistics and names in almost a monotone. He tried to look through her eyes to see if there were visible transistors. He made the mistake of asking her whether she drank and the statistics on whiskey were shot back, without emotion, for five minutes.

Christian saw promise, both for the campaign and for his libido. As a game, though, he was determined to break through to this girl machine because machines didn't look and smell as good as this one.

"What do you enjoy doing when you are not in the mission?" he asked.

"I like to read the Bible and have sex," she answered without hesitation or emotion.

Christian looked around nervously to see if anyone had heard the remark. She didn't look around.

"Do you do a lot of both?"

"No I just read the Bible. I haven't met any attractive men but Brother Tracy and he won't do me anymore. He asked me to stop selling sex because it would be bad for the mission. I kind of miss the extra money, though."

Christian looked around again. "Do you remember the last time we met?"

"Of course I do. We met at the Pine Rest Motel, room seventeen. Big Jim paid me to see you."

Another glass of milk, another cup of coffee, and soon they had negotiated a secret arrangement in which Windy would keep Hugh sober and charge only for sexual favors. Christian was to get a monthly invoice based on time and frequency. The arrangement was written twice in a small notebook from Windy's purse, one copy to Christian. After the contracts had been exchanged, there was silence while Windy drank the rest of her milk.

"Would you like to sign this with a kiss?" Christian asked.

"Would you like to do me? I have thirty minutes before I go back to the mission."

"Do you?"

"Yes, Brother Tracy says not to say the F word."

"You don't say it when you go to bed with him?"

"Oh, I haven't been to bed with him for more than a year."

Christian pulled out the envelope and the photos. "This isn't you?"

Windy picked up the photos and examined them with some interest. "This can't be me. I don't have a mole on my right breast like this woman and I don't own a black garter belt. Come on and I'll show you."

"Where?" Christian looked around.

"In the storeroom behind the health-food store but now we only have twenty-eight minutes. Hurry, Christian!" She pulled at his sleeve and was racing across the street before Christian could pay the check.

The "Closed until 2:00 P.M." sign was still in the front door but it was unlocked. When Christian rounded the corner and found the supply-room door, she was sitting on three crates of bottled wheat germ. Her blouse was off, her skirt pulled around her waist. "See, there's no mole." She pushed her breasts up with her hands toward Christian's mouth. She wrapped her legs around his waist and breathed heavily. "Hurry, Christian!"

They used all of their remaining seventeen minutes.

# 14

Hugh's Aunt Betty owned an ancient, fine automobile with a red-faced, helmeted explorer on the hood that lit with the headlights. At least it had lit up when both the car and the aunt were in their prime. The car and the explorer were both named DeSoto. When her old black driver, Jericho, died and she grew too weak to wrestle the huge steering wheel, she gave it to her favorite nephew. He drove it proudly to high-school dances and later to bayou bars and whorehouses in Opelousas. It had long running boards to stand on and seats high enough to give a eagle's view of the countryside. It was named the "Blue Monster" by high-school classmates and was in much demand for parades and school outings. Four people could stand on the running boards and seven more could fit inside.

It became a totem to modify Hugh's behavior. When he misbehaved, the car was padlocked in a sturdy garage. After Hugh swore repentance and showed Aunt Betty an abnormal amount of attention, the lock would come off and the dinosaur of a car would be liberated. Soon after Hugh graduated from high school, the car began to spend more time under lock than it did under Hugh. Two of Hugh's friends solved the problem by carefully removing the back wall of the garage and reassembling it to open when only three nails were removed. They drove the car into the alley and away while the old aunt reassured herself that her sentence was being carried out by glancing at the locks. This ploy ended when a building was constructed so close to the rear of the garage that the escape route was sealed. Hugh weaved home late one night after a lost week of debauchery to find both of his entrances closed off. Aunt Betty considered it a sort of miracle that the car had been locked outside a garage. She even opened the door to see if the car had a twin.

A priest who was familiar with young Hugh's habits finally convinced Aunt Betty that the car appearing outside the garage could in no way compare with the virgin birth. The car was impounded and the old building was wrapped with a double thickness of chain. Periodic special appeals freed the car for campaigns. When Hugh entered the institution where one goes who becomes too proficient at drinking, Aunt Betty double-wrapped the garage again for what appeared to be the last time. And there the old car sat on flat tires until Hugh's conversion.

The DeSoto had been locked up for five years when Hugh called Christian with his strange request. He needed transportation for his date with Windy Dawn. Aunt Betty was unrelenting until Christian swore on her family Bible that Hugh was a new man and had been sober for more than three months. As a Roman Catholic of the old school, she was not overjoyed that Hugh had been saved by Dick Tracy. She muttered at Reverend Dick when he was on television, said Hail Marys constantly, and made the sign of the cross to ward off his evil. But watching the preacher had become her Sunday ritual. After consideration, she thought if her nephew stayed sober, she could get him back to Father Gilbo later by taking away the car until Hugh turned to truth and the Holy Virgin. She still considered the car one of her best tools for the salvation of Hugh.

"Ain't she a beauty?" Hugh asked Christian. The members of the steering committee, anxious to be part of Hugh's romantic involvement, had voted to accompany him to the garage and put the car in running order. It was covered with five years of bird droppings and dirt. The younger committee members stepped cautiously up on the running boards and peered inside. "This motherfucker's a motherfucking tank," a newsboy said with admiration. "It even got a sign with Mr. Crazy Hugh's name on it." Indeed it did. On top was half a sheet of plywood standing erect, held in place by triangular boards and piano wire. "Elect Hugh Conklin for . . ." After the "for" was a blank blister of paint that had been built up in campaigns since high school. In front of the sign was a huge metal speaker with a wire running through one of the side-vent windows.

"This be a fucking Batmobile," the other newsboy said in some disbelief. "Do that metal thing on top suck the air like a jet and make the car go?"

Soon the car was on blocks while the four wheels were rolled to a neighborhood service station for repair. Sonny and Matsu stole a battery from an electric utility truck and Edmund appeared three times with a five-gallon can filled with gas. Christian noticed a rubber hose dangling from Edmund's pocket.

With soap and water and a deafening amount of profanity, the old car came slowly back to life. Its metamorphosis complete, the speaker began spitting a scratchy version of "Good Golly Miss Molly." Then the steering committee piled into or clung to the running boards of their new campaign vehicle as it rolled down the drive and crept down the street.

With car in hand, the committee became fashion consultants to Hugh. He had to be dressed and trained for his date. Aunt Betty found one of her late husband's old suits. It had strange, wide lapels and bold white pinstripes, but it was sound wool "from a time when things were made to last." It smelled of twenty years of mothballs. A committee shoplifting trip produced a blue shirt that almost fit, two red ties, three pairs of socks, and a tweed golf hat.

Soon Hugh was walking back and forth in the living room of campaign headquarters for general inspection. Sonny would pretend to find a piece of lint and Happy would pull down Hugh's coat in the back. His uncle had been a tiny, dried-up old man and the suit was a little tight, making Hugh look heavier than he did in the gathered trousers and coats he normally wore.

Christian gave Hugh three twenty-dollar bills and a lecture about his behavior in church. Happy sulked. His life was being changed too quickly. An interest in girls would mean Hugh being gone more at night, absent from the prized afternoon conversations. Sonny, Matsu, and Edmund gave Hugh obscene advice.

"That car has a big armrest. You put her head up under that rest and it won't be hard to hold her down," Sonny advised.

"If she won't kiss on first date, ask her 'bout copping your joint," was Happy's suggestion as he tried to join the levity.

They laughed and slapped backs, following Hugh to the car. They all waved as he drove away. The committee was in good spirits, being part of something important. The morning newspaper had even included Hugh's name in the list of rumored candidates. It was the first time any of them had seen a friend's name in any place but the police reports. Without saying anything to each other, each put the folded clipping in their wallets. If Hugh became important, they were important. Already they walked straighter. Sonny had begun reading the front sections of the newspapers and the newsboys assumed quiet arrogance at home. Their parents presumed the boys were dealing dope. Happy wore a tie daily to the newsstand. The weight of responsibility was settling comfortably on their shoulders.

Hugh was proud. He had never even been in the company of so beautiful a woman. She wore a long white dress that became transparent in strong light. Hugh imagined that he could see the dark sensual areas of her body through the clinging dress. Of course, he could.

She and Hugh both bowed to the Bible in the center of her apartment and backed out the door. Hugh liked that. Ceremony was something he missed in Brother Tracy's church. The "With It" church didn't have candles or mysterious rituals involving incense.

Hugh's car/campaign vehicle looked like a skyscraper among the small foreign cars that had won acceptance while the Blue Monster was serving time for Hugh's bad behavior. The couple circled it in admiration. Hugh loved the old car.

"Builds name recognition." Hugh pointed to the red-lettered sign. The DeSoto fenders and doors were covered with what drinkers call "whiskey rash." Those are dents from backing into lampposts and other cars. One back door was wired shut. The hood stood an inch or so above its intended place because of a broken spring.

Hugh held Windy's arm as they walked. He explained the function of each component. The strong trunk was a platform he could stand on to nail his posters high above his competitors'. The great road clearance made it possible to campaign in regions of the Atchafalaya Swamp that would be inaccessible to other candidates except by pirogue. "This speaker," Hugh said, "is mass communications." He explained the tape player and the mike and then demonstrated the volume.

Windy liked the speaker best. As they bumped down the highway toward the church, Windy recited Bible verse at high volume. Her John 3:16 made Hugh weep. Then they sang "The Old Rugged Cross" almost cheek to cheek so that they could both be heard through the small mike.

They stopped at a Sonic Drive Inn for root-beer floats and Hugh startled the carhops by blasting his order through his PA system. He let Windy call for the check. They attracted attention. Neither noticed.

When Hugh pulled into the church parking lot, they were just finishing the last verse of "Love Lifted Me."

". . . loooove lifteeeed meee."

They stayed cheek to cheek as the last notes died away. As he began to notice the tight fit of her warm flesh against his body, love began to lift a long dormant part of Hugh. Windy noticed almost as quickly. "Hugh, will you do me a favor?"

Hugh, taken with the woman and the moment, would have agreed to anything. Windy took his hand and moved it under her dress. "Press right here and wiggle your finger," she said in a throaty voice. She was still holding the mike when Hugh's finger did its work. The sounds coming from the car were of joy but those who heard it were told by Brother Tracy that Sister Windy had been shocked by the mike.

Perhaps it was her natural generosity or a contribution to the campaign, but Windy never billed Christian for that night.

# 15

Windy moved in with Hugh. That solved two problems and created another. She was insurance that Hugh would stay busy and away from the bottle. But Happy was crushed. It was bad enough that Windy moved in and came between them, because now Hugh spent most of his time in the bedroom. But, worse, she threw away Happy's dope and chained his chair to the bed at night so that he could not go out for more. She forgot him one day and left for work without unchaining his chair. He couldn't make it to his newsstand. Christian had to step in. The steering committee used Happy's incarceration as an excuse to vent some of their frustrations.

Christian knew it would be a troubled meeting when he found the chairs set, the claw hammer in place, and the battered *Robert's Rules of Order* on the table. In defiance of the new house rules, Sonny put a full bottle of Thunderbird on the table and Edmund lit a blue cigarette.

"Hammer the cocksucking meeting to order," Sonny demanded. He looked at Christian and then at Hugh and took a long pull of Thunderbird. He wiped his mouth on his sleeve and belched. Edmund blew smoke at Christian and tried to belch, but failed.

Hugh asked for the floor first and was recognized. "Gentlemen, I want to remind you that we don't use drugs in this

house and we don't use dirty words like 'cocksucker' and the
F word.''

"F, fucking word. Mr. Chairman, did you hear that cocksucker say 'F fucking word'? He's talking just like that bitch
that almost killed you by chaining you to the bed.'' Sonny
did not like to have his vocabulary questioned.

"Come to order. You ain't got the floor.''

Edmund stood to make a point. "Mr. Happy, you was
almost dead when I come in here and found you.'' There was
much discussion about the courage and vigilance of Edmund,
who had discovered Happy after he didn't show up at the
newsstand. In truth, Happy wasn't chained, only his chair
was. He had simply turned over and went back to sleep. But
Edmund's role in the campaign was growing. It was he who
had successfully stolen the shirt and the golf cap. It was Edmund who had known how to siphon gas. Saving Happy was
simply another in a series of accomplishments.

At Lincoln High Edmund had joined the Young Democrats
club and tried to show up for class at least four days a week.
At Lincoln, the Conklin committee had gained great stature.
Sonny Clinton had become "one of the last great white fighters, but his chance at the heavyweight title was stolen by a
Mexican referee on the take from the mob.'' At least that was
the way Sonny had explained it to Edmund. Happy had become "one of the richest news dealers in the nation with
plans for expansion to Washington, Fucking D.C.'' Of course
Hugh was the next U.S. senator and a rumored candidate for
president. Christian was a strange genius who had been ordered
by "people at the fucking top" to make Hugh a senator.

Happy began to dig half-moons in the table with his hammer to get attention. The bottle of T-Bird was getting dan-
gerously near the line of violence. Actually, it was more an
illusion of violence. Oh, Sonny sputtered and screamed and
broke things. But Christian began to understand that he could
find no example, past or present, of the fighter actually hurt-
ing a person. It seemed he had never hurt anybody in the ring

either. A sportswriter said that Sonny had been a punching bag for fighters on their way up who needed an easy victory for their records. Sonny told Edmund that he had been called the New Orleans Mangler. In truth, a sportswriter had dubbed him the New Orleans Dangler because of his tendency to tie up his opponents and hang on around their necks to avoid punches. His reputation was that he could take a punch and stay on his feet for five rounds. Because of that, Sonny always reminded Christian of a blowfish. Two chairs lay in splinters in a corner from a previous meeting. They had made a splendid, satisfying crunch against the wall, but both were aimed away from the Royal Brothers of the Broken Table.

"Mr. Chairman. What we gonna do with this cunt who moved in here and messed things up? My fucking hands is sore from pushing a fucking broom. She even yelled at Edmund for not putting down the toilet seat. We can't fucking drink. We can't fucking talk. 'Sides that, Hugh was a better man when he drank a little. . . ."

There was much discussion and general agreement at the table that the quality of life had slipped at campaign headquarters. There was a doormat outside on the porch and fresh flowers in the middle of the meeting table. Four or five pieces of furniture had been brought in, killing the ambience of the room. They didn't like the way it smelled, the way it looked, and they certainly didn't like the new house rules.

"Mr. Chairman, can I have the floor?" Hugh stood until the room was silent. "You are my friends. I'm sorry about what's happening but I want to beg you guys to get along with Windy. She's been here three weeks and she done a lot of good. Now things ain't the same but in some ways they's better. Sonny, how many times you had a good hot meal at my table? Edmund, how many times she helped you with your homework and let you sleep on the porch when your mother has all-night visitors? What I'm saying is she turned us into a family. Each of you is my brother. Admit it, Sonny. You ain't been in jail since she got here. She patched the windows and put in glass. She painted the bedroom and the kitchen. All she wants is that you drink outside the house and blow your dope in the streets. She loves Happy. Happy, when's the last time you didn't have a clean shirt?''

The committee members studied the table. Edmund wanted to ask why Windy chained Happy's chair if she loved him, but didn't. He was feeling a sadness that knotted in his chest.

"I'm asking my brothers at this table to help me be a U.S. senator. All my life I've wanted to be elected. I know I can never be a great man like Huey, but I can try. I've studied him for years. This is my last shot. Please help me. When they tried to impeach Huey, his friends stepped in and defeated them. They stood like a stone wall.'' He pronounced "stone wall" as though all the letters were capitalized. "Please don't leave me when I need you. I'll talk to Windy. I'll sweep so Sonny don't need to. I'll tell her about the toilet seat. But I beg you to keep her rules. I ain't asking much.''

Hugh was sobbing. That soft but deafening sound froze the room. Sonny looked at his fingernails. Happy twisted his red tie into a string. Edmund ground his cigarette under his foot.

Sonny stood and half raised his hand as a gesture to *Robert's Rules*. His head was down. "Hugh, I used to be a great fighter. At least I was the best in New Orleans. And I always was gonna make a comeback. But I kept drinking that wine and pretty soon I ain't even a middleweight anymore. I was a heavyweight with short arms. Now I'm old. Too old to fight. I know I ain't making no comeback. Happy there, they tell me, was a good soldier, a sergeant, but he ain't got no legs. Old Happy ain't making no comeback. Edmund ain't making no comeback. He ain't never got started 'cause he's a nigg . . . black. I never knew any . . . any nig . . . blacks except in the ring. Edmund's a smart kid. If I had a kid, I'd want him to be like Edmund. But Edmund ain't got much of a chance. You Edmund's maiden fight and his comeback at the same time. Mr. Simmons back there is nice enough but he can't be too good or he wouldn't be here with us. I been thinking about it. We all missing a little part of some kind. Every morning we get up and say 'What can we do for Hugh?' But what we really saying is 'What can I do for me?' You our comeback, Hugh. I ain't gonna fuck it up.''

He stood silently for a few seconds, still staring at his feet, and then sat down. Christian leaned his chair against the back wall and lit a cheap cigar. He truly needed something to do with his hands. Then the committee filed outside and sat on the porch, where they silently watched the sun go down over the refinery. The cottonwood shook in evening protest.

Windy came home and, as though there was a hidden signal, kissed each silent man on the cheek. Christian met later that night with the happy couple and Happy and negotiated an agreement that there would be no dope smoked in the house and in return she would not chain Happy's chair. Happy agreed because he had learned to eat the plant mixed with food. The result was that his consumption doubled. He smoked all day at his stand and ate the weed at night.

Soon Happy was the terror of the sidewalks. With a freshly charged battery, he would run through flower beds and over dogs. He often showed up at the shack with roses in his wheels and leaves in his white beard.

Windy decided Happy was just careless and they developed a strong friendship bonded by their love for Hugh. In private, Happy called her Mrs. Conklin and talked about how she was going to be the first lady. Windy only smiled.

**16** For Christian's class, the room had been arranged to resemble a schoolroom. There was an easel and a circle of chairs. Windy sat almost in the middle with Brother Dick Tracy to her left. Darleen, who was beginning to develop a friendship with Windy, sat on her right and whispered confidences. Hugh and fifty people from other churches sat scattered in the other rows. A dozen read Scripture. An old man cleaned his fingernails with a small knife. Two women without makeup cross-stitched Bible verses.

The remarkable thing about the men in the group was that they all used the same barber, or at least Christian reasoned they did. They wore what he called "preacher helmets," blow-dried and varnished hair swept back from their foreheads. Looking around, Christian also decided that Jesus only called those to preach who had low foreheads. Most hairlines started an inch above the eyebrows.

And they shared a fashion consultant. The material of their coats sparkled in the light, ablaze with metallic thread. Many of them wore mismatched plaid coats and trousers. The women wore their hair piled atop their heads and sacklike dresses that buttoned around the neck. That is, except for the beautiful Flora Tracy, the preacher's wife, who sat in a back corner with a serene look on her face.

Christian was late. He had stopped at the 7-Eleven for a second quart of orange juice in an attempt to replace the fluids in his T-Bird-wine–damaged body. He had spent most of the afternoon at Ernie's cut-rate liquor store, sidetracking Sonny so that the fighter didn't show up drunk and profane at the meeting of preachers.

"I want to go to the cocksucking meeting. I'm on the fucking committee and I need to go and look those broke dicks in the eye. I want 'em to know that if they fuck up, they got to deal with me. Once you tell them cocksuckers about how I beat the shit out of that Mexican, they always toe the fucking line. The enforcer has to go to the meeting. How can they be scared of me, if they don't know me? And besides, I need to know more about this plan."

As a compromise, Christian set up a private school for Sonny at Ernie's Cut-Rate. They had been drunk and sober twice during the day as Christian attempted to explain his campaign technique. Sonny objected to almost everything except the endless bottles of white port with the eagle on the label. All they accomplished was naming Thunderbird the "official Hugh Conklin campaign drink." It was Sonny's idea. After election he intended to sell Hugh's endorsement to the wine company.

"Every cocksucker in Washington will be drinking T-Bird when Hugh and me get there," he explained. "We'll get Hugh's picture holding up a bottle of blackberry T-Bird with the Capitol Dome in the background." Christian was in no position to disagree. " 'The Juice of Winners,' it'll say. 'It goes down smooth and don't cost much.' " Sonny stood and held up his glass with two fingers and smiled for an imaginary camera. The drinkers at Ernie's who had been there so long they were furniture, began applauding. They knew a good ad campaign when they heard one.

So Christian was a little late and a little drunk.

"Mr. Simmons, I think we need to open this most important meeting with prayer," suggested Brother Dick Tracy, who stood and spoke to the ceiling for ten minutes. Christian nodded off twice but wasn't caught because all eyes in the house were closed. He fortunately didn't snore as he often did when tired and drunk. Christian fought sleep until it was his turn to speak. His eyes were still slightly out of focus when he drew a large circle in black and put a small church, complete with steeple, in the middle. He then drew an arrow from the church to the circle and wrote "25 miles" on the line.

"Each of you represent five churches. And I, ah, ah . . ." Christian stuttered. Both Darleen and Windy had crossed their legs, exposing an expanse of white flesh and hidden silk. Both at the same time. Both smiled.

"I have a package for each church that contains, ah . . . ah . . . ah . . ." Christian stared at the ceiling to collect himself. "I have a package for each church in your association. The package contains a list of every voter within twenty-five miles of each church who participated in all of the last three elections." He continued to address the fluorescent lights. "The first thing you must do is phone each of the people on the list and identify them by church affiliation. Then we—"

"May I interject something here?" Reverend Tracy stood. "This is a wonderful opportunity to expand the income of your church. You will find some people who don't have church homes. I want to remind you that every new member brings in about seven hundred dollars per year. If each of you manage to get just ten new members out of all of this calling, that is seven thousand dollars more per year for the collection plate. You bring in that kind of money and I just bet . . . er . . . think, your board of deacons will look more kindly on your next raise." He smiled and sat back down.

"Yes, ah," Christian continued, "there is great potential for all of us in these lists. I, ah." Darleen had her hand on

Windy's thigh. "I ah, will now explain how the phone banks work." He stumbled through the next hour explaining proper phone technique and follow-up letters keyed to the phone calls.

Thighs flashed, fingers were sucked. The two women, who already knew all of Christian's "Cottonwood" political technique, created a sexual fantasy, aimed only at the speaker. Christian began to sweat. The T-Bird rumbled in his stomach, fighting with the orange juice.

Hugh raised his hand and stood. "College . . . ah, Mr. Simmons, this computer business is good but, ah, but what does the candidate do? You ain't talked about the candidate yet. I was thinking maybe these folks would like to hear a few words about my plans for the United States of America. The committee has come up with a platform."

Christian panicked. Part of the committee's platform was the legalization of marijuana, the recognition of homosexuals as a third sex, and a new boxing commission with Sonny as its director.

"Ah, Mr. Conklin. This is intended as a training session. Don't you think we should refine that platform before we release it? These people know that basically it calls for a return to morality in government and traditional family values—"

"Amen," "Amen," "Amen." A dozen "Amens" were heard in the room.

"These people know that your platform is based on solid Christian values with the Bible as your authority."

"Amen. Amen."

"And, none of these folks need to be reminded that they will each have a key to your office door in Washington." Christian was improvising. He liked the key idea.

"Well, ah . . ." Hugh sat down. "I just . . . ah . . . wanted everybody to know where I stand." There was polite applause in the room.

Christian was getting slightly ill and excused himself from the last hour of the session. One of his computer whiz kids was to demonstrate the use of a program written for the church people. Christian's participation was not necessary.

Darleen and Windy followed him to the parking lot.

"You don't look well, Christian." Darleen put her hand on his forehead and leaned over to smell his breath. "You were right, Windy."

"I saw him leave with Sonny."

"Windy agrees with me that you're drinking too much."

"Any is too much," Windy corrected.

"It's just the pressure of the campaign" was the only defense Christian could think of at the moment. His head hurt.

The women drove away in the MG, leaving him standing in the parking lot. They were laughing and waved as they turned the corner. Only then did Christian realize he didn't have a ride and he had not had time to ask them about their antics in the classroom. How much did Darleen know? What new complication was being introduced that would detour him from fame and fortune?

Hugh took him home in the Blue Monster.

Christian tried. He truly did. He drank less and made it home for dinner on time three consecutive days. He made another list of proper behavior and kept it in his shirt pocket. Both Windy and Darleen had brushed aside his sexual advances, emphasizing his need for reform. They got his attention. He reasoned that he was now a much better and more wholesome man. At least that's what Darleen said and she seemed to understand about such things.

When T. Boy knocked on the door, he interrupted a character-betterment lesson by Darleen. Christian was learning about his being self-centered and calculating. Earlier he had learned about not delivering phone messages and "staying out too late chasing whores." He nodded at each of her points. Darleen was mostly right. Christian was tempted to take notes but he tried that once and became a target for small but heavy airborne items in the living room. He wanted to ask Darleen if whores and prostitutes were the same thing. It seemed an important point. He thought of Windy as a prostitute but not a whore. She had far too much character to be a whore. Besides, her billing procedures and conduct proved her to be a trustworthy professional. The sort of women described by Darleen seemed low in character and morals. Windy must, he thought, fit in a separate category because she and Darleen had become friends who talked daily on the phone and ate lunch together twice a week.

But Christian was learning. In fact, except for the recent drinking problem, he and Darleen had had several peaceful weeks. He had made little mental notes about things that disturbed her and tried to improve. She had rewarded his efforts with peace.

Darleen kissed Christian good night, knowing that he would never return before daylight from a Big Jim meeting that started after 10:00 P.M. He in turn patted her fondly on the behind.

T. Boy, usually a barometer of Jim's highs and lows, cursed slow drivers who had the bad judgment to stay under ninety miles per hour. He screamed insults at bewildered drivers and jerked the wheel instead of guiding the car in his usual fluid movements. T. Boy was usually a skilled driver. He could bring the huge car to a quick stop without spilling a drop of his passenger's scotch. This night, though, Christian bounced around the car and was forced to hang on to a strap. He lowered the glass between the seats.

''What's wrong with Big Boss, T. Boy?''

T. Boy chewed his cigar for a few moments trying to decide what he should say. He was hesitant to even give an opinion about the weather without Big Jim's approval. T. Boy's hero was the Nixon guy, G. Gordon Liddy, who testified that he held his hand over a candle flame to demonstrate his toughness. He knew he would take a bullet instead of ratting on Big Boss. T. Boy had two scars on his hands from practicing the candle trick. In fact, he would be happy to languish in prison again if the other inmates knew that he was there because of his loyalty. "Loyalty," Big Jim had told him, "is the noblest human virtue."

"All I can say is Big Boss says you took us all out on a limb and he's some pissed."

"Last time I saw Jim we laughed our asses off. Remember?"

"I can't say no more. It's just he thought you knew more about politics than you do. That's all. Big Jim says he got a lot of money invested in your skinny ass and all you doing is shucking and jiving."

T. Boy puffed on his cigar and defiantly rolled up the window between the two seats, isolating Christian. Christian pushed the button and the window started down again.

"Why did he change his mind? I thought . . ." He stopped because the window had rolled back into position and was locked.

Christian pushed a Hank Williams tape into the backseat player to find troubles greater than his own. Hank sang about being too blue to cry.

The blueness of the country singer matched Christian's. He was constantly aware that his Conklin campaign was a giant balancing act requiring each piece to stay in place for months longer than was natural. And to fuel it he had to have the cooperation of Big Jim. So he justified becoming a court jester, laughing on cue, drinking beyond his capabilities, sleeping with white black girls, and listening to lectures from Darleen. It was all part of the price. And Christian had not yet found a price he would not pay.

Christian saw Baton Rouge as a dark, deep hole with Big Jim and Hugh standing at the top holding the end of his rope.

Neither had a strong grip. His escape from Louisiana was delicately plotted and required some luck. This was not good luck.

Hank Williams cried about being lonesome.

It was a strange kind of crowded loneliness Christian felt. He was surrounded by people but they were only temporary flickering film images projected across his vision. He walked through them and around them without touching. And he danced and laughed. A political Bojangles. Holes in his shoes, a grin painted on his face. Sweet sadness. An operatic tragedy. A noble young man fighting to escape his roots. Playing clown. He ejected Hank and inserted Richard Tucker singing about the unhappy clown of *I Pagliacci*.

The big car pulled into the ranch gate and began to wind down the long drive. The sweetness of "I'm So Lonesome I Could Cry," the drama of *I Pagliacci*, fought for attention in his romantic head. A young man washed in an ebb of important events, delivered in limousines. Sweet sadness. The stuff of novels and of conquests. Truly, Christian was more impressed with his dilemma than frightened of his future.

Big Jim was sitting in his huge living room at the ranch. He still wore a bright green western hat and didn't get up when Christian walked in but waved him into a chair and yelled for a bottle of scotch and a glass of ice. He had his own bottle of bourbon, and the guest, sitting to Jim's left, had a bottle of Booth's gin.

The other man looked like he had been dressed by the legislature's style consultant. His suit was of some light blue Du Pont fabric discovered while trying to develop a new flak jacket. It shined and was held together with darker blue metallic thread. His hair was a stiff, sprayed halo, cut square in the back. Of course he wore alligator shoes. Most of the better-dressed legislators and their lackeys like this man bought their suits from a shop in Lafayette, Louisiana, that, they boasted, "stayed about two years ahead of New York." Christian always thought that there was a manufacturer someplace who, as a joke, made suits just for the Louisiana legislature and country preachers. He imagined it was an act of vengeance by a suitmaker who had contacted a social disease from a B-girl on Bourbon Street.

"This here is Bobby Sutto. He was electing politicians when you was still pissing in your pants, College Boy. Bobby here's talking about how we wasting our money and you don't understand Louisiana politics."

Big Jim crooked his finger toward Christian. "Bobby, this here is Christian Ahab Simmons. Everybody calls him College Boy. They tell me he's the brightest son of a bitch to ever graduate from LSU."

"Book learning ain't everything, Jim. No college boy made you rich. You did that with a third-grade education."

"I been trying to tell Bobby 'bout your computers and your lists. He thinks you're crazy. And the more he talks, the more sense he makes. I think we got big trouble, College Boy. Tell him where he's fucked up, Bobby."

"You just don't understand how things work. You got to have the tax assessors, the sheriffs, and the legislators or you're fucked. Them kind of people ain't gonna support a wino who's biness is selling donkeys with the red ass. How many sheriffs you got?"

"None."

"How many assessors?"

"None."

"Same number of legislators?"

"Yes."

Christian was amused by this New Orleans hack but he feared the doubt he saw in Big Jim. But he had long expected to be challenged by someone from the old political establishment. They had to stick together and guard the fiction that they mattered.

Bobby Sutto leaned back and took a long swallow of his gin. He had a smug look on his face. He winked at Big Jim. "Son, this here is Louisiana. You ain't got a chance without the support of those folks. Senator LeBlanc has got the endorsement of every one of those groups. When he hums, they dance. How many nigger votes you bought with all that money Jim says you spending?"

"I haven't bought any. However, part of our organization is black."

Bobby Sutto slapped his knee and laughed, then he shook his head at Big Jim. Jim winced every time Bobby said "nigger." He had a wide stretch of basic human decency. Score an infield hit for Christian.

"Son, the senator has bought every nigger leader. You won't get ten votes for your rummy. That means you gonna lose, automatically, about thirty percent of the vote."

"Eighteen percent," Christian corrected.

"Bullshit. Where'd you get that number?"

"The voter lists are broken down by race because of the voting-rights legislation of the sixties. I matched people who actually voted with the voter list by race. The result is that only about eighteen percent of blacks will vote in this election. But besides that, the south is no longer a plantation. These are intelligent people who can make their own decisions."

Jim leaned forward. "Bobby, them numbers come from them computers that College Boy has."

"Well, do them computers tell you what you get when you don't have a single sheriff or tax accessor?" He laughed and winked again at Jim.

"They don't matter anymore. Those guys have trouble delivering the votes of their families." Now Christian was being a little smug.

"That's what I'm telling you, Jim. This kid don't know shit about elections." Bobby Sutto picked up his drink and moved to a chair closer to Jim so that Christian was shut out of the circle.

"Jim," the hack said earnestly, "do you want to go tell Earl Long or Jimmie Davis or John McKeithen or Russell Long or Edwin Edwards how all a' them people don't count? They'd have you committed."

Christian realized that he was losing the argument and he was getting a little angry. "Look, Edwards didn't need those endorsements. He just didn't know it. He was still playing by the rules set a generation before. We'll never know for sure until somebody gets elected without all of those guys. People like you are living in the past. Look at the rest of America. They haven't believed in machine politics since the advent of television. You know what a political rally is now? It's three people gathered around a television set."

"Listen, you little cocksucker. Louisiana knows more about politics than any state in this union. They should come here to get lessons."

"The rest of the nation marched past Louisiana politically years ago. Like in everything else."

The two men were screaming. Big Jim kept pouring down drinks. But he had begun to enjoy himself.

"You step outside and I'll whip your ass." Bobby Sutto and Christian both stood.

"Boys, now we just gonna have us a little political discussion. We don't need no ass kicking. Show College Boy what you got, Bobby." Jim motioned toward a thick brown envelope. His face was grim.

"You got to swear on the lives of your children you'll keep this secret. I ain't supposed to have it," Bobby warned.

Christian swore.

"I got a poll taken by a professor at Tulane." He opened the envelope and pulled out a printout. "Senator LeBlanc has thirty-two percent of the vote. He's in first place. Second is the Congressman Milton Fulton. He has sixteen. Third is

former governor Gremillion. He has twelve. Fourth is a busi-
nessman named Hays. He has six. Baton Rouge Mayor Laurent is at five. I could go on with the rest of these broke dicks,
but I want to get to your man Hugh Conklin. He's got zero.
That's zero. He gets no votes. There are only ten men in the
race and he barely gets to be number ten. And you tell me
you got no sheriffs.'' The man was screaming again. He threw
the pile of papers on the coffee table.

Christian took a long swallow of scotch. "Sounds correct
to me."

Big Jim exploded. "Sounds correct to you. Sounds correct
to you? Do you know that I got about three fucking hundred
fucking thousand dollars in this fucking campaign in fucking
expense money and bets and you say it 'sounds correct to
me'?''

With Jim an apparent ally, Bobby faced Christian again and
lowered his voice. "Them computers is good to add up sums,
boy, but they can't vote. Now I think Jim's got to cut his
loses and get on with Senator LeBlanc. This pussy business
with the Washington stripper is gonna blow over and he's
gonna be reelected. He's got every elected official in this
state. He's kinda low now, under fifty and all, but when those
political groups kick in, he'll do fine. You can't poll things
like that. I'm really here because you're fucking with us.
Three times yesterday we had some church people tell us they
supporting your drunk. They don't count for much, but we
want the senator to win big. Every vote he loses in holy-roller
North Louisiana hurts." Bobby lowered his voice as though
he had told a great confidence. He winked again at Big Jim
but there was a sharp edge to his comments, like the warning
rattle of a coiled snake.

"Look, I don't disagree with you. Senator LeBlanc may
win the whole thing. We're not even trying to win. I'm sure
Jim told you we're trying to make some bets and sneak up
on some people." Paint on a grin. *Tu sei pagliaccio.* "I know

that I can bring Crazy Hugh in about fourth place. He doesn't show in the polls now because we haven't done anything yet to make him show in the polls." Grin! "I want to wait until the last minute. Then we'll call those people on those computer lists and get just enough votes to win the bets." Christian smiled again. His mouth was beginning to ache. "Your man will win and Jim and I'll make a few bucks." Smile. Palms held open and up.

"Tell Bobby how you gonna do it," Jim commanded. "Maybe he can give you some advice."

"No."

"No? I got three hundred thousand in this cocksucker and you say *no.* "

"Forgive me, Jim. How's still a secret. If it gets out, it could be stopped. No matter how much money you give to Senator LeBlanc, my future is on this one. Remember, I get half of the winnings. I have a big stake in this."

"Tell him what you told me," Jim said to the hack.

"Senator LeBlanc has a place on his staff for you. He'll make you his press secretary and pay you more than you're worth."

"I'm honored, but I want to continue what I'm doing. I'll win this bet or I'll go into another business." Christian looked at Jim. Christian never needed a lecture from Darleen on guts and determination. Like the thugs on that summer night outside Hugh's house, Bobby Sutto saw the cold eyes and the set of the chin. It was a look of violence from a man who seemed too soft to fight. But those eyes. Jim saw it too.

"Listen, you little cocksucker, you're playing with the big boys. A little pimple like you gets mashed. You fucking with some votes that ought to go to the senator. And you're smart-talking me. People in this state know better than to smart-talk Bobby Sutto. You fuck with me and I'll whip your ass." Bobby clenched his fists and moved toward Christian.

"If you boys gonna fight, do it in the yard," Jim demanded. Christian was angry. He threw open the door and walked outside. Bobby Sutto was half a step behind him. Christian had barely cleared the steps when the heavy fist hit him in the back of the head, hurling him into T. Boy's car. He braced himself in time to be hit again in the face and once in the stomach. He crumbled to the gravel and was kicked in the shoulder and ribs. Blood covered his shirt. His nose was broken.

Rage boiled in Christian. And the rage masked the pain enough that he was able to sustain two more body blows before he attacked the political hack. Suddenly Bobby Sutto felt terror. Christian was a machine that pounded the soft politician in the face and head. There was no grace to it. Nothing about the fight resembled photos in *Sports Illustrated*. Christian used his fists and elbows and knees and head. When Bobby Sutto fell to the gravel and covered his head, Christian used his feet, kicking him until both T. Boy and Jim pulled him away. The man lay terrified, bloody and wheezing in the gravel. Slowly he pulled himself to his hands and knees.

A shot exploded. Bobby Sutto had pulled a pistol from a shoulder holster. The bullet went through Christian's trouser leg and the door of the black car. Bobby Sutto managed only one shot before T. Boy crushed his gun hand under his foot. An even larger pistol had jumped into T. Boy's hand. He looked at Jim for permission to shoot. He was angry that Bobby had shot his car. Jim shook his head calmly no. Still angry about damage to the car, T. Boy shifted his weight until he heard bones crack.

Christian leaned against the car and caught his breath. He had a broken nose and bullet hole through his suit. He ached everywhere. But later the pain proved to be worth the price. When the bones broke, Jim had become Christian's accomplice. Without knowing it, Jim had chosen between the past and the future. Later the senator sent a representative with an offer to fire Bobby, but Christian's plan had begun to work and Jim refused. Christian always knew that Jim would have to decide between his friendship with "College Boy" and blind loyalty to old politics. Christian had always wondered how he would persuade Jim to select the future when he was a citizen in good standing in the world of Bing Crosby.

It turned out to be the pistol. Jim knew that Bobby Sutto had a gun and assumed that Christian knew also. When Christian went into the yard to face the gunman without his own gun, he earned Jim's respect. Even T. Boy added a hero to his Watergate models. "The little fucker is tough," he told Jim. And Jim was proud. If he had ever had a son . . .

Darleen screamed. Christian's nose tilted to the side and one eye was swollen shut. When he stumbled through the door, she caught him and held him close, her face wet with tears, her body shaking. Big Jim had called to warn her but he had only said that Christian had been "in a little fight." In reality, he was covered with blood. His hands were swollen.

T. Boy took off his hat and tried to ease her pain. "I don't think nothing's broken. You think he's bad, you outta see the other fuck—eh, feller. He's got a broke hand and—"

"I'll take care of him now."

"You want I should drive him to the hospital?"

"No, you and Jim have done enough. I'll take care of him now." She led him to a chair. "Oh, Christian, did you do this for me?" Darleen wept.

He was drunk and wounded but he could still reason.

"Yes," he said.

Everybody seemed happy about Christian being beaten and shot. Darleen took him to the hospital to have his nose set and later attended to his every need. Happy built the story into a legend at Ernie's Cut-Rate. It grew into a gunfight similar to the one at the O.K. Corral. Windy rubbed his body with sweet-smelling salve. Sonny talked to him about his nose and gave advice on how to slip a punch. Sonny had obviously not been successful with his own advice. And best of all, Big Jim bet another $100,000 at five-to-one odds. He did it more as a reward for Christian's valor than as an endorsement of Hugh. Jim still had grave doubts about Christian's plan.

**17** Christian had a problem. Oh, Christian had many problems with Big Jim and Darleen and a dwindling bank account and a sore nose. So this could be more accurately called "another problem." His problem was the steering committee.

They stayed in perpetual session. They had nothing else to do. But that was not good for Christian. A committee in session has to have a purpose. That purpose usually ends in some sort of action to justify the hammer pounding and the "Mr. Chairman's" and the "that cocksucker's already got the fucking floor." The intentions were always good but the results were usually disasters. One of their meetings had resulted in their building what they described as the "biggest fucking sign in Louisiana." They hung the sign illegally between two utility poles and it had blown into a police car, causing extensive damage. Big Jim fixed that one.

A political rally in Ernie's Cut-Rate had seriously threatened the campaign and had been responsible for two broken arms and Sonny spending two nights in jail. It was a wine-tasting rally. For a five-dollar ticket one was allowed to sample from a selection of Sonny's favorites. The table was laden with five flavors of Thunderbird, four white ports, Mad Dog 20-20, and Boone's Farm Zapple. Ernie had kicked in a couple half gallons of strawberry brandy made by his relatives in Amite.

Ernie's had been transformed into something that looked like prom night for winos. Edmund had stolen some paper tablecloths with large red hearts from a greeting-card store. "When you care enough to steal the very best," Edmund explained. Ernie, to make the event special, had payed Edmund's brother, Matsu, to sweep out the bar. It was splendid when they turned out all of the lights except for the neon beer-and-wine signs. It gave all of the guests a certain Coors Beer orange glow. And during the first part of the evening, all of the paying guests, and the few who had sneaked in through the back, were on their best behavior. It was truly an event of decorum and class.

The unfortunate fight started when Happy caught Bernie Pense "lipping the bottle and not using a cocksucking glass." The gallon of Zapple was halfway down his throat when Happy, his chair on full power, flattened Bernie. He made a high-speed turn around the pool table and hit him again as he wobbled to his feet. Bernie fell over the pool table and Happy was thrown from his chair. The chair continued to run amuck in the bar, terrorizing the drunks. Edmund hit Bernie over the head with a pool cue, and three men and V. D. Gertrude, who had sneaked in with them through the back, picked up armloads of wine and tried to escape. Sonny punched Gertrude with his fabled uppercut and both companions jumped on his back. Edmund lost a tooth and Hugh briefly reacquainted himself with strong drink.

Because of the rally at Ernie's, Windy had to stop traveling out of town to the headquarter churches. And that hurt Christian's plans until Darleen began to pick up the slack. Later Christian discovered that at least two preachers and three deacons were also disappointed when Windy's overnight campaign trips stopped. When the authorities raided Ernie's, they discovered he didn't have a liquor license and incarcerated him.

The committee's next official act was churning out red and white bumper stickers demanding "Free Big Ernie." Ernie weighed 311 pounds.

They deemed the party at Ernie's a success because after damages and being wonderfully drunk, they had still shown a seventeen-dollar profit. So they began planning what became the legendary fundraiser. As they gained confidence and solidarity, no task was too great. Raising money to finance the campaign was well within their self-perceived limitations.

Originally, the committee had seemed a sound idea. They had become a troop of self-interested bodyguards who would watch over the candidate to keep him sober and occupied until it was time to play his part in Christian's play. But the committee had begun to meld into a tight unit, a cell of well-intentioned subversives. And as they grew cohesive, strong personalities emerged. Sonny stopped going to wherever he called home and slept on the front porch of campaign headquarters or under the cottonwood branches. After a month, the committee passed a resolution asking that he stay on duty twenty-four hours a day to secure the "health and well-being of the next United States senator." "Health and well-being" was something Edmund introduced. He had gone beyond the school texts and was reading American history. After he got an *A* on an exam, the history teacher tried to have him expelled for cheating. Edmund's highest grade previously had been a *D*. After school he would join Sonny on the porch. He began to walk and stand like the fighter. Occasionally Edmund would even screw up enough courage to take a hit from the bottle of rotten but fortified Thunderbird.

Happy began closing his stand two hours early so that he could cook meals for Hugh, Windy, and the committee. He had begun reading cookbooks on nutritious diets that Windy brought home from the health-food store. Matsu, who was actually a half-brother to Edmund, would stand watch at the street while Happy smoked and Sonny took pulls from his bottle. Matsu had red hair and freckles. In fact, he looked a lot like the man who owned Handi Shop on the next street. When Windy turned the corner, Matsu would take Sonny's bottle and hide it in its place under the porch. Then he'd put Happy's dope back into the small metal can that stayed with Sonny's bottle. Matsu was slight and could maneuver under the porch like a possum.

Campaign headquarters was a center of order. It had rules and rituals. It was a dry place out of the elements, and at the end of the day, there was a hot meal, even if it was healthy. They all would have liked pickled pig's feet, fried chicken, okra, corn bread, fried catfish, or alligator stew. Regular food. Instead they got vegetables not cooked enough for their taste, baked chicken and fish, fresh fruit, and little cups filled with natural vitamins C, E, A, and B that Windy supervised their taking. After dinner there was usually a committee meeting. It was here that Christian's troubles always began.

Christian, who had been invited for dinner, was concerned. There was no conversation. Each committee member sat staring at his beets and green beans. The only question in Christian's mind was the gravity of the problem. Windy was bright and beautiful and attempted to keep a conversation flowing. She asked Sonny when he had bathed last and lectured Edmund on homework. She asked Christian about Darleen and why he had not brought her to campaign headquarters for dinner. But the rest of the committee, including Hugh, stared at their plates, and moved their half-cooked but healthful green beans from one side to the other.

Though the meeting was glum, Christian had little to fear. Hugh had been sober for two months, Darleen let Christian sleep in the house every night, the churches were organized, and their phone banks working as planned. Big Jim's new doubt was a problem. Several times Christian had fantasized about sending his enforcement chairman Sonny Clinton to call on the New Orleans hack who had created his dilemma but feared the fighter's enthusiasm for the project. He wished Bobby Sutto a broken arm, not a broken head . . . or worse. Christian intended to give Jim several more days to cool down before he pleaded his case. In the meantime, though, he knew it would be useless to ask Jim for more money.

The meeting began after Happy, Sonny, and Edmund retired to the front porch for fifteen minutes. Christian could hear someone rooting around under the dark house for the wine bottle and could see the flare of matches under the cottonwood. Like Indian war councils, this one was getting ready for battle.

Windy had assumed the title of "Women's Chairman" and had a tent card. Sonny's new card showed only a boxing glove and his first name. Edmund had changed his title to "Chairman, Minority Relations. Edmund G. Washington." The card was more than a foot long. Hugh's card now read "U.S. Senator, Hugh Conklin." Stars were on all four corners.

Sonny took the floor first and read haltingly from a small card in his hand. "Mr. Chairman. I would like to move that that house rules be s-u-s-p-e-n-d-e-d during meetings as they p-e-r-t-a-i-n to language." He looked up and over at Windy. "It's hard to do business when about half your words ain't allowed. We got to worry so much about F words and shit like that we can't say nothing." He was nervous because he had violated house rules before they were officially suspended when he said "shit."

After some nods and winks between committee members, Windy's rules were suspended and freedom of speech restored. Encouraged by his victory, Sonny tried a motion "to allow a little wine drinking" during meetings but was voted down because Windy threatened Hugh. Happy pounded his hammer a couple of times and Sonny asked to recess for ten minutes to "take a leak." All committee members ignored the noise under the house. He returned with dirt on both knees and a shine in his eyes.

"Mr. Chairman," Sonny began again, "I think we got to do something about this campaign. It just ain't going nowhere. Three of the cocksuckers got TV commercials. All of 'em got signs with their picture on 'em. All of 'em got buttons and bumper stickers. All of 'em get their names in the *Morning Advocate* and the *Times Picayune*. We don't. We sit around on the front porch eating raw beans and jacking off while we losing this race."

Though Sonny's new diet at campaign headquarters had taken about ten pounds off him, his belly still overlapped his New Orleans championship belt buckle. The scar tissue over his ears, eyes, and nose still made his face look like a mistake. But Christian could see a change.

The old fighter's trips outside had left him slightly drunk, but the wine did not mask a new determination and self-confidence that he must have had at one time in the ring. Edmund showed proud approval of his hero's resolve. Happy looked stern. Whatever was going to happen had already been approved in some closed session before Christian arrived.

Sonny reached into his jeans pocket and pulled out a piece of lined paper covered with some primitive-looking marks and with some numbers written at the bottom. Christian could see four lines with slashes indicating groups of five.

"I got me a poll. I know it's right 'cause I took it myself. Now this ain't no jack-off poll. I personally went to ten different places and asked ten people each. I went mainly to bars 'cause that's where everybody hangs out. And except for Ernie's Cut-Rate, where Hugh is got one-hundred-percent recognition 'cause he hung out there for so many years, nobody even knows he's in the race."

Happy, with great enthusiasm, pounded his hammer. "What we voting on, Sonny? Get to the point. You know,

Sonny.'' Happy stammered, trying to get him to follow the script. He rapped twice more for effect.

''Well, I vote that we change things. I make a motion that we get a new political consultant or that we ask Mr. Christian Ahab Simmons to get off his ass and do something. Hugh don't even go out an' campaign.'' The fighter looked over at Edmund's younger brother, who wrung his hands trying to remember his part. The room waited.

''I second the mention,'' Matsu recited finally, and looked around triumphantly.

Christian didn't have a chance. The rebels had swooped down out of the mountains and captured their objective. The vote was four to two. Windy voted against the motion because she was the only one not afraid of Sonny and she worked for Christian. Happy joined her because he knew that Sonny would never hit a cripple. There was never doubt about the vote of the two blacks. They appreciated raw power, and Sonny had promised to ''beat the shit out of anyone at school who fucked with 'em.'' That sort of protection had made their lives much easier. Edmund's peers even stopped kidding him about reading books. All it took was for Sonny and his big belt buckle to walk around the school yard for ten minutes with the two brothers. They loved Sonny Clinton.

Christian had a dilemma. He had tried to keep the committee busy without involving them in the campaign. They had produced the pictures of the preacher and the blonde and had helped get the Blue Monster ready for the road. But the rest of their time had been spent in meaningless meetings and porch speculation. With three months left before the election, they were getting restless. Attempting to look contrite, Christian stood.

''May I have the floor, Mr. Chairman?'' He paused and looked at his shoes. ''You're right, Sonny. It's time for some changes to be made. I'd like to keep the campaign. I surely would. It's actually in better shape than you know but I've failed to tell you what's happening.'' His voice took on an exaggerated good-ol'-boy tone that helped put them at ease. He explained the web that started with him and branched out to the headquarters in Baton Rouge, to the churches, to the block workers, and to the voters.

"I understand," Edmund contributed. "It's like the Mary Kay lady. She gets other Mary Kay ladies and makes money off all of them. They get more Mary Kay ladies until the first Mary Kay lady get rich."

There was a lull in the meeting while the members discussed various Mary Kay and Avon ladies they had known. Windy knew one who was a prostitute and used the home meetings to get a stable of part-time housewife call girls. It took considerable pounding to get the meeting back to business. A final blow sent the hammer through a weakened place in the plywood. The meeting stopped while the tabletop was turned around so that Happy had fresh wood.

By force of will, Christian finally got their attention.

"The reason we don't have television and radio is that we are broke. B-R-O-K-E. You need me to spell it? You guys want to fire me? Who's gonna fire you? The job of a steering committee isn't to sit around a table. Your job is to raise money. How much have you raised? What you raised at Ernie's didn't even cover bail." Christian was getting angry.

"Mr. Chairman." Sonny asked for the floor again. After a little hammering, he said, "College Boy, I didn't mean to crawl your ass so bad. I'm sorry. But we on the ropes. My poll proven it. Now we decided to give you another chance." He looked around to acknowledge the applause. "And I tell you what else we gonna do. We gonna raise money." He winked. "I got me a plan."

Sonny's plan wasn't original. It had been discussed for years with other drunks when the level of wine neared the bottom of the bottle. It would have taken a lot of work and Sonny and his friends never had the energy. But now the scheme had a noble purpose that somehow affected the future of the Free World and Sonny's chances at becoming boxing commissioner. Besides that, now he had good, dependable friends. Sonny's jaw squared and he strolled into the yard under the cottonwood to have another swallow of inspiration. Sonny Clinton had a mission in life. The responsibility weighed so heavily on him that he sent Matsu to Ernie's for two more bottles of white port. But he was a changed man.

# 18

In any other place in America this funny lot would have attracted attention. A man with Buffalo Bill Cody–length white hair and beard in a wheelchair pushed by a flat-nosed, hooded-eyed man with twisted ears, a red-haired black youth without shoes, and a coal-black sixteen-year-old smoking blue cigarettes. But this was New Orleans' French Quarter. A neighborhood that finds a woman followed by a duck commonplace and a leather-fetish transvestite just another good citizen. The steering committee was hardly worthy of a second glance.

It was early Sunday morning. After swearing to a rigid code of conduct and taking driving lessons for almost two hours, they borrowed the Blue Monster for the eighty-mile trip to New Orleans.

"Now, no fucking with the mass media, and no driving fast, so that the mass media speaker blows off," Hugh had warned. Edmund, the designated driver, with a James Brown tape already in his back pocket, nodded. Happy raised his right hand as though to swear. But he didn't. Edmund had been chosen driver because he had so much experience at driving different cars. Usually, according to his taste for the weekend, he simply picked up transportation in the shopping-center parking lots.

They didn't disobey many of Hugh's driving rules. They

drove slowly. In fact, it took them more than seven hours to complete the two-hour trip. That seven hours, though, included four stops for wine and one for boiled crawfish. And they were afraid of the interstate highway, so they stayed on back roads. All their lives had been spent on one sort of back road or another. The narrow, winding River Road with all its dust and bumps was most comfortable to these travelers. James Brown, shrieking for the love of his lost woman from the big speaker, gave advance notice of their arrivals. In Louisiana many thought the blue DeSoto was the first float in a parade. Several times young children screamed, "Throw me som'thin, mister." Indeed, this crew looked like a small-town Mardi Gras parade, but somewhat more colorful.

They spent Saturday night at the Salvation Army shelter, where Sonny drank with old friends. Now the dew was on the pavement and weekend drunks still slept unmolested on Jackson Square Park benches. A policeman tipped his hat to the Baton Rouge delegation and two short-skirted hookers, still warm from courtyard tricks, asked them for a light and then paid Edmund five dollars for one of his blue cigarettes. Pigeons cleaned up crumbs of discarded po-boys and Lucky Dogs. Across town the homosexual priests, busted the night before, were being released from jail in time to hear confessions. Tourists had not yet begun to line up for breakfast at Brennan's. An old black man polished the brass on their entry doors. Brennan's sous-chef blackened the *roux* for the day's gumbo. The smell of browning flour mingled with street smells of soured wine, spilled scotch, and warm beer. The *Times Picayune* lay untouched before courtyard gates. A baby cried. A Franck violin concerto seeped out of courtyard blackness. A boat whistled on the Mississippi. As the delegation marched on, the violin music faded and the slight squeak in two-four time created by one of Happy's wheels marked cadence. The French Quarter sleeps late on Sunday.

New Orleans is not part of Louisiana or part of this nation. It is a Latin outpost that somehow wandered away and grew like a barnacle on the tip of sediment and sludge accumulated by a million years of the Mississippi vomiting the leavings of a continent. It is a nose-deep fog that assails the senses and leaves the brain almost untouched. Here orgasms are longer, drunks more exciting, angers more terrible, food hotter, relationships stronger and at the same time more temporary.

"Make us feel good," the citizens demand. So the music plays. And the shrimp boil. And the bourbon is poured. And the whores laugh and roll over on their backs. For there were no *Mayflower* pilgrims in this city. There were no scarlet letters, no stocks, no school primers saying "In Adam's Fall, We Sinned All."

The French Quarter has the sweetness of a fine French sauterne, the wine created by "noble rot," the grapes picked hours before they spoil. Just before their death they are best. New Orleans truly has the sweetness of noble rot.

They rolled on past Brennan's, past the Greek bars on Decatur whose drinkers had not yet discovered morning, past a new luxury hotel filled with Jaycees, and finally up the levy. Edmund helped Sonny pull Happy backward up the steep incline. The Mississippi lay at their feet. "There's that cocksucker," Sonny announced in triumph. He pointed to a paddlewheel boat, the *Huck Finn,* that bumped gently against a wharf hung with signs and banners. "See Historic Plantation Homes, Gamble for Charity."

"This cocksucker's got roulette wheels, blackjack tables, dice tables, and slot machines that take little plastic quarters. People wear funny hats and little string neckties and buy paper money to gamble with. Then they trade their paper money for toasters and shit like that. The real money goes to the symphony and church people. They rent the boat from a guy. After the spick cut me, I worked on the boat cleaning ashtrays and shit like that. Shit, there was free whiskey everywhere. Me and C. C. Turner would take new drinks off the tables and pour 'em in jugs. We had us a scotch jug, a bourbon jug, and a jug for all of the clear shit like gin and vodka. Then we'd get bottles off the street and pour in our stuff. For fifty cents we could sell a stumblebum a pint of hootch that didn't taste half bad.''

Sonny waved at a black man on the top deck of the boat. The man waved back with a red cloth. They waited while he walked the gangplank to the shore and up the levy to where they stood. He had a broad, toothy smile as he approached.

"The champ! My Lord, I never thought I'd see the champ again. I thought the champ had died or something. When Marie answered the phone, I told her, 'No, woman, the champ be dead. He go to Baton Rouge and get killed.' But here he be, looking ready for a comeback. I ain't had me a fighter since you, Sonny. We ain't got no fighters now. It ain't like it was when you and Tony Graphia and Will the Snake pounded the shit out of everybody. No sir, I told Marie, the champ be dead.'' He laughed and the two men embraced. A tear rolled down his face.

"This here is C. C. Turner, the best corner man in the biness.'' Sonny held C. C's hand in the fashion of ring victory. The committee members each shook his hand. To Edmund and Matsu, C. C. was a famous man. That he was a janitor on a riverboat didn't detract. . . .

"Next Thursday night, Champ. The boat be dark next Thursday night,'' C. C. said with his hand still in the air and a smile still on his face.

"That's fucking quick.''

"That be the only night, Champ. Harry be in Las Vegas with his woman and the crew be off.''

"You get the dealer.''

"Yep, but the dealer want five hundred fer himself and two hundred dollars per man. And that be in advance. And Champ, I don't like to say it, but I gots to have two hundred like we said on the phone.''

Sonny looked indignant. "I got something better than that for you, C. C. I got a hundred joints of Thibodaux Blue. This shit'll take off the top of you head. You sell 'em for two dollars each, you got you money. You sell 'em for three dollars and you make a ton. Some cocksuckers pay much as five dollars for Edmund's shit. It's famous. Show C. C. you shit.''

Edmund dug out a cigar box almost filled with the blue cigarettes. He was proud of his product. He borrowed a professional roller so that each joint was perfect. Near the end was a small *E,* his signature. They watched C. C.'s face as he lit up and took long drags, waiting for the desired effect.

They struck a deal. C. C. took the dope and a heavy bag of coins to pay the dealer. They all hoped College Boy wouldn't notice that his little car drove lighter. They had been forced to reclaim Happy's good-faith money.

''Sonny, all them cats be old who gonna deal. They coming out of homes and shelters. Some of 'em on crutches. All of 'em over seventy. The gambling halls be closed for thirty years.'' C. C. had tears in his eyes. ''Don't fuck with 'em. Pay 'em the money you promised. I told 'em the champ never threw a fight. That he stood with blood all over 'im to keep from going down. This will be the last time they ever gonna deal. It kinda a comeback for 'em.''

C. C. left with his bag of coins and his cigar box of free enterprise. The committee felt the heavy weight of responsibility to C. C., to the old dealers, and to the Free World. They had a lot to do in a short time.

As the committee made its deal, Christian watched the new and improved Hugh give his first major public address to the huge congregation of the First Baptist Church in Shreveport. Hugh had begun by speaking to Sunday school classes in legitimate but small Baptist and Methodist churches. He had three different speeches on the ''Need for God in Public Office.'' Hugh explained to the congregations that he had run for several offices but God had not willed a victory because Hugh Conklin needed to be taught a lesson. He explained that he had once held one of the highest offices in Washington as the administrative assistant on the powerful Energy Committee of the United States Senate.

Christian found some dead politicians who had been bad fellows and laced Hugh's little talks with their sins. The men's Sunday school classes particularly liked talk about loose women, so he even threw in John Kennedy's conquests. They had all heard of his exploits, but none had ever heard Hugh's new material. In fact, JFK had never heard of it. But Christian remembered him fondly as a president with a sense of humor and was sure he would not mind.

Hugh graduated to Class-B Lions Clubs in small towns and their second-largest churches. Hugh had found an old picture of himself leaning drunk against a pole, and Christian had it blown up to use in Hugh's talks. Another picture was faked to show Hugh standing between Robert and John Kennedy.

In six months, his three little talks had grown to five and another couple of photos. Hugh graduated to larger Lions Clubs and even small high-school assemblies. Christian began sending press releases on Hugh before each speech, and attracted larger crowds. The only place this didn't work was Baton Rouge, where Hugh was too well known as a derelict to engender much respect.

Christian had worked carefully with Hugh. He considered Hugh's speaking manner sufficient but not worthy of the response the little drunk was getting. Someone had even written a letter to the editor on the power of God as demonstrated by Hugh Conklin. The master plan for Hugh's election that Christian had romantically titled ''Cottonwood'' was going much better than he expected. Hugh called every morning with glowing reports of his success.

''College Boy, this is Hugh. How're you and the little lady doing this morning?'' He always called Darleen the ''little lady.''

''How's the candidate?'' Christian always responded.

''Sober another day'' was the conditioned response. It was a ritual that gave Hugh time to listen to inflections that might denote displeasure in Christian's voice and Christian an opportunity to listen for slurred words. Then they would discuss Hugh's day. Christian had been careful to schedule Hugh so there was little chance of being covered by major newspapers and television stations. As Hugh began to get invitations on his own, he carefully cleared them with Christian. He treated Christian as though he were a loaded bomb that could explode and ruin his campaign. He was right except that the stakes were higher for Christian than for Hugh.

"I got a big one for us."

"That's what you told me when you were asked to speak to the Chaneyville gays."

"Well, cocksuckers vote, too. But this is in Baton Rouge. I got an opportunity to speak to the second-largest Civitan group in Baton Rouge. They got more than a hundred members."

Christian thought about it briefly. It was too fast. Hugh was still a drunk in Baton Rouge, and this was a group of middle-class slobs who needed to suck the dignity from a poor drunk in order to preserve themselves. He could imagine catcalls and insults. He could even imagine that Hugh, who was now existing on a euphoric diet of sobriety, religion, and ego, could be forced back to drink. And Hugh going back to drink would ruin his and Big Jim's little scheme.

"No, Hugh."

"Please, College Boy. Give me a break. I can handle it. The people like me. They listen to every word. The speech you wrote is beautiful and they like me." Hugh was about to cry. The seven months of sobriety must have seemed like a lifetime. Christian's "too much, too fast" attitude was "too little, too slow." He wanted respect in his hometown.

"I'll go to your speech Sunday in Hammond. That big church is a real break for us. Give our new speech, and I will decide about the Baton Rouge speech."

The new speech was designed to eliminate much of the religious fundamentalism. It was time to progress to a talk about morality without a lot of the amens. It was a speech that could be given in front of such groups as Civitan Club—but not in Baton Rouge. Hugh had spent too much time in jail there and too much time walking the streets with his fly open.

Christian and Darleen sat in the back of the huge church. He didn't want to be seen. Slightly to one side of the podium was the poster illustrating the drunken Hugh that could be revealed at the most dramatic moment. It would show him in his splendor, with a broken wine bottle beside him, a whiskey bottle in his hand, and his tie hanging like a hangman's noose from his neck. But what made the photo great was the lamppost he rested against. The stereotypical drunk is always leaning against a lamppost. On the other side of the podium was the Kennedy photo, also covered.

Hugh was late and Christian was concerned. Could Hugh be drunk? Christian always worried Hugh might fortify himself for a new situation.

But as the speaker finished the introduction, Hugh bounded two steps at a time onto the stage. His blue blazer and conservative tie didn't look anything like a drunk's uniform. Darleen had dressed him. Hugh was sober. And Hugh had a few surprises.

"It's great to be alive," Hugh said without the benefit of a mike. He walked over to the stage steps.

"I used to stagger up steps like those or even sleep under them. But that was the time when I lived in the twilight zone. And tonight I want to talk about that twilight zone. I want to talk about what happens when we turn ourselves over to anything that robs us of our dignity and our intelligence. I let alcohol ruin my brain and corrupt my life. But your life can be corrupted by other things. Life can be corrupted by fear or dishonesty."

It was good but it wasn't in their script. It took Hugh about five minutes to get into the speech Christian had written. All of the preliminaries were a shock. The steps were a brilliant introduction to a speech about moral decay. But Hugh had a few more surprises. He flipped back the cover of the drunk photo and simply referred to it as an example of the decay of whiskey. The poster was a centerpiece in the rehearsed speech. But not now. Hugh went immediately to the other side of the podium to what should have been the Kennedy photo and revealed a montage of headlines about politicians being caught stealing, fornicating, and lying.

"This is an example of moral decay."

He was faithful to the rest of Christian's speech. Waving his arms in moral indignation, Hugh paraded around the stage shouting and whispering. The result was astonishing. The audience was on their feet at the end of the speech. He had shouted and he had whispered. The audience seemed glued to their pews.

Christian knew at once how Dr. Frankenstein must have felt when his creation got up from the table. He was both amused and angry. If Hugh could change or add to his material, he might make some terrible mistake that would end the little game and Christian's large investment in time and money.

After Hugh had shaken every right hand in the house, Christian cornered him outside.

"It looks like you don't need me anymore, Hugh. You have gone out on your own."

"No, College Boy, I just put on a little show before I started your speech. I didn't mean no harm. Me and Happy thought you would like it. Please don't be mad at me."

"For me to elect you to office, you must be an extension of my brain. If you defy me, I can't be responsible."

"I'm sorry."

"I think we had better call it a day. I'm getting tired of our little game. There's nothing in it for me. You get all the profit. All I get at home is my wife bitching about me fooling around with an old drunk and not working for a legitimate living.''

"I'll behave, College Boy. I'll never change the speech. If you say so, I'll never even think again. Please, don't be mad. Please.''

Hugh sat on the curb and wept as Christian and Darleen watched.

"What are you doing to this poor man?'' Darleen whispered.

"I am maintaining complete control. Play along with me. He'll heel.''

They drove Hugh back to Baton Rouge and told him that Christian would think about their relationship. It had been a good morning. Christian had gained even more control and he had also learned something. Hugh was good, damned good.

Darleen, though, was pensive and quiet. She seemed to be studying Christian's face.

"Christian, just how far will you go? You left that poor bum in tears. When you jerk a string, he hops.''

"I'm doing what I have to do. I want to change our future. I want to get out of this town and this state. I want respect and recognition. I want money. If I soften up, he ends up drunk. If he drinks, I . . . we lose. Before he met me, he slept in gutters. Now he eats a nutritious diet and—''

"Sure, a diet you select. He even sleeps with the woman you selected. He wears the ties you tell him to and the suits I buy. What is left of him? You're God and no person can question your commandments. You have toilet-trained a poor, desperate human being.''

"I'm as desperate as Hugh.''

"But Hugh is not cold-blooded.''

"You think I am?''

"Let's just say I wouldn't want to be in your way. I wouldn't look good with tire tracks across my ass.''

"And such a lovely ass.''

"Yep, just the size you like, decorated in just the color of silk—not nylon—you like. A few inches above the stockings you like, slung below the garter belt you like. A lovely, lovely, lovely ass. I like that it's a lovely ass. I don't like that it is *your* lovely ass. I would like for it to be *my* lovely ass. And what about my lovely tits? Now you want to talk about my lovely tits?"

"Darleen, what can I do to make you like me?"

"Come up with a plan. Put *As*, *Bs*, and *Cs*, beside the paragraphs. Get some college kids to put it in a computer. Get Big Jim to finance it."

"I'm being serious."

"I am too."

"So where do we go from here?"

"I decided that months ago when I became part of your plan. I'm going to be the best organizer you can imagine. I'm going to keep my ass the size you like, decorated the way you like. I'm going to dance while you pull the strings. If Hugh can come in fourth and you can make a pile of money, I'm going to stay in for my share. I want money too," she said.

"Another reason I'll stick, though, is I owe you. I've been a bitch during all of our marriage. I'm going to spend the next three months doing it your way. Then I'm going to make a decision. One of my options is to take this beautiful ass and market it while it's still young and firm. Another option is to become a perfect Darleen Andrews that is owned by Darleen Andrews. The third option is to blindly say, 'I love you' and continue with the Simmons Perfect Wife, Plan A."

"I'll try harder to be what you want."

"I feel sorry for you, Christian. You are always trying to be what I want. If I could come up with a plan, I have no doubt you'd follow it to the letter—at least until there was another project or another goal. Christian, I think I love you, but you are what you are. That will never change. I have every confidence that if you fail as a political consultant, you'll be famous as an astronaut or ballet dancer. You'll be a success. But you'll always leave human rubble behind. I'm not sure I want to be part of the wreckage.''

That night Darleen cooked perfect red fish and oysters and later spun bedroom fantasies that demonstrated her creativity and resolution. The following morning she fixed fried eggs with slightly browned edges, as Christian liked them, and kissed him twice at the door.

Once again he felt comfortable that his marriage was headed in the right direction. Christian was a happy man on Monday morning.

# 19

The little car began to protest the eighty-five-mph pace by making a strange sound. Christian almost complained to the driver about the excess speed but realized that he was driving. He had a lot on his mind. It was hard for him to save democracy, carve out a national niche for himself, and remember details like thumping off cigar ashes or driving. Only an hour before, he realized that he had gone fifty miles past Bunkie, where he was scheduled for a meeting with rural preachers. He stopped to call about being late and left his car keys in the phone booth. When he found his car keys, he ran out of gas and had to flag down a car.

Christian was one of those people who needed watching. He had been born too late for women who devoted their lives to the care and comfort of a man. And he was too poor for valets and drivers. He made little notes to remind himself to go home at certain hours and to eat. But he couldn't write notes about things like glancing occasionally at the speedometer or the gas gauge. So, often, he drove too fast or ran out of gas. He followed his notes enough to take shirts to the laundry, but later forgot which laundry. This cost him about twenty shirts per year.

It wasn't that Christian wasn't intelligent. All evidence contradicted that.

No, Christian was intelligent. Darleen didn't mean it when

she said he was "dumb, dumb, dumb." She also didn't mean it when she said he didn't care about anybody but himself. In truth, Christian cared a lot. He just forgot to show it. He would turn and walk away in the middle of a conversation, leaving the impression he didn't care. He cared. He just forgot. Something electrical sparked between two connectors in his brain and he shifted gears. But it was disturbing to Darleen, and Happy, and Brother Tracy, and the people who were attempting to break through and see a light come on in his eyes. It wasn't the same when Christian talked with Big Jim because the big man seemed never to have long conversations. Christian would forget he was talking on the phone to Windy and wander out of the room. With Big Jim a telephone conversation was seldom longer than thirty seconds. Details didn't concern Jim and details sort of missed Christian.

Despite the almost flawless execution of the Cottonwood Plan, the printout on the seat next to him was troubling. Hugh had moved from tenth to eighth place. It was too soon. Big Jim was someplace in Mexico hunting doves and Christian didn't know how much money had been bet. It was time to load up. He took another silent vow of vengeance and reminded himself to wait down the road for the Bobby Sotto, the political hack from New Orleans who had broken his nose, almost shot off his balls, and endangered his project. He picked up his notebook to write the note of vengeance and the car ran off the road and across about half an acre of soybeans before finding its way back between the yellow stripes.

Christian, covered with dust from the detour, stopped to relight his cigar and discovered he had left Darleen at home. He had gone out to check the car and had left her, baggage and all. "Oh shit," he said aloud, and made a note to call her when he found another telephone. But he forgot. When he called her that night, item number four on his "end-of-day checklist," a baby-sitter said she had "left for the night with friends." Christian couldn't think of any friends with

whom Darleen would want to spend a night and made a note
to call her again the next day.

Finally he found the turnoff to the "Ol'-Time Religion
Campgrounds" where the Association of Independent Evangelical Churches was meeting. Rural preachers from splinter
churches all over the state were attempting to write some sort
of theological agreement that justified their own theory of
theology. Until they came up with some sort of structure,
their preachers would be "called by the Lord" as they had
been in the past.

Dick Tracy had heard the call while standing behind the
lead guitar in a rock band. Several of the preachers had been
mechanics under cars reaching for wrenches when they found
Jesus. "Come out from under the Chevrolet and preach" was
the exact language the Lord had used on one of them. "THE
CALL" was one theological concept on which they already
agreed.

Christian liked the camp. There was a large meeting shelter in the center of what looked like a parade ground. Around
the perimeter of the parade ground were small frame cottages
with eight bunks in each. Also in the parade ground were a
swimming pool and a dining hall. The dining hall looked like
the meeting shelter except that the insects were screened out
and long picnic tables ran from end to end. Cut-over pine
trees and red dirt circled the entire compound.

Because the camp had at one time been a World War II
training area, there were also concrete machine-gun bunkers
spaced around the clearing. In fact, the campground was
sometimes called "Camp Christian Soldier." There were only
men in the camp. Women, by another theological agreement,
were mainly for procreation and cooking. Besides, men and
women could not "mix-bathe" by using the pool at the same
time. The Bible strictly forbade men and women swimming
together. Yes, women would have complicated the scheduling. Christian was curious about "mixed horseshoe pitch-
ing" and "mixed softball playing" but didn't ask. He did,

however, make a note of the question for a later conversation with Brother Tracy.

The camp meeting had been a great convenience. Darleen and Windy had been going from church to church training the volunteers, and this meeting gave Christian an opportunity to talk to more than a hundred of the ministers at the same time. The preachers were a rough bunch who had been drafted by God from some rather unusual jobs and situations. There were tattoos of naked women and some even had scars of earring holes. A couple of them walked with the rolling gait of merchant seamen. Christian's part of the program came after a seminar called "Jesus Speaks Loud on Radio and Television." Earlier that day there had been a seminar on methods of increasing collection-plate income by special offerings.

Christian didn't talk to the group about moral reform or the need to move Jesus to Washington. Instead he talked about power and the potential of political and economic growth because of his training and techniques. He started at the bottom and explained the campaign organization, step-by-step.

First he handed out complex position papers, too complicated for Christian or any of the preachers to understand. He explained that these papers were to give the "illusion of substance." When reporters asked or when respondents on the phone bank wanted more information, they were to be sent these university-written-and-inspired documents. Christian had not really read them, but had the word of some of his LSU whiz kids that they were solid and harmless. One of the papers actually called for a new form of Marxism but no one ever noticed.

Christian explained his plan and sprinkled financial incentives throughout his talk. "We found one church that has already increased its collection by more than twenty thousand dollars per year," he lied. Every mention of enhanced contributions brought scattered "Amens."

The uniform of the day out here at Camp Christian Soldier was preacher-helmet hair, jeans, and old dress shirts that had become too frayed to wear to church. All of them carried red Bibles. When he asked, Christian found that the red leather books were status symbols that cost more than a hundred dollars each. They were filled with yellow highlighted passages and bookmarks from the Holy Land. If their hair had not been varnished, these men could have been described as ''letting their hair down.'' Had they truly let their hair down, it would have shattered on the floor. They wore sneakers and combat boots and slumped in the pews.

Even Christian was bored with his speech. Soon he was getting smart-ass remarks from the preachers. ''Boy, if I wanted a sermon, I'd get ol' Rufus here to scare the devil out of me.'' There was much laughter and some ''Amens.'' ''Tell me how to make money.'' ''I'd like one of them long black Pony'act preacher cars with a foxtail. Tax-free, of course.'' More laughter. More ''Amens.'' Soon they were so disruptive Christian had to hold up his hands in surrender.

The heat in the shed building was stifling. Christian's coat turned a darker shade of blue.

''One last thing.'' There was much hooting and clapping. ''I have some gold pins here. The symbol of our campaign is a large *C* with an arrow through it. Some people will think that stands for Conklin. But we know that it stands for Christian Power. Now I want each of you to guard this pin and put it in a safe place every night. We paid about fifty dollars each for these pins, and they can only be worn by you preachers. It is our symbol of power. Before long, you walk into a political gathering wearing one of these pins and politicians will kill . . . ah . . . fall all over you to be nice.'' There was much laughter. Christian had lied. The pins cost about two dollars each, but he wanted to make the preachers feel special.

As each preacher came forward to have his pin put on his shirt, he was also supplied with a kit containing reprints of the newspaper clippings Hugh and Christian had collected during the past months. Also in the kit was a badge that read ''State Chairman for Hugh Conklin and Reform.'' Each preacher was made a member of the steering committee. The same steering committee that was, without Christian's knowledge, at that very moment gambling and whoring on the Mississippi River in the Big Easy.

A tall, good-looking man stood in the middle of the congregation. Before he was "called," he had been a tennis pro in a country club in Monroe. "Mr. Simmons, I'm called to speak. I want to relate the Lord's word as it came to me last year. 'Edgar,' the Lord said, 'I'm gonna send you a messenger to change this great nation. He will be like us but not necessarily of us. He will be a shining light and you will meet him in the darkest forest. Listen well to his word, for it is my word. Work for him, for ye will therefore be working for me. Doubt not. I hereby command ye.' It was like he grabbed me by the throat. I fell down on my knees and told him I would obey. Now I see it all. Mr. Simmons, you have been sent by the Lord.''

"Amen," the congregation began chanting. "Amen, amen, amen." Soon competitive preachers began praying in different parts of the auditorium.

Christian raised his hands in the air for silence. He knew this could go on for hours and he had scheduled a romp with Windy Dawn that night and he was more than eighty miles from Baton Rouge.

Slowly they became silent once more and turned to Christian. "I have to leave you. I have an important mission in Baton Rouge. I have left more kits on the table for distribution. I recommend an hour of prayer.''

"Amen.''

Christian could still hear the praying behind him as he reached the MG. The preacher with the vision was sitting in the passenger's seat.

"Brother Simmons. Before you got here, some of the brothers had started to talk about your motives in leading this nation back to the straight and narrow. Some actually felt that you were taking advantage of their good Christian natures. I knew it wasn't so because I had discussed it with Miz Windy Dawn. She had . . . she had . . . lifted me up to greater heights of awareness. She said that I should attend this meeting and try to help you in some way.''

''I can't tell you how much your help has meant to our cause.''

''No, I guess you can't.''

''And I don't guess I can repay you.''

''I wouldn't go that far. You can give me a ride to Baton Rouge.''

''You have business there?''

''You might say that. In fact, I took the liberty of scheduling my important mission there after you are through with your important mission with Miss Dawn.''

The drive to Baton Rouge wasn't bad. Christian stopped and bought a quart of gin and a six-pack of tonic. The night was hot and the gin and tonic made the air cooler and the ride shorter. He had four. His new best friend had five. Then they shared some breath freshener. Windy had firm rules about drinking.

Christian registered the tennis-pro preacher in a Howard Johnson's motel at the corporate rate and then drove to the phone-bank offices to find Windy. He was only about an hour late, but the huge room was empty except for Windy working against the far wall. Chamber music was playing over the radio instead of Windy's normal gospel music. Bach instead of ''The Old Rugged Cross.'' Christian crept behind her, cupped her breasts, and bit her lightly at the edge of her hair on her exposed neck. ''Sorry I'm late.''

Christian knew instantly it was wrong, something about a familiar feel that was not familiar. The woman turned her head up slowly. It was not Windy. She was even more beautiful, but she was not Windy Dawn. He straightened up in shock. He had molested Flora Tracy, the preacher's wife.

''Windy said to tell you that she had to leave early.''

''I'm so sorry. It was just a little joke. Windy and I kid

around a lot. Er. I was just kidding.'' Christian was stammering.

The woman had turned completely around. She was blond like Windy. She was about the same size as Windy. Later, when she stood, Christian found she was an inch taller. She had blue eyes instead of brown and her nose was slightly different. But she could have been Windy's sister.

''Windy said for me to tell you that she had to break the appointment because of a problem at campaign headquarters. I told her I would wait. I really wanted to have a chance to talk to you when you're not concentrating on eating cupcakes. I've heard so much about you and I've been working here for months.'' The woman had a soft whisper voice that came out of bloodred lips. ''The women who work here never get to meet Christian Ahab Simmons.''

Christian had expected to be slapped. Instead, she offered her hand and he shook it vigorously. Christian was not so shocked to ignore the fact that she jiggled when he shook her hand. But he tried not to look. ''Remember, I'm Flora Tracy. Dick Tracy's wife.''

Bach played on and Christian numbly held on to her hand, though he stopped shaking. Then he noticed and immediately dropped his hand but could not decide what to do with it. He rubbed his own sleeve and then put his hand in his pocket. ''I'm so sorry. That was just a little joke between Windy and me.''

''I saw you come in the door or I would have screamed.''

''I'm so sorry.''

''Don't be sorry. If I kept a diary, I would record this scene. That's never happened to me before.''

''I'm terribly sorry.''

''No, don't be. Once I wondered what a cigarette would taste like, so I tasted one. It was terrible but I wanted to know. Another time I took a swallow of wine because I never had. It wasn't really bad. Someday I might do that again.

Now another man has kissed and touched me, and I've recorded two more firsts.''

What an opening Christian had with her last comment. Clever retorts about the losing of various virginities flashed through his mind but froze on his lips. And it wasn't that he feared her or her husband. For a woman like this one Christian would normally take any risk. But a flashy remark would have been as vulgar as throwing a beer can on the White House lawn or drawing swastikas on synagogue walls. For once in his life, Christian was in a holy place. His holy place.

"I . . . I . . . I . . . would like to get you a cup of coffee or a soft drink or something. Anything.'' He had to hold her in place.

"I unplugged the coffeepot hours ago.''

"Wait here and I'll go across the street to the 7-Eleven. Don't leave. I'll be back immediately.'' Christian began backing up and fell across a table. She smiled at his awkward situation but didn't refuse his offer. He ran down the steps and was back with steaming coffee in minutes.

Christian sat staring at Flora. His coffee grew cold as the Bach washed over him, leaving small bumps on his arms. Flora took small sips of her coffee. He watched her heart throb in the base of her throat. It was the single most beautiful thing he had ever seen. He studied each swallow, each heart beat. The Brandenburgs played on and on, the tape automatically reversing. The gin wore off but Christian stayed dizzy.

"May I get you another cup?''

"No, it's after ten and I had better go home.''

"Some other time?'' It was almost a prayer.

"If you will tell me about things.''

"Like what?''

"Tell me about your plan for Mr. Conklin and my husband. He's so excited about what you're doing. Tell me about the kind of life that allows you to touch a woman like you touched me . . . a woman who isn't your wife.''

"I'm terribly sorry.''

"No. Don't be sorry. I don't want you to be sorry. I just want to understand things. I got married when I was fifteen and I've lived a sheltered life. I'm a senior in college now. I'm older than the other students, but they seem to know so much more. I can't ask them questions about life and experience. I don't really know enough to ask questions. I know what the sermons say and I know what the King James Bible says, but I don't know much more. I don't know if I am supposed to tell my husband about meeting you. For some reason the way you touched me makes it a secret. But there's no need for it to be a secret. Is there?" Christian had to lean forward to hear her.

"I do not want your husband to get the wrong idea. Perhaps you should not tell him." He noticed that his words sounded stilted. Each was carefully chosen and shyly delivered. Christian also whispered.

"I have so many rules. The other ladies can't see me talking to you. My husband is a great man and I don't want to cause any kind of talk. The other ladies say you have a . . . a special relationship . . . with Windy Dawn. They say we have to be careful around you. But you seem sweet. Maybe we can meet here again one night for a few minutes after everyone has gone. I think I would like that. You're not like they say."

"Do they think I am a bad person?"

"I don't really know. The ladies give you special consideration because you're so intelligent and you're doing so much good for the Lord and for our church. They say we should not question the Lord's decisions. On Wednesday night they pray for you."

"Do you pray for me?"

"Sometimes when they pray I hear Bach in my head. I want to hear the prayers and Bach keeps flooding them out. That happens in my husband's sermons, too. Sometimes I do a terrible thing on Sundays. A terrible thing. I put a tape player in my purse and run a tiny wire through my blouse to

an earpiece under my hair. All during the sermon I listen to
Bach. It makes the sun so beautiful coming through the
stained glass. So beautiful. It is like God talking in strings
and harpsichord. I weep a little. And then it's like a lie because my husband thinks I weep at the power of his sermon
and I don't tell him otherwise. I have never lied to my husband before. But it seems important to him that I am moved
by his sermon. And my husband is a good man and I want
so much to make him happy.''

''Do you love your husband?'' Christian asked, careful to
not mention his name.

''I must. I've been married to him for eleven years. He's
good to me. He tries so hard. But I seem to want things he
doesn't want. And I think things he doesn't think. He protects
me. But he seems to have lived up all of his life when he was
in rock and roll. Life was bad, he told me. There was illicit
sex and drugs and foul language. So when he was *called,* he
changed all of that. Only church magazines come to our home
and we only watch the Christian Broadcasting Network on
television. There are no hidden corners in our life. A few
times I tried to invent some . . . some . . . sexual excitement
and he tried to satisfy me, but it was disgusting to him.''

Mrs. Tracy walked to the door and Christian followed. He
continued to ask questions to slow her down, but she continued to walk. When she got into her car, she rolled down the
window and patted his hand.

''Now I have a secret. When I go to bed tonight, I'll think
about our secret.'' She drove away. Christian's hand burned.

**20** Christian drifted in the direction of campaign headquarters. First he stumbled into Ernie's Cut-Rate and had a
double scotch, trying to untangle his feelings about Flora
Tracy. He was confused. He almost didn't hear Big Ernie say
that Sonny and Happy and the boys had been in that afternoon. Bach kept dancing through his brain.

"Them cocksuckers is some happy," Ernie taunted. But
Christian didn't hear. "They all dressed like kings and covered with gold jewelry."

Far away, Christian could hear Ernie but no contact was
being made. He tapped his finger on the bar and hummed the
strings. "De dumm . . . de dumm . . . de dumm . . ."

"I got to get into politics. I never seen such a pile of
money as them cocksuckers had. You boys sure doing okay
for yourself."

"Pile of money?" Christian began to leave the eighteenth
century. "Pile of money?" Ernie had gone to the end of the
long bar. "Ernie, bring that scotch bottle back here." He
returned with the bottle of rotten scotch, the best he carried.
His customers were Four Roses and Old Crow drinkers, those
who did not drink white port and Thunderbird.

"Pile of money" was the best Christian could manage. He
fought Bach and the whispering goddess to the back of his
mind. "Pile of money?"

"Look at what they left me for a tip." Big Ernie pulled a hundred-dollar bill from his shirt pocket. "They had thousands of these. They had a bag so full of this kind of shit it almost wouldn't close at the top. They gave Sailor Jim a hundred for holding open the door and gave Dumb Tom a gold watch for cleaning their windshield 'fore they left. They bought drinks for the house five or six times. They was rolling. And you should have seen 'em. New suits and shoes. And hats. They all had new hats, even Happy. They was high, wide, and fucking handsome. You politicians know how to live. Yes, sir. I'm gonna run for office."

Christian was already halfway out of the door when Big Ernie told him his drink was "on the house."

Windy Dawn was sitting on the porch when Christian drove up. She had been crying. "They're drinking in there. They've got Hugh drunk. Sonny's drunk. Happy's drunk and is smoking dope. They gave me five hundred dollars to sit on the porch." She held up a wad of bills. They were all hundreds.

"Where did they get all the money, rob a bank?"

"They say they put on a fundraiser in New Orleans."

"I'll see what I can do."

"Don't go in there. I think they want to fire you."

"Fire me?"

"They say they have enough money to hire a professional from Washington to run their campaign."

"What does Hugh say about that?"

"Hugh's passed out in the bedroom. He can't even walk."

Bach kept pushing to the front. The harpsichord trilled. Flora was even more beautiful than Windy. Perhaps not in every detail. Windy had a better chin and nice cheeks. Christian pushed back the music. Windy changed to Flora and back to Windy. There was silence and then loud laughter from inside. The crash of glass.

"What are you going to do?" Christian asked.

"I have an appointment."

"With the preacher."

"With a preacher. Yes."

A cab pulled up and Windy left Christian standing on the front steps. He watched her get into the cab, and worked up enough courage to enter the campaign headquarters.


They were glorious. Except for Happy, they all wore Bogart-type hats with wide brims and bands. Edmund's was yellow with a white band and a large black feather. It matched his jacket. He wore a plaid bow tie and a cummerbund to match. And that's all Christian could see above the table. Sonny's hat was black and the brim was turned down low over his eyes. His coat was black and had red checks. He wore blue-tinted glasses. Happy wore a western hat with a snakeskin band and a matching western coat that could have been made for Big Jim. The shoulders were brown and the bottom of the coat was tan. The pockets were brown patches. Matsu, the eleven-year-old hero of the hour, made their dress look conservative. He wore a peach-colored tux, red hat with a white band, red glasses, and smoked a long cigar.

The meeting table was stacked with piles of cash and gold jewelry. Matsu was standing at attention at the table while Edmund retold the story of his heroics. ". . . so my brother here sees the bus full of cops a block away. They was waiting to raid our boat. So Matsu goes to the K-and-B Drugstore and buys a lock and locks them police in their bus. Then he goes and unties the boat and lets it drift out in the river. The band was still playing and the gamblers was still gambling and the hoes was still screwing and it all just drifted out in the fucking river. You should 'ave seen them cops with they guns drawn, standing on the dock. They looked like they all had they dicks in they hands."

Christian was too stunned to interrupt. And they may not have heard him if he had tried. Each point of the story was punctuated by table pounding and laughter. "Tell it again, Edmund," they would scream.

"Then the drunk undercover cop with the secret radio in

his coat dives into the river because one of the hoes stole his pants and threw 'em in the Mississippi. He was getting him a little bit of poon afore he called in his friends.''

They had all told their tales fifty times but the stories improved with each drink and each retelling. The whores grew more beautiful, the heroics of Matsu more brilliant, the bag of jewelry the gamblers lost heavier, and Sonny braver. But Edmund had become the chronicler.

''So I drove our little getaway boat over to the cop and let him hang on for 'bout a mile to the bank.''

''Tell him what you said,'' Sonny urged Edmund.

''I say, 'Mr. Police, buy youself some new pants,' and I give him back his gun he had left with the hoe and 'bout a thousand dollars. I just picked up a fistful. I didn't count.''

''Tell us what he say,'' Matsu, the new hero, suggested.

''He say, 'White boy, you and them Italians better get the hell out of here quick.' He call me white boy and Mr. Sonny and Mr. Happy Italians.''

Bach was firmly back in the eighteenth century. Christian was, for once, speechless.

''Well, lookie here. Here's College Boy. Matsu, give College Boy one of them foreign cigars and pour him a drink of this Raymond Martin brandy. The cocksucker's late. Edmund, look at your fucking Rolex fucking watch and tell College Boy how late he is.'' Happy pounded his hammer a couple of times for effect.

''My solid-gold Rolex say it be midnight. What do your solid-gold Rolex say, Happy?''

''My gold and silver Rolex says it two hours since this meeting was called.''

''My solid-gold Rolex say tick, tick, tick.'' The hero contributed and all of the table laughed uproariously. A huge gold watch slid around on his arm.

''Now, College Boy,'' Sonny said. ''Money talks and bullshit walks. You gonna get off your ass or you gonna walk. We got a few bills less than forty thousand dollars here. And that's after expenses.'' He cast an admiring glance at the attire of the committee. Later, Christian would find that Matsu even had a pair of shoes, his first. Matsu lit Christian's cigar and handed him a new bottle of brandy from a stack of cases against the wall. Christian broke the seal and took a long swallow. It burned going down. He took another. Sober was not a good condition in this crowd. There was silence as they watched Christian pass the initiation for their club. Hugh could be heard snoring in the back room.

''We start shooting television commercials next Monday. I have scripts and a crew lined up. All we lack is money. Now we have that. We can produce and get this campaign in gear.''

''College Boy,'' Happy said rather pompously, ''we got to review the scripts. We ain't putting up all this money for bullshit. We been talking in the car on the way back. We got some ideas for you. We did a little writing.''

''And we not gonna waste it all on TV either,'' Sonny added. ''We want signs and bumper stickers and T-shirts with Hugh's name.''

''And we gotta have some signs on buses,'' Edmund added.

''And buttons with Mr. Hugh's picture,'' brother Matsu added. Locking up the police had earned him a front seat at the table.

''And College Boy,'' Sonny added. ''People don't listen to radio unless there's music. So we wrote a tune with some words for you. All you got to do is get some musicians. Sing it, Edmund.'' Edmund got up from the table and began to sing in the style of James Brown.

''Hugh, Hugh, he's for you.
Send him to D.C. and
He'll know just what to do.
Hugh, Hugh, he's for you,

A senator you can count on
Through and through.''

''It was better in the car when we was all singing, but you get the drift, don't you, College Boy,'' Sonny asked.

This was Christian's first steering-committee uprising. In later years he would learn this was rather typical and had nothing to do with the education or social standing of the members. All committees would want billboards, and T-shirts and bumper stickers and catchy radio jingles. All steering committees would consider themselves experts at producing television. All committees would resent paying an outsider to do what they knew they could do better themselves.

But Christian had learned his early lessons well. ''Brilliant,'' he said, applying the Miz Molly Pierce rule of never disagreeing. ''I think that jingle is simply brilliant. Sing it again slowly, Edmund, and let me write it down.'' Edmund stood and slowly recited the lyrics as Christian wrote them on the back of an envelope. The committee nodded among themselves. They had won the battle. But they forgot to ask for the television scripts until the shooting was finished. Christian left that night with thirty thousand dollars in hundred-dollar bills and a gold bracelet that had been lost on a boxcars throw of the dice. The rest of the money was kept for what the committee called ''operations capital.'' Bach fought back to the top as Christian drove home to the compliant arms of Darleen. She liked her bracelet. He didn't sleep well that night or for many nights to come.

# 21

". . . and if it were not possible for man to change, we would be without hope and simply animals swept along in the currents of life . . . helpless, and without purpose.

"Hugh Conklin decided to make the world a better place. He started with himself. Before he is through, he will return morality to Washington. Because one voice for right will be heard loudly in the deserts of our nation's capital." (Hugh rubs small child's head as helicopter shot begins to move back once again showing children with Hugh picking up trash in the park.)

Christian looked around as the house lights came on and the projector flickered off. Every eye was wet. There was silence while the audience regained its composure. Then the praise began that did not stop for more than a year. For years after the election, Christian was known as the creator of that "wonderful Hugh Conklin television program."

During the showing, he had watched the light flicker off Flora's face, lighting her tears as they welled in her eyes and then ran down her cheeks. Glittering prisms. There had been two other meetings in the phone bank between this sheltered woman and the humbled consultant. Meaningless comments whispered across the table seemed intimate secrets. But the only real secret was that they met. Just met. Nothing more. And they talked. Nothing more.

Once, Christian's hand lingered, barely touching hers. An accident? he wondered. He was afraid to breathe. The warm touch vibrated through his body. As their flesh parted only an eighth of an inch, Christian felt rejected. I pushed too fast, he cautioned. He used that discarded hand to drink his now cold coffee. To keep it busy. Was it rejected? Perhaps she didn't intentionally move her hand. He wanted to hold her hand, to touch her face. Was that too bold? He would settle for cold coffee with a table between them.

But reality was calling. And the reality was the woman's husband. "Mr. Simmons. Mr. Simmons. Over here. What I said was if I could preach that well, I would have the largest congregation in the United States," contributed a wet-eyed Brother Tracy.

"I just know now that Brother Conklin will win," volunteered another woman.

Christian had the same feeling. He had produced thirty minutes of emotional pap. There was not ten seconds of substance in it. In fact, he could not even think of one truth it contained except that Hugh was a dried-out drunk. And Christian included that truth because it was necessary to meet the gossip and the critics head-on.

He was confident that this film combined with the organization work would lift Hugh from his current tenth place to fourth and make Christian a rich and famous man. He had found that television was the campaign tool by which political consultants were judged. To break out of Louisiana he had to have a great reel of television and an upset showing of some kind. Fourth place for a drunk would suffice, he thought still.

After getting the church-group approval, he arranged a private showing for Big Jim and Susie at the ranch. He thought the film would be the key to restoring his relationship with them. Jim still lacked the commitment necessary to contribute more money. He seemed more willing to bet than to make the bet work. Christian thought often that Big Jim was paying a huge price to force him into a business relationship. But, despite the importance of the meeting, Christian scheduled it early so he could return to Baton Rouge for a late-night meeting with Flora.

The showing went well until the lights went on. Susie was at once hysterical. The story of the drunk making a comeback stirred the dark hooker guilt in her heart. She cried and prayed on the floor next to the sofa. She swore she was going to change her life. Big Jim looked at her in disgust. She was still small and hard to replace. Besides, he was now engaged to her and he was too busy to go out and look for another girl.

"Have a couple of drinks and forget about it," Big Jim shouted. He looked at Christian for help.

"It's all bullshit. Everything in the film is bullshit," he said, trying to calm her.

"You may have dried up every whorehouse and liquor store in the district."

"It won't last long."

"Just till they get thirsty or their dicks get hard," Jim observed.

Of all days that Christian wanted brevity, Big Jim was talkative. He had on a tan cowboy suit with red trim. His boots were tan suede with "Big Jim" stitched in red across the top.

"Now, you tell me we're broke and can't run the film," he repeated for the fourth time. Bach was again crashing through Christian's mind, so he didn't hear the first two comments.

"I have three women on the phone trying to raise contributions."

"You've heard about snowballs in hell?"

"Every dollar helps," Christian said.

"Where is Crazy Hugh in the polls?"

"Tenth."

"Tenth . . . tenth . . . why, I got all that money invested

and it's five weeks out of the gate and you tell me we're tenth.''

''Trust me.''

''Goddamn it, College Boy, I think I've trusted you too much already. I can do simple math. You got to move two places a week. You got only thirty-five days. You want me to figure how many minutes that is.'' Big Jim was so upset he turned into a mass of red and tan. ''Now you tell me we can't win without more fucking money.'' There was no need for Christian to say anything more. Without the film, Christian didn't know if Hugh could be pulled to fourth. He worked to push back Bach.

''I'll make you a deal, College Boy. How much money can you raise if you hocked your car and your furniture and everything else you owned?''

''I guess about ten thousand dollars.''

''Then do it and I'll match you dollar for dollar,'' Big Jim commanded. Christian thought, I shouldn't have made Susie cry. It put him in a bad mood.

As Christian opened the door, Jim had one final comment. ''College Boy, it's the best fucking film I ever saw.''

Christian raced to the phone bank. He was wet with sweat. She sat calmly on the opposite side of the table. His heart pounded. Over a five-minute period he increased the pressure until the edges of their hands, both holding coffee cups, were in firm contact. Her flesh burned him. Without moving his paralyzed right hand, he reached across with his left and removed the coffee cup. Then he put his hand lightly on Flora's. She didn't move. They sat for ten minutes almost without breathing. She stared at the table under their hands. He watched the throbbing of her throat.

''I want to help you, Christian.'' She continued to look down. He watched her heart pump in the tops of her breasts and in the white, soft skin of her throat.

''Help me what?''

"I want to help you like yourself. You're driven and usually a robot. But now you're holding my hand and I can feel warmth. There is potential in you for love and great decency. When one of the ladies praised you the other night, you simply walked away. She was giving you something and you didn't know how to accept."

"I guess I've never been given much. Early in life I learned to live by ducking and staying out of the way. I would climb high up in an old cottonwood tree and stay for hours, safe and untouchable. The tree seemed to hold me. It was always better when there was some distance."

"Tell me more about your boyhood."

"I didn't have one."

She smiled. "Does that mean you were a man from birth?"

"No, I wasn't a man until I was about six. I don't remember all the years before that. I was just a short adult who was left with an old jailbird Wobblie to raise."

"He raised you?"

"No, I raised him."

"Wobblie? I'm not sure I understand."

"Me either."

"Was he a relative or a guardian?"

"No, he was just an old IWW union guy left over from the thirties that my daddy met in jail. When my daddy died, he moved into our house and stayed. At least he used the house for a base. Sometimes he would be gone for a couple of months and sometimes he would be in jail. He cared about things. He and my daddy both cared about things. They just burned at injustice."

"It's nice to care."

"Sure, caring killed my daddy and burned the guts out of Caleb. Caring kept us too poor to buy shoes. When there was a strike, we would take our food to men who were wavering and considering crossing the picket lines. 'We're strong,' my daddy would say. 'We can stand up to an empty stomach, but the weak ones can't.' I never—" Christian's voice caught and a tear formed in the corner of his eye. He quickly turned his head toward the window.

"I care about you, Christian. My husband cares about you. I think your wife cares about you. Take off the armor. Give us a chance." She squeezed his hand.

All Christian could raise was seven thousand. Sadly he concluded that thus far, his life had come to only seven thousand dollars. It was depressing. Big Jim matched the money, but Christian had lost two more days.

He went back to his manual to check progress. All of the television being run by the other candidates was beginning to frighten him. The months until election had become days. The fourteen thousand was spent on Baton Rouge, Shreveport, Monroe, and Alexandria television. It had to be spread thinly but it was used as proof to the church organizations that the campaign was making progress and was competing with the other campaigns. Each of the churches called their select list of decided voters and urged them to watch the late-night and early-morning programs. Christian could afford only fringe time. After the programs ran, the phone banks called again asking for contributions so that they could run again. This tripled the coverage in the four markets, but still didn't give the campaign the media punch it needed.

The campaign committee had spent all of its remaining money on pictures of Martin Luther King, Jr., that changed to Hugh Conklin when the light shifted, T-shirts with Conklin misspelled "Conlin," signs on stakes that glowed in the dark and engraved nameplates for the table.

Windy, through Hugh, had regained some control as the money was depleted. The wine and spirits were once again hidden under the porch and there was no smell of dope.

Ravin' Dave of the Tower of Power, the most popular radio-morning-show personality in New Orleans, lay in a huge bed in the Baton Rouge Oak Manor Motel with Betsy Lavell, the station's most beautiful salesperson. Her territory was Baton Rouge. Between their toes, through the cigarette smoke, the television turned from a temporary diversion to a riveting emotional experience. Betsy lay sobbing as a visionary Hugh Conklin rubbed the head of a small black child. A man in a wheelchair speared park litter in the background. Bach swelled up under the sound of laughter and a New York announcer with a tear in his voice almost whispered, ". . . and if it were not possible for man to change, we would be without hope and simply animals swept along in the currents of life . . . helpless, and without purpose. . . ."

Ravin' Dave wiped away a tear and got up from the bed.

"Where are you going, we're not nearly through." Betsy sat up.

"I'm going home to New Orleans. I just got a great idea for my show. I'm gonna wave the flag and make this bum a superstar. I'm going to talk about the trashy behavior of our political leadership and the loss of traditional values. The nuts out there can swell my ratings back to the top. What an opportunity. Get dressed and go on home to your family."

"I am, just as soon as we're finished. Come on, Dave. The only half of this roll in the hay we've finished tonight is your half. Besides, my husband is staying with the kids and doesn't expect me home for another two hours."

She kicked off the sheet. She was a little plump but not bad. "Look, Dave . . . you can't do anything at the station tonight." She ran her hands seductively down her body. Dave continued to pull on his pants. It was obvious that Betsy was losing.

Dave snapped his suspenders and began tying his left shoe. "Look, Betsy, I've had a long and firm conviction that our station needed some cause. This could be it."

"Come on, Dave. I want a little more of that long and firm conviction." She reached out to him. Dave paused and then began taking off his suspenders. Betsy wasn't the station's best salesperson for no reason. But Dave didn't forget his obligation to his station.

The Blue Monster's old tube radio could pick up the clear channel transmissions from New Orleans, so the steering committee all piled into the car every morning to listen to Ravin' Dave. He had been mentioning Hugh's name on the air. He talked about the campaign and used lines from the program and created an incredible demand for the show in the New Orleans market. Soon listeners, who could also call in to the station and express themselves on the air, had donated enough money to broadcast the show three times on the huge New Orleans television stations. Thirty percent of Louisiana's voters lived within viewing distance of New Orleans.

"Dave, this is Old Bill. How are you this morning?"

"I'm fine, Old Bill. You're on the air."

"Dave, I know I can't mention names on the air but . . ."

"This is America, Old Bill, and the hot line is yours. What's on your mind?"

"Well, out by Algiers we set up a 'Morality in Government' fund. If folks out there want something other than our state's representatives"—*beep* . . . *beep*—"in the tidal basin with a"—*beep* . . . *beep.*

"Old Bill. This is America but we still have some rules here at the station. We have a three-second delay and our engineer just beeped out a few of your words but I'm sure we all get the drift. What's the address of your group?"

"Let the cocksucker talk," Sonny screamed. They had been holding the mass-media mike close to the radio speaker so Happy could hear the broadcast on the porch. "Cocksucker" rang throughout the neighborhood.

"Sounds like I'll be buying another TV show tomorrow," Happy screamed back.

Hugh was worried about the committee's activities. They bought television without telling College Boy. Hugh would have said something earlier, but he liked the development of the campaign in New Orleans. He feared, though, that College Boy would find out what was happening. There was some danger he would quit again.

"Happy, don't you think we ought to tell College Boy about all of that money we're spending in New Orleans?" Hugh asked in almost a plea.

"Fuck 'em. I think that cocksucker wants you to lose. He didn't do our music and he didn't let us see the television script before he made the show."

"But everybody says it is a great show."

"Could have been better. Me and the boys had some ideas."

Christian was in love. He had drifted through the days after production of the television program listening to Bach and writing poems that he never delivered. For days he had not gone to campaign headquarters. The committee was driving him crazy.

Darleen was spending her time on the road, coordinating the churches and doing advance work for a tour by the candidate. Christian had finally caved in and scheduled some stump speeches on courthouse steps like the other candidates. Darleen had taken over all of the organizational duties from Christian and Windy. She even bought a briefcase and had business cards printed.

Hoping to get a glance at Flora, Christian hung around the phone-bank headquarters. Twice a week she would stay after the other women left.

Christian crashed out of his lethargy when one of his computer whiz kids brought a printout from their latest poll.

"Your candidate is in a firm fourth place and climbing," the student reported. Christian studied the printout. Blood rushed to his head. Of the people polled who had seen the television show, Hugh received sixty percent of the votes. Coupled with the voter-turnout operation in the churches, and without any more growth from television, the numbers wizard predicted that Hugh would run no worse than third.

"What do you mean, 'no worse than third'?"

"I think Hugh could run second."

"Bullshit. As soon as the other candidates see this growth, they'll butcher him with their money. I didn't want to run better than sixth this week. This could be a disaster. How—"

"If you want to slow down the growth, take your television off in New Orleans. It's—"

"I'm not running television in New Orleans. Your numbers must be wrong." Christian was relieved. "You got a bad sample."

"Nope, we have unaided recall of thirty percent in New Orleans. In the open-ended comments a lot of people quote directly from your script."

"I don't understand. . . ."

"It's simple. The people of this state are frustrated and angry. Supporting Hugh is like kicking sand in the eyes of the political establishment. This anger is being translated—"

"No, I don't understand how our program ran in New Orleans."

The graduate student began folding the printout. "Congratulations, Christian. You may be in the process of one of the greatest upsets of our time."

Christian had mixed feelings. It had to be the steering committee. There was satisfaction in knowing that his campaign philosophy and techniques were working, but he knew the Bobby Suttos of the state could not afford to have an outsider win. It would destroy the illusions that kept them in power. "The fucking steering committee," Christian muttered to himself as he sat clutching the cold cup of coffee.

" 'Lo, Ravin' Dave, this here is Alfred Newman in Baton Rouge."

"You're on the air, Alfred. What's on your mind?"

"I just want to say that Mr. Conklin is a wonderful man and, even if his TV show could have been better, it convinced me and my friends. Good-bye."

Happy handed the phone and a quarter to Edmund. "You call 'em now." Sonny took a hit from his bottle. "We'll show College Boy and all them cocksuckers a thing or two about telephone banks."

The steering committee was truly out of control.

**22** They held hands for much of their allotted hour. Softly. Christian's thumb floated over the smooth skin on the back of Flora's hand. She didn't withdraw. Silence. It was their first night on the same side of the table. He could smell the perfume and the starched freshness of her.

"I'm sorry about the other night," Christian whispered.

"Did you hurt your head?"

"No," Christian lied. There was a gash in the back of his head from her car's window frame. He had leaned in to kiss her good night but she had jerked her head aside, startling him. It had been a mistake. He had gone too far. And he hit his head as he tried to undo his mistake.

"You frightened me. I've never been kissed by another man."

Silence. A large clock ticked. The Bach tape had run its course and hissed quietly.

"I'm sorry."

"After I got home I thought about it. About what it would have been like. I didn't sleep." She searched their fingers and carefully put her other hand on his. "Later I was sorry."

"Were you sorry that we didn't kiss or that I hit my head?"

She continued to look down and didn't answer for long seconds. "Both, I think."

Christian gently put one finger on the pulse at her temple. Slowly he traced the outline of her eyes, her chin, and then her lips. She raised her head and closed her eyes. Her body shuddered faintly. He kissed her gently on the lips with almost no pressure. She leaned slightly into him, a sweet signal of response, and then withdrew.

"Christian, I feel like we're sitting in a fish bowl."

"May I turn out the lights?"

She nodded yes, looking squarely into his eyes. Her lips were parted.

Street light coming through the blinds threw vertical slices of brightness across her body, turning her skin pale blue, her white silk blouse even whiter.

They kissed again. This time she put her hands on Christian's shoulders. Their tongues met cautiously and then withdrew. Christian reached for the first of many small pearl buttons. She froze, but the button slipped free. Then another. It revealed the swelling of her breasts, and Christian glided his fingers over the exposed lighter skin, carefully, as though he were reading a difficult passage in braille. She leaned again toward his lips. Her mouth opened. A third and fourth button worked free. She helped, only slightly, by leaning forward. His fingers began to explore. A sigh of surrender and then . . . then . . . with the prize within his grasp, Christian's telephone pager exploded with sound. The sanctity of the holy place was defiled.

*Beep. Beep.*

"College Boy, this here's Sonny. If you can hear me, come quick. The little cocksucker's got drunk and run away. Come quick, Coll—" The time limit on the beeper had expired. Flora was refastening her buttons as she rushed from the room toward her car. Christian recovered and ran after her, but she was driving out of the lot when he got to the last stair.

* * *

It's amazing how one can remember the bad times in life better than the good times. Christian would remember forever every breath and step he took during those five days and nights. It's those times that form scar tissue on one's soul, and if one survives, the soul is harder to penetrate the next time. Maybe there are no hard men, just experienced men with scars.

When Christian found Happy, the news vendor had gone up and down the neighborhood streets so many times, the battery in his chair had run down. He was moving along slowly by hand. The dirty old derelict was crying. But the tears were angry. His hands were bleeding from blisters he had acquired after the battery had given its last spark. Christian had to walk beside him because he wouldn't stop.

"I did it, College Boy," he sobbed. "I ruined the only man who ever took me in. Me and that woman. If that woman hadn't moved in, we would've been all right—just Hugh and me."

"What did Windy do?" Christian had to follow him for almost a block before he would answer. Happy was panting and wet from the exertion.

"Nothing. She didn't do nothing."

Christian stuck his foot under the wheel and stopped the chair. It pivoted sharply toward him. "Come on, Happy, I don't have time for this. You got to tell me what happened. We have to find Hugh."

"We just tried to do what's right. We didn't mean no harm. We heard you was out of money. The woman said if I would bring her men, she would raise the money—you know, whore for it. We was just going to raise money for the campaign."

"And Hugh found out?"

"Yeah, he found out."

Christian couldn't understand Hugh's objection unless he thought taking money for sex was worse than what she was already doing with him and a couple of preachers. He knew that Hugh considered a prostitute just another professional like a lawyer or doctor or truck driver.

"Who did you fix her up with, Happy?"

"The legislature. I took a naked Polaroid picture to my newsstand and showed it to the legislators."

That made it simple. Happy had told them that the woman was trying to raise money for Hugh's Senate campaign. Hugh was politically embarrassed. Christian thought for a moment and decided that he had to first get Windy Dawn back to home base. But Windy had checked out of the hotel and was gone.

Happy had already called a meeting of the steering committee. They were waiting at the shack. For once, Christian was glad to have them. But before they would listen, they made Happy use the hammer and officially call the meeting to order. *My life and future are on the line and they want their own, perverted* Robert's Rules of Order. *Shit!* flashed through Christian's mind.

Edmund spoke first. "Mr. Chairman. Who gives a flying fuck if Mr. Crazy Hugh get drunk? Everybody get . . . gets drunk. We used to let him sleep it off and go back to campaigning. My whole fucking Boy Scout troop get . . . er . . . gets drunk."

Sonny saw the complete logic of Edmund's position. "Shit, if the little cocksucker don't get run over by a truck, he'll come home. We don't give him but twenty dollars at a time. Even if you drink T-Bird, you can't stay drunk but four days on twenty dollars."

"First," Christian explained, "three terrible things can happen while he is drunk. Getting run over by the truck is the least painful for all. I want to remind this committee that Hugh is a candidate for reform. If a reporter finds Hugh drunk and puts it in the newspaper, it'll wreck the campaign. The third bad thing, worse than getting run over by a truck, would be for Hugh to show up at the church or the telephone bank. If he stumbles drunk into my volunteers, we're through, because we need all of those church women to get out the vote.''

Happy began to weep again. Sonny and Edmund were, for once, humbled and offered no smart-ass comment.

Christian organized the ragtag group and gave each of them simple duties. Action Chairman Sonny Clinton was to stand outside the headquarters door to stop Hugh from going in, should he show up. Edmund was assigned to take his friends and comb the black bars. Christian had highest hopes of finding the candidate there. Blacks don't tell. They had been offering and receiving sanctuary for hundreds of years.

They solemnly shook hands and agreed to meet again at midnight, hopefully with the lost candidate. Christian began a tour of the legislative hangouts, thinking he might also get information. From his experience with Big Jim, he knew a lot of the legislators and their bars.

Nothing worked. One at a time, the committee members staggered back into headquarters. Hugh was lost. They sat glum and remarkably sober around the conference table. Happy tapped his hammer lightly against the plywood. Midnight.

''Hugh's changed,'' Sonny mumbled almost to himself. '' 'Bout a year ago he wouldn't have cared if some woman sold pussy. He woulda been proud.''

Sonny's statement reflected their own thoughts. None of them could understand Hugh's consternation. They each offered comments similar to Sonny's. Each comment unnecessary, little more than filler for the morning hours.

''You puts it in and you takes it out and don't nothin' change. It goes right back to the same shape, ready to be used again. It don't hurt a woman none,'' Happy reflected aloud. Each, in turn, after being recognized by the chair, offered comments as profound. It was a riddle beyond their understanding that Hugh would mind a simple act of commerce with a reusable resource.

"Gentlemen, I think our candidate is in love," Christian explained.

The startled committee looked up. The thought had never occurred to them. Christian was beginning to understand love. Flora's white flesh and tiny buttons fought for time with his concern about Hugh. He shook his head to drive away the thought of Flora lying next to her husband.

Happy moved to adjourn until morning because "Hugh always passed out before midnight and was safe until he needed a drink the next morning." An exhausted Christian drove toward home, first going slowly past Flora's large house, where one light shone in an upstairs window.

Darleen knew the old bromide about asking questions one didn't want answered. But she had to get her marriage out of its buffeting stall. For weeks it had all seemed so good. Christian had spent time with the children and confided his hopes and dreams. They had truly become a team working together. It was almost storybook quality. He had cut back on his drinking and had helped Darleen develop her career as a political organizer. He celebrated her successes and seemed to care about things. The distant man from the cottonwood had made a landing in her home. He had become a human instead of a machine. And then, slowly, a fog had crept between them. He still smiled. He still patted her on the head. But something was wrong. And Darleen was afraid the new man had found a new woman. "No," she said. "It couldn't be Flora. No." She screamed loud enough to disturb the children. *"No. No.* Even Christian wouldn't do that." But she had to know. She had to start a new life—with or without Christian.

When she heard his car, she arranged herself in bed. "I have to know if he truly loves me," she said aloud. Her face was wet.

Christian found his wife sitting in the middle of the bed,

fully dressed. Five hundred-dollar bills lay scattered around her feet.

"There's a note for you on the table. Flora Tracy called but said you could reach her tomorrow."

Christian tried to act casual at the mention of Flora's name. Darleen watched his face carefully.

"I have some money for Hugh's campaign." She motioned to the money. "There's another fifty in my purse I'm keeping for expenses."

"Where did you get the money?" Christian asked, glad to leave the subject of Flora Tracy.

"I sold my services. I went into business with Windy. Do you care?" She continued to watch his face.

"Did you use your real name?" was Christian's reflexive response.

"That's what I thought. You don't really care. You don't care that I might have sold myself to a bunch of legislators. All you care about is whether it could reflect on you and hurt your chances in your insane search for stardom. You don't care. You don't care that I've become the best organizer in the state. You don't care that I'm pretty. You do care that I'm a great piece of ass. But you would just as soon have Windy or Flora Tracy or any other woman that looks good and has the proper techniques."

Christian stood speechless. How could Darleen have suspected Flora? He had hardly even touched her. Darleen looked good sitting in the middle of the bed with her skirt pulled up over her stockings to the top of her legs.

"Do you know where Windy is?" he asked.

Darleen began weeping. She pointed down the hall, her body racked with sobs. "I'm through, Christian. I'm through, you son of a bitch."

Windy was asleep in the other room. She sat up when Christian turned on the light. The sheet fell around her waist.

"Christian. I have the greatest news. I have three thousand dollars for the campaign." She picked up a leather purse from a bedside table and emptied it. She sat nude in a sea of hundreds and fifties.

"I have twenty-five hundred here and Darleen has another five hundred."

"Did she earn it the same way you did?"

"No, I just lent it to her. She said she had a joke to play on you." Christian could hear sobs in the other room. And a child had begun to whimper.

**23** Christian Ahab Simmons hurt. He blinked his eyes three times and the strange green spots floating through a yellow void became cottonwood leaves against a humid polluted sky. He moved one leg and the other. Christian balled his hands into fists. Despite the pain, his inventory proved that everything worked.

Next he flexed his mind. The recent past was blank. Christian didn't know if the void was hours or days. But there was a black hole in his mind. A loud horn from a tanker scolding an encroaching tugboat put his position close to the Mississippi River. That meant the cottonwood floating above him was in Hugh's yard. Christian had slept under the tree. If one could be in such great pain and be pleased, Christian was pleased. He was in friendly territory. And friendly territory was shrinking as Hugh's campaign grew more successful. The Bobby Suttos of Louisiana did not give up easily the illusion of their power.

Trying not to move, Christian began to assemble the puzzle pieces of his yesterdays.

Monday, Darleen kicked him out. Oh, she didn't exactly kick him out. Rather she left a toilet-paper box on the front steps filled with a tangle of shirts, suits, and underwear. A note was taped to the box: "Christian, you son of a bitch, get out of my life."

Tuesday, Windy failed to keep a motel appointment with Christian. Instead, she moved in with Darleen to escape campaign headquarters. In Hugh's absence the old house had turned again into a den of vice and lassitude. Windy also left a note: "Christian, you should be ashamed of how you treat Darleen. We will not have sex again until you make amends."

Wednesday was a terrible day. Flora called. "Christian, I'm leaving town for ten days with my husband. He's been called to preach a revival in Tallahassee." Christian thought he and Flora were only one meeting and a couple of buttons away from bliss. The trip could set them back. Then on Thursday, the MG died. Christian had forgotten to add oil and the engine sort of melted together.

Now Christian focused his eyes. He feared the pain of turning his head. He remembered moving his toilet-paper box of possessions into campaign headquarters. The ramshackle old cypress house was his last refuge. He was broke. With the last money available, Windy's three-thousand-dollar contribution, he had made a five-to-one-odds bet. The coins were in the trunk of the car but they belonged to Happy, and Christian still held tightly the pride that he had never resorted to theft.

Once again he proved to himself that his arms and legs were indeed intact and clicked off his sorrows. Darleen had kicked him out, Windy had rejected him, Flora had left with her husband, the MG had died, and Christian was broke. By making neat columns of sorrows in his mind, he was able to mask an even greater problem. Hugh was still missing. Thinking about Hugh lured him into a deeper swamp. Their premature rise in the polls threatened his plan. To complicate matters, Big Jim and his bankroll were somewhere in Mexico. Had Big Jim actually made the bets? It was too much to bear. Christian slid those thoughts over behind his left ear and turned off the projector in his mind. Soon he snored.

When Christian woke again, he was covered with clear sap

from the tree. There was a hole in his slacks and a knee peeked through. Each day a torn cuff, a frayed collar, a scuffed shoe made Christian almost indistinguishable from Hugh and the committee. But it wasn't fair to lump Hugh in their sorry group. In the past weeks he had begun to wear blue blazers with silver buttons and a jaunty hat with a silk band. Christian, though, was becoming a sartorial equal to the cripple and the fighter with the mashed nose. Their attire was usually supplied by Mr. Hank at the Salvation Army.

Christian's campaign had changed the orbits of some of God's lesser planets, and he was being pulled into their path as they rearranged themselves.

There was a division in the committee. Edmund and Matsu had followed Hugh's lead. What the two boys lacked in taste, they compensated for with flair. Matsu's peach tux was always clean and well pressed. Edmund had begun wearing large horn-rim glasses filled with clear glass. He was making an effort to distinguish himself intellectually. His speech had slowed so that he could test each word in an attempt to escape his ghetto vocabulary and grammar. He often carried a history or foreign-language book as part of his ensemble. Sonny's menacing tour of the school yard had given the two boys license to pursue something other than male posturing and hanging out on street corners with boxcar-sized radios.

It was late afternoon. Christian looked up and saw the old fighter, Sonny, sitting close by with his back against the rough bark.

"College Boy, you one smart cocksucker."

"Thank you, Champ."

"Yep, you one smart cocksucker. It took me eleven years to get to sleeping under the tree. You did it in a few days. It took me months to develop a taste for T-Bird. Shit, you did it in hours. Last night you did about two bottles of black-berry. You one smart cocksucker."

"Look, Sonny, why not? My wife kicked me out of the

house, my car committed suicide, and Hugh is on a drunk or dead or something. It's all come to shit."

"And you fucking the preacher's wife. The campaign's over, you say, if Hugh shows up drunk at the phone bank. What happens if the preacher catches you with his woman wrapped around your dick?"

"It's not like that."

"No, College Boy. You invisible. The T-Bird does that. Drink a quart of that shit and you can walk right in the preacher's house and fuck his woman in the bed next to him. You fucking invisible."

"How can you lecture me about drinking?"

" 'Cause I'm a fucking professional. I know where to get the best price on a half gallon and how to hide the bottle so nobody finds it. And you fucking beginners need to notice that when I pass out, it's always in a soft spot. I know blackberry and peach wine makes me puke. Look at the front of you shirt and see you ain't even learned that lesson. Nights I drink Concord grape. Mornings I drink white port. I know my fucking wine. I'm a fucking professional."

"Did I talk about Flora?"

"Some."

"I've never . . . I've never had sex with her." Christian found he couldn't use the big F word in connection with Flora. That proved again he was truly in love.

"I know. You will. Why don't you just fuck Windy or get some whore down at the Cut-Rate. When the preacher catches you, it's all over for us professional drinkers. I'll never be on the boxing commission. Happy'll never have that newsstand in the White House. Edmund never be head nigger in Baton Rouge. When the preacher's woman gets fucked, we all get fucked. But you the only one who's gonna enjoy it."

Christian drew himself to his knees and vomited downwind from Sonny. "You're one miserable cocksucker," Sonny said, and took a deep drink of T-Bird so that Christian could see.

It made Christian gag again. Edmund sat on the steps and read *American History's African Roots.* Happy was on the porch smoking a blue cigarette. Neither seemed interested in Christian and Sonny.

It was a gentle afternoon of warm breezes and only the faintest smell of sulfur from the chemical plants. As the streetlights began to hiss to life, Christian worked up enough strength to go inside, shower, and put on his cleanest dirty shirt and suit. He shaved and washed out his mouth with Old Spice. Darleen had neglected to put a toothbrush in his traveling box, so he put toothpaste on his finger and ran it around his gums. Soon he was as good as he could be under the circumstances.

He found an old loaf of bread and ate the parts of four slices that didn't have green spots and washed down his drunk's meal with water. Because his pockets were empty, he walked the two miles to the phone bank. Christian Ahab Simmons was determined to put his life back on course.

Christian was shocked. There were so many cars parked around the headquarters it looked like the parking lot of LSU's football stadium. Hundreds of plywood half sheets leaned against alley walls, waiting for paint. In the side alley, thirty or more people were painting signs. A man in a white painter's suit followed a blue-and-red-splattered old woman as they rushed from sign to sign with a silkscreen cutout that read "Conklin." She would position the screen and the man would slap at it with his brush, leaving paint on the sign, the wall, and the woman. Inside, the phone-bank headquarters was frantic and electric. The room roared with women and men making phone calls.

Sonny was already back at his post outside the door when Christian arrived. Edmund had driven him in the Blue Monster, passing Christian on the street. They didn't offer to pick him up. Sonny didn't speak as Christian walked by him.

Christian ignored Sonny's snub and pushed through the door. The entire crowd paused, stood, and applauded.

The painters working outside put down their brushes and moved into the large room. Palms slapped his back. A dozen women kissed him on the cheek. He stood, stunned, in the center of the room. Applause turned to cheers. To add to his amazement, Christian saw Flora working her way through the mob. She stopped midway and began applauding. Christian questioned reality. Perhaps this was a cottonwood dream, where reality had become dream and dream reality. But he could still taste the vomit and Old Spice in his mouth. A man in front of the crowd held up a *Morning Advocate* with a banner headline. UNKNOWN CANDIDATE SURGES IN SENATE RACE. "Shit, it's happened. Our secret is out," Christian hissed to himself, still watching the lovely Flora. He grabbed the paper and worked his way amid kisses and backslaps to the tiny office he reserved for his own. Flora followed him.

"When did you get back to town?"

"About an hour ago. I came as soon as I heard. Our assistant pastor read the article to Dick this morning. You don't have to read it. It says that a brilliant media campaign by a brilliant young man, one Christian Ahab Simmons, by name, has changed the direction of the campaign."

"I've missed you."

"And I've missed you. The article just gave me an excuse to come home five days early. Hold me, Christian."

Their bodies crushed together. Flora left no doubt as to her intentions. Christian reached behind her and locked the door. This time she didn't withdraw when he began working on the buttons. This time there were only three. And she helped him with the catch on her bra. As her breasts fell free, he saw a dark mole.

She was the woman in the photographs. The pictures the committee had taken through the motel wall were of Reverend Tracy having sex with his wife. "So that was one of her games that the preacher didn't like.'' Christian felt a moment of anger when he thought that her husband had touched her and the committee had violated her body with their camera.

"I want to spend the next five days with you," she whispered as he ran his hand down the back of her skirt.

"I don't have a place to take you. To be honest, I'm broke.'' Honesty was one of the resolutions of the new and sober Christian Simmons.

"I know a place. Meet me in the family-counseling room at the church tonight. I have the only key and there's a private entrance in the parking lot.''

A loud knock froze them. "Mr. Simmons. There's an emergency phone call for you. He said you need to go see Mr. Conklin. And oh, Mr. Simmons, tell Mr. Conklin how happy we all are.''

The phone call was from Matsu. "Mr. Happy says that you better get down to the legislature quick. They done found Mr. Crazy Hugh.''

The legislature was out of session. Happy met Christian at the bottom of the forty-eight steps where he had started the project. Happy reeked of dope.

"I saw him go in there, but I can't get my chair up the steps.''

"Is he bad drunk?''

"I don't know. Run see.''

Christian saw two reporters walking toward the steps. If they turned left, they would enter the press office through the door under the steps. If they turned right, they would go up the steps and perhaps find Hugh. They stopped and talked. Christian waited. Then they turned toward the newsroom. Christian sprinted up the forty-eight steps. The ever-alert reporters were in their basement offices, unaware of the little drama.

The house side of the capitol was built like an auditorium.

Desks formed semicircles around the speaker's platform on different levels like stairsteps. Massive windows went from near the floor to the sixty-foot ceiling. On the front wall was a voting tally board that lit as each representative pushed the red or green button on their desk. At the moment, every green bulb was glowing.

Hugh stood under the huge voting board. Or rather, he slumped against the speaker's stand. Christian stood for a few moments in the dark so that he wouldn't startle the candidate, as though Hugh was a rabbit caught in the garden. Christian didn't know Hugh's mental condition and thought the little man might bolt and run. Also, he knew that in his hung-over condition he didn't have the strength to chase a drunk rabbit.

"College Boy, is that you?" Hugh's voice echoed in the marble hall.

"Yes."

"I'm sorry."

"You drunk?"

"No, I kinda wish I was."

"Where you been? We've been looking all over for you."

"Oh, I was drunk a bit, 'bout a day or so."

"Where you been since then?"

"Praying."

"Where?"

"I found me a Catholic church with a big cross and pretty windows. There was little stools you could kneel on. I stayed there and prayed about what I done to you and Windy and Happy and all the citizens."

"We were worried about you."

"So the Lord told me to kill myself. He kinda whispered it in my ear, and I walked to the top of the bridge and jumped."

Christian was astonished. Only a couple of people had survived the jump from the bridge.

"You jumped from the Mississippi River Bridge?"

"No, I jumped from the Amite River Bridge."

"Shit, Hugh, that's only fifteen feet into a slow river."

"I know. I even pick the wrong bridges. Did I cost you much, Christian?"

"What do you mean, did you cost me much?"

"Did my losing cost you much? I know I didn't pay you."

"Hugh, the election is almost three weeks away."

"I musta had the dates wrong. I remembered it was a Saturday."

"It's a week from Saturday."

"Oh."

"What are all the 'yes' lights on for?"

"Them's all the legislators who fucked my girl. I lit every one of 'em up."

"No, Hugh. Only fifteen or twenty fucked your girl."

"No shit?"

"No shit."

"How much she make?"

" 'Bout three thousand."

"No shit?"

"No shit."

Hugh thought about Windy for a few minutes. With glassy eyes, he turned toward Christian. "She's a fine girl. How many women you think would do something like that for you?" He didn't pause for an answer. "None . . . that's how many. She's class, real class. I'm going to ask her to marry me. A senator needs a first lady."

"Shit, Hugh. Let's go home."

"I got to first go outside and thank Huey. If you can give me a little boost, I can climb up and kiss his face."

When Christian knocked on the church door, it was opened immediately. Flora had changed to a dress with only one button.

"I'm not sure I know how to do this."

"Come sit beside me on the couch."

She sat close but with her hands in her lap and her knees together.

"Close your eyes."

She complied. "Maybe I can't, Christian. I love my husband. I think I—" Christian covered her mouth with his. His hands explored her body and began to pull her skirt from beneath her. She raised her hips so the material could slide around her waist. His hand continued its journey of discovery over flesh, over silk. Finally she opened her legs to admit Christian's hand. Then wider. She began to move her hips in rhythm with Christian's. She opened her eyes to watch.

A violent kiss.
They fell together
in a tangle of
limbs and lace.
Street light
flooding through
stained glass
made a crimson icon
of her body
that was offered
all night
without reservation
or restriction.

Lust.
Fulfilled dreams.
Cries.
Wet bodies.
Unspoken oaths.
Answered prayers.
Christian's future
was washed over

yet
another cascading fall
in a swift and
i-r-r-e-s-i-s-t-i-b-l-e
c-u-r-r-e-n-t.

# 24

"When does your husband come?"

"Seldom ever."

"Be serious. I was trying to say 'come home.' "

"He arrives on Delta flight eighty-six at two-fifteen today."

"Today! *Today!* That's only two hours from now."

"Right. Come here."

"Don't you think we should put all of the Bibles and stuff back into the bedroom and wash the sheets?"

"Sure, in a minute." Flora began her well-practiced enticements.

"I feel funny about being in his bed knowing that he'll soon be back home."

"Does this feel funny?"

"No, that feels great. I guess another half hour won't hurt," he said in languid surrender.

"Flora." A door slammed. Christian rolled from the bed to the floor. His pulse thundered. Caught. The preacher was home. It was all over. "Flora, are you home?"

"He's home early," Flora whispered, and quickly gathered her new lingerie scattered around the bed. She stuffed it into a drawer while Christian crawled around looking for his pants. Two days earlier, he had left his pants hanging on the end of the bed. Now they were tangled in discarded covers.

"Flora, are you decent?" The preacher was now outside the door.

"No, dear. I'm indisposed for a moment or two. I'll be right out. You're home early." She pulled a sweater over her head and stepped into a skirt.

"No, I'm on time. It's two-fifty."

Christian, in a reflex action, looked at his watch. The preacher was correct. The bedside clock had been unplugged by some innerspring gymnastics. Flora motioned Christian toward the window. "I'm almost decent."

"Don't get too decent, I've been gone a long time."

Christian dove through the open window into a bush of purple azaleas. His shirt and shoes were in his hands. His socks were still missing.

"How was the revival?" Flora continued the conversation through the door as she adjusted the draperies.

"I brought home a love offering of more than two thousand dollars. We can make a down payment on that new car you want . . . and, oh, I led thirty-seven souls to Christ."

Flora closed the window.

By the time the preacher had pulled Flora back into the still-warm bed, an azalea-stained Christian had scaled two fences and was headed for the safety of the cottonwood.

"Where you been, cocksucker?" Sonny, as usual, was snarling.

"I've been working in the campaign."

"You been working in something but it ain't the campaign."

"Leave me alone, Sonny. I've had a hard day."

"I bet you have. You smell like a cathouse. 'Sides that, the senator is pissed at you. I think he's getting your number."

"Pissed about what?"

"Some fucking big shots from the Democratic Party headquarters in the Capital of the United States of America been looking for your skinny ass."

"Why?"

"I don't know. I told 'em you was probably fucking the preacher's wife."

Christian felt pain in his chest. He couldn't bear the thought that the preacher had replaced him in bed. "Where'd they go?"

"To the governor's office. You 'sposed to meet 'em there at three."

"It's almost four. Maybe they're still there." Hugh's house was only eight blocks from the capitol. "I'll jog over and try to catch them."

"You gonna put on some socks?"

Christian looked down at his naked ankles. "I'll go inside and get some."

" 'Member to stay downwind."

Two leather Hartman briefcases leaned against two sets of pin-striped legs. Both men wore yellow ties. Both had small wire-frame glasses. Another man in a safari jacket sat on the edge of the governor's desk with the calm indifference of a man who sat on the edge of a score of governors' desks. Bobby Sutto leaned against the wall in a corner. He had a cast on his hand. The pinstripes looked stern. Bobby Sutto curled his lip in contempt. The great white hunter and the governor laughed loudly. None of them spoke to Christian. Heeding Sonny's advice, Christian stayed close to the door under a downdraft from the air conditioner.

Safari Suit paused while Christian entered and then continued his story. "So I said to the president, 'You have your choice. You can go downstairs and visit with those twenty governors or you can stay here and make a television spot that'll reach fifty million. And Mr. President, I'm a genius at TV commercials and not good at math but I think fifty million beats twenty every time.' That's why he missed the meeting with you guys. He had to chose between you and me. Ha. Ha. Ha.'' They both laughed. Safari was obviously very funny.

"Well, I'll just be damned. I thought he was talking to Russia on the hot line. We felt sorta honored to have even been in the White House during such an important event."

"Well, Governor. You were in the White House during an important occasion. That television spot saved the presidency for the Democrats. Ha. Ha. Ha.''

The governor looked up. ''Are you Mr. Simmons?''

Christian fumbled in his pants pocket until he found his shirttail and pulled it down to eliminate the bulge that revealed a missing button. It was then that he noticed his left sock was blue and his right was brown. His shirt stuck to his back from the jog to the capitol.

"Yes, Governor.'' Christian bent slightly at the knees, hoping his pants would cover his shoes.

''Well, I want to introduce you to these gentlemen from the Senate Campaign Committee and to America's most famous media consultant. You might have seen him on TV.''

The introductions were made. Christian promptly forgot the names of the two bureaucrats. The consultant, Richard Gentry, was featured in all of the books Christian had read while he worked on his Cottonwood Plan. He thought Gentry's work was trite but had decided already that talent wasn't the most important ingredient for Washington media consultants. Christian had a fool's smugness in the knowledge that Richard Gentry had a divine gift for the spotlight and had been extraordinarily lucky during one election cycle. Yes, Christian thought, give me luck and I'll be sitting on the edge of a governor's desk in a ridiculous safari jacket.

Bobby Sutto didn't bother to shake hands, but he did sniff a couple of times like a dog looking for the first sign of a coon.

"Mr. Simmons," the governor said, "these gentlemen have come here on a mission of utmost importance to the future of the Democratic Party and perhaps even to the future of the Free World." The governor, a Tulane man, spoke slowly, pronouncing each word as though it were a challenge. He waved his hands in grand theatrical gestures. "They are going to take over Senator LeBlanc's campaign. As you perhaps know, he has fallen in the polls and now leads by only ten points. If Senator LeBlanc is defeated, this state stands to lose the chairmanship of the powerful Armed Services Committee. These gentlemen are here to ensure that doesn't happen. And—"

"To be brief, we're here to declare war." Gentry impatiently interrupted the governor. He hated to share the spotlight. "The next chess moves will be made by us. We have two polls that show us that through some fluke of name identification or something, your candidate has moved into third place and is taking some votes that should go to the senator. If we can get your candidate to bow out gracefully for the good of the party, we are confident that Senator LeBlanc will be elected and the chairmanship will be saved for Louisiana."

"Mr. Simmons." The governor leaned forward in a confidential manner. "These gentlemen are prepared to give you a job on the Senate Campaign Committee. And Senator LeBlanc said he will put Mr. Conklin back on his staff here in Louisiana." Both bureaucrats nodded.

Gentry added another incentive. "Tell you what else, sport. You can go with me on a couple of film shoots and observe the business." He sniffed twice.

"Now I understand that you have some small difficulty with Mr. Sutto, but he's agreed to join the team for the good

of Louisiana. He's here because he has something to say."
There was silence and then the governor said, "Don't you,
Bobby?"

"Yea . . ." The rest of the sentence was unintelligible.

"I didn't hear you," Christian said.

Bobby looked at the governor, who raised his open palm,
asking for more volume.

"I said I'm sorry we had that fight." He looked back down
at the floor.

"Well, now that we have that little problem out of the way,
I'm sure we can work out the details," the governor said,
terribly pleased with himself. He sniffed.

Christian stood looking at his blue and brown socks. An
azalea blossom peaked out of his cuff. There was a long silence punctuated only by the governor's tapping a pencil on
the desk. One of the bureaucrats spotted the flower and whispered to the other, who noticed the contrasting socks. Both
looked at Christian's feet, directing the attention of Gentry
and the governor. Sutto still stared at his own shoes.

Christian was only seconds away from using his practiced
technique of agreeing with anything and working out the details later when he noticed the two bureaucrats smile and stare
at his feet. He saw their lips curl in superiority. In their world,
matching socks and yellow neckties were more important than
creative thought.

Christian's desperate lifetime of dodging and weaving to
survive was suddenly symbolized by a flower peaking from a
cuff. Once again the bully was in the school yard. Once again
runners were between him and the finish line. Fuck 'em, he
thought.

"Governor. Bobby Sutto shot me with a pistol. We didn't
just fight. He tried to shoot off my balls. He tried to murder
me."

"I just wanted to scare him a little, I shot to miss and—"

"Sutto's a criminal. He should be in jail, not hanging

around the governor's office.'' Christian was angry. The two young bureaucrats were horrified at the new tone of the meeting, the brutal frankness and violence of Louisiana politics and the anger in Christian's voice.

''And Hugh Conklin isn't getting out of the race. He's going to win the race. He's going to be Senator Conklin and I'm going to move his entire steering committee to Washington. Wait till Washington sees that.

''And these experts''—Christian pointed to the two well-groomed young men—''hold their jobs by virtue of not being qualified for a respectable deadhead job in the administration. Or maybe they have rich daddies. I once had a yellow dog who knew as much as guys like these.'' He wasn't sure about his last statement but it proved to be a good guess.

''And Gentry. I don't want to watch you perform, you pompous ass. My work is already better than yours. You need to spend more time behind the camera and less time in front of a mirror.'' Christian had strafed the room. The only person left standing was the governor, so he turned and made another sweep, guns blazing. He would leave no survivors.

''And Governor, if you oppose us, you'll find a man named Sonny Clinton as your reelection opponent. And I'll do his media.'' Christian simply couldn't stop. His mind searched for new and better insults. The veins on the sides of his neck throbbed blue. The room was petrified by shock. But the governor recovered first. For despite his Tulane manners, he had been in more back rooms than a legislature whore.

''You better win, you little son of a bitch. Because you're going to need a new place to live. You'll wish that Bobby Sutto had been more accurate. We're coming after your wino. Then we're going to look at you and the rest of your organization. I have auditors looking at Big Jim's banks.'' He slapped his desk with an open hand. ''Now, get out of my office. No, get off the capitol grounds.''

Christian slammed the office door on the way out. There

was nothing to do now but win. Fourth wasn't good enough. Money wouldn't heal wounded pride. Christian felt hate and hate needed revenge. For a full ten minutes he didn't think of Flora.

**25** The headline and the photo didn't agree. TOP CONK-
LIN CAMPAIGN WORKER ARRESTED FOR POSSSESSION OF DRUGS.
The photo was of a helpless, old, dirty cripple selling newspapers. There must have been conflict between the editor who
wrote the headline and the editor who selected the photo.
Christian and Big Jim studied the picture. The story explained that the reform candidate and ex-drunk lived with the
dangerous dopehead Howard "Happy" Bolliver, in a North
Street den.

"Where's your dope addict?" Big Jim asked glumly.
Christian had borrowed money from Jim to bail out Happy.

"Me and the boys hauled him to the second floor of the
Howard Johnson motel so that he can't cause more trouble.
There's no elevator."

"Might be better for all of us if he rolled his chair down
the stairs and broke his head." Big Jim was angry. "Hey,"
he screamed toward the kitchen. "You hatching them fucking
chickens?"

A huge Cajun cook in a long wraparound white apron
backed into the room with a mountain-sized platter of fried
chicken. He had a balloonlike belly, a long black beard, and
a bald head. "No, sir, Mr. Big Jim. I was making it crispy
like you likes it. You can't hurry good chicken. I'd just as
soon throw all this chicken in the yard as to serve it soggy.

You gotta let T. Sam do it his way or T. Sam's gonna throw the whole mess into the yard. Now, you want T. Sam's good chicken or you want a whole yardful of soggy chicken?''

Christian never understood why so many Cajuns called themselves ''T'' something or other. At times it seemed a term of endearment, but they were also likely to refer to a black person as ''T. Nig.'' Somehow ''T. Nig'' didn't sound like a term of endearment. It was another of those annoying riddles of South Louisiana.

He put the mountain of chicken on the table between the foothill of biscuits and the lake of cream gravy and then defiantly put his hands on his hips. ''You had stuffed peppers and crawfish bisque to tide you over till the chicken was cooked. And why you think I put that platter of sausages and mustard on the table? I'll tell you why. So T. Sam could have time to fix the chicken right. That's why.'' The cook backed through the kitchen door, grumbling under his surly breath.

''Why do you keep such an insulting bastard around here, Big Jim?'' asked hooker-turned-girlfriend Susie, for perhaps the twentieth time.

''A man who can cook like this has got job security in this house,'' Big Jim explained with a shrug of his shoulders. ''If I ever get rid of him, I'm gonna open a restaurant in New Orleans so people can pay for his insults. People pay big money to get insulted in New Orleans. 'Sides, trouble makes me hungry.''

Happiness, sadness, sex, everything made Big Jim hungry.

''So what you gonna do about your rummy and his friend?'' Big Jim held chicken legs in both hands. The underside of his yellow hat brim had circles of grease where he had missed his mouth and hit his hat. One of the chicken legs had knocked it to the back of his head.

''I'm going to meet the problem head-on. I've called a press conference for tomorrow. I'm going to get Happy to take the rap. He'll explain that Hugh didn't know about the dope.''

Christian watched Jim eat. He decided to tell his friend about the audit.

"Jim, the governor said he's auditing your banks."

"Yeah, I know. I sent him a hundred thousand dollars. He'll call off the dogs tomorrow." Jim calmly spooned cream gravy over three biscuits. Christian ate little and tried to ignore the cream gravy. It always reminded him of library paste. Except for the addition of milk and meat drippings, it had the same ingredients and tasted much the same. As a child, Christian had eaten a similar substance while he pasted cows in blue pastures and birds in green skies. Christian was colorblind but didn't discover it until he was in his teens. His teachers thought him eccentric and feared stifling his creative freedom.

"I'm sorry I cost you so much money."

"Oh, don't worry 'bout that. The governor agreed to ask the legislature for a bill abolishing the minimum price for liquor. The liquor boys will bring sacks of money to the legislature to beat that bill. I'll make back my hundred grand several times. Then the governor'll withdraw the legislation so we can save the issue for another day when we need it. He'll make another hundred thousand or so out of that. The consumer folks will be happy because the governor made an attempt to do the decent thing. The legislators will be happy because of all the new money. The liquor boys will talk about how smart they were. All of their lobbyists will get raises. Everybody wins."

"What about our bets?"

"Now, that's something else. I got a lot of money scattered out 'cross this state. Some of it is two-to-one. But most of it's at four to one. I even got some five-to-one. But none of that matters if we come in fifth." Jim put down his fork and looked angrily at Christian.

"When you got me into this, you said you'd watch those lunatics full-time. But you didn't. You gotta go fuck the preacher's wife. You gotta piss on the governor's foot. You

gotta show Bobby Sutto and all this state how fucking smart
you are. If you was really smart, you'd have kept your fucking
mouth closed. Now you gonna cost me a ton. College Boy,
I'm having a brass plate made for your office door. You going
into the lobby business with me. Your future is secure."

Jim was so upset that he picked up two chicken breasts and
began gnawing at both of them.

"Jim, we're not out yet. If I can work the spin on this, we
can maybe hold on to fourth place."

"You finished eating?" Jim asked.

"Yes."

"Then get the hell outta here. I'm tired of looking at your
face. Go back to work."

Christian walked slowly to the door. He knew he deserved
the abuse. As he pulled the door open Big Jim called out,
"College Boy. Susie and me is getting married. I want you
to be best man."


"You're on the air."

"Dave, this here is the old golfer. How are you this morning?"

"I'm fine. What's on your mind?"

A loud screech blasted Ravin' Dave's eardrums. "Golfer,
you've got to turn down your radio."

"Sorry there, Ravin' Dave. As I was saying, Thelma,
God"—*bleep* . . . *bleep*—"down the"—*bleep*—"radio.
Sorry, Ravin' Dave. I was telling my wife to turn down the
radio. I ain't been on your show for about a month. Me and
Thelma went up to Eureka Springs, Arkansas, for a little
vacation. Left the camper at home and stayed at a motel. I
won't make that mistake again. You know what they charge
for two eggs and a—"

"Golfer, I'm sorry, but we're discussing the arrest of Hugh
Conklin's friend in Baton Rouge. We're running a little poll.
Do you think Hugh Conklin should drop out of the race for

the U.S. Senate? Let's vote and move on and make some
airtime for the next caller.''

"Well, my mind is still where it was when we discussed
this subject in February of last year. Maybe you remember
the last time I called? Remember, it was about leash laws for
cats—''

"Golfer, we have to move on. Can you tell me how you
vote?''

"Well, I keep records of my appearances. A lot of folks
call me for advice since I got to be a regular on your show.
Now, listen close. This is the old golfer speaking. I think we
should put every dope addict and dope dealer in the 'lectric
chair. Fry 'em. Teach 'em a lesson.''

"Thank you for your opinion. Our open phone lines are
running five-to-one for Mr. Conklin dropping out of the
race.''

Dave leaned into the mike and cued "America the Beautiful'' on turntable B. "What's wrong with you listeners. Have
we forgotten about 'innocent until proven guilty'? And what
about 'old-fashioned American fairplay.' Is this man guilty
by association? I fought for my country on bloody beaches
so the Hugh Conklins of the world could have a fair trial. I
fought so that every son and every daughter of every citizen
could have the right to run for office. Have any of you considered that this may be nothing more than a political trick
by Senator LeBlanc's henchmen? Does this in any way change
the fact that Senator LeBlanc embarrassed the Bayou State
when he chose to compromise himself in the Tidal Basin?
And I'll give you one more thought before I open up the
phone lines. Is this maybe a conspiracy by the rich and powerful to hold down the working people?''

"Fourth and slipping.'' The whiz kid had made a tube of
his printout and sat on the loose boards of the front porch.

Christian sucked on a cheap cigar and looked at his feet.

The cottonwood rattled and wept some leaves. "Does Happy taking the fall help us recover?"

"Maybe a little. We read the respondents several different scenarios and that one seemed to work best."

"What about his being crippled and using the dope for medication?"

"Our poll shows that most people don't consider marijuana medication."

"Fourth and slipping," Christian murmured to himself. "Fourth and slipping."

"You dropped ten points in the first twenty-four hours."

"We were on the front page of every newspaper and the lead story on every television news program."

"Maybe you can have Happy jump off the top of the capitol building."

"Happy can't jump." Christian brightened slightly and then sagged. "Did you test that?"

"No."

"Oh."

They both watched a line of ants carrying leaves to a hole under the roots of the cottonwood.

"He weighs about two-fifty."

"What?"

"Happy. He's too heavy to lift over the edge."

"You're on the air."

"Ravin' Dave. You going to that press conference?"

"Yes. This is a good time to tell our listeners that Station WHAM will be there in full force. Tomorrow we will be live from Baton Rouge. After the conference we'll open our mikes to the listeners. No matter what happens, Louisiana, the truth shall set you free."

"I hear he's gonna drop out of the race."

"I've heard that, too, but I understand the Reverend Dick Tracy and his entire congregation have gone into their church for a 'Power of Prayer' meeting and promise to have a twenty-four-hour-long prayer."

"I'm a Catholic myself, Dave."

"Well, I am too. But I have respect for prayer, no matter which denomination."

"Well, there's even a story that some gambling money was used in the campaign. Now, that's both dope and gambling."

"Who is this? Do you work for Senator LeBlanc?"

*Bzzzzzzzzzz.* The phone was dead.

"Well, listeners, does that last caller tell you anything about how some of these rumors got started?

"Hello, I'm Ravin' Dave and you're on the air."

"Christian, this is Darleen."

"I still recognize your voice."

"May I help?"

"Yes, I have a part of the dutiful wife for you to play, if you're up to it."

"I've played it like a champ for years."

"Show up tomorrow at ten A.M. for the press conference. Tell Windy to dress in one of her Sunday-school dresses and to keep her legs together."

"Since when have you started wanting Windy's legs together?"

"Do you want to fight or help?"

"Both."

"I don't have the energy to fight."

"I understand you got into religion."

"What do you mean?"

"I mean that I heard you got into something religious."

"I don't even know what you mean."

"Of course you don't. I'll see you tomorrow, sweetie pie."

*Bzzzzzzz.*

Hugh had come in from his stump tour of the state and was sitting at home having committee meetings about the next steps to take. The table in front of his place card was dented in hundreds of places from his gavel.

"I guess it's all up." Hugh was downcast.

"I'd be lying if I told you it looked good, Hugh." Christian spoke into his lap. He chewed the remains of a short cigar.

"Happy blew smoke in the cop's face, you know. When the cop stopped to buy a paper, Happy blew smoke all over him. Choked 'em," Hugh explained for the fifth time.

"It was a bad break."

"Weren't no bad break. That cop is related to Bobby Sutto. He's been watching the house for two weeks. Why you think that reporter and photographer just happened to be by Happy's newsstand? It was a frame. You didn't do this campaign any favors when you picked a fight with Bobby. He's smart. Fact is, he's about the best." Hugh got up and paced around the small room.

Christian ignored the insult, but he had noticed a change in Hugh. But that was a future problem. Now he needed a miracle. "Fourth and slipping." Besides the newspapers attacking in every edition, the other candidates already had new television spots on the air showing the newspaper clippings and asking questions about the "reform candidate." Big Jim was angry and called every thirty minutes.

Christian began to think about other professions. The night before he had a vivid nightmare where he went from door to door looking for a job. Behind every door was Bobby Sutto.

"Do you think Windy will still want to marry me if I'm not a senator?" Hugh asked. He stared through Christian.

The room was the largest Christian could find at an affordable price. A table with a large urn of coffee and paper cups hugged the wall next to the door. A speaker's stand was positioned to allow room for television cameras in front and twenty chairs in the rear but in clear view of the lenses. A desperate and sweating Christian was determined to fight back, until election day. And election day was close. The clock was ticking on his future.

In the first two chairs he positioned Brother Tracy and Flora. Next to them was Windy Dawn. Miss Dawn was holding a Bible. She was accompanied by ten teenage girl drugettes dressed to look like something out of a Baptist Sunday-school book. They had on no makeup, but wore ribbons in their hair. Christian glanced over and saw Flora holding hands with her preacher-husband. His chest felt heavy. Darleen patted Windy's arm.

As the reporters came into the room, they simply smiled or laughed. It was theater to them but deadly serious to the people behind the podium. Sides were drawn.

Hugh was in his blue blazer with silver buttons, and a scrubbed and dressed Happy sat in his wheelchair beside him. Christian shook a few hands and beat it to the back, out of the way. A PR man should never be in front. He watched until he felt the cameras were all in place and signaled Hugh to begin.

"Ladies and gentlemen. I have a few remarks to make and will then answer questions. It has been our policy in this campaign to be honest with you at all times. I promise you that there will be nothing evaded and nothing off the record.

"A friend of mine, you know him as Happy, was caught in the act of smoking marijuana. We think this is serious. We think part of the problem of this country is dope. And we are doing everything we can to stamp it out. I hope you will see that our actions speak louder than words.

"Behind me is Brother Dick Tracy. A good man, my pastor, my friend. It is his church that runs the mission to help our young girls who have wrecked their lives using dope.

"Sitting next to Brother Tracy is his wife, Flora. She is my campaign chairman and the most Christian woman I have ever known. She is a sample of the high moral tone we have tried to keep in this campaign.

"Next to her is a special lady. This is the lady who actually counsels the girls. Her name is Windy Dawn. I'll tell you how much I think of Miss Dawn. We are going to be married on election day. And all of you are invited to the church for the wedding . . . after you vote, of course. Behind her are some saved girls. They have been taken off dope by the people who are really responsible for running this campaign."

It was going well. Hugh was delivering the speech as though he were a robot being pulled by strings from Christian's mind. Windy Dawn had managed to keep her legs together, and Darleen looked concerned and loving. Happy sat very still looking at the floor.

"Now, my friend is accused of smoking that terrible narcotic marijuana. We are going to do something a little different than is being done in the halls of justice today. Happy admits that he committed this terrible crime. Do you, Happy?"

Happy never looked up. He nodded his head. "Yes," he said.

"And Happy wants to make amends. Happy is guilty as charged. Happy tells me he didn't know what he was smoking. He tells me that a stranger gave it to him and he smoked it because he didn't have any cigarettes. And we don't want to accuse any of our opponents of such a low tactic, but we have reason to believe that we know the man who did it. But that is not why I am here.

"There are those who tell me this has hurt me in the polls and has ruined my chances to be elected. One man told me I should renounce my friend. What have we come to? Renounce an old friend? Never.

"Why, this man was my friend in the bad times. I don't throw away men because they are weak. If that were the case, our Savior would have deserted this earth generations ago.

"Never let it be said that Hugh Conklin runs out on a friend. . . ."

At this moment came the consultant's dream, the stroke of luck, the single moment that often changes a campaign. Consultants take credit for these magic blips and wear them like badges on their campaign tunics. But they are never more than luck and fuel for insider speculation. Later Christian would claim "I made my luck," but it was a lie. He had no idea that the old cripple would take charge and give history a double bank shot.

For at that magic moment Happy raised his head and almost shouted, "Let me talk, Hugh." This wasn't in the script, and Christian, who would later take credit for the ploy, tried to signal Hugh to stop Happy. The cripple rolled his chair to the center of the room. His face was wet from tears.

"Put the camera on me. I got a few things to say." All of the cameras swung over to Happy. On the monitor Christian could see the CBS-affiliate camera on a close-up of the lined, gray face. A forest of boom mikes hovered around his head.

"Happy, you don't need to say nothing," Hugh said, departing from the script.

"I got to say it. I got to tell the truth and then you can roll me to jail." He wiped his face with his sleeve.

"I knew that was dope. I've smoked it before. You see, I'm old and crippled and I hurt. I take the dope to get over the hurt. Lots of people do that. It was wrong, but it just hurt, and I'm an old cripple who's not gonna live a lot longer. I didn't give it to nobody else."

He stopped for a moment and sobbed. Now Christian signaled Hugh to leave him alone. Christian could see a woman reporter wiping away a tear.

"And now I done a bad thing. I done hurt Hugh. And he's the man who took me out of the rain and let me live in his house, and I don't pay no rent. He built me a ramp up to his door and let me move in. I don't mind going to jail, but you people don't not vote for Hugh 'cause of me. He's a good man."

Happy once again looked down at the floor. There wasn't a dry eye in the house. Christian's tears, though, were pure joy.

"This is Ravin' Dave in Baton Rouge and you're on the air."

"Dave, is it true that the cripple feller lost his legs trying to put up that flag on Ioa Gemo? I had a first cousin who was there and he says the first time they tried to put up the flag one of the guys got shot in the legs."

"Well, we don't have much information on how Mr. Bolliver lost his legs, but I'll tell other Americans this. The true heroes never talk. I'm a veteran. I know."

"Dave, they tell me you was a war hero."

"I don't want to talk about it." He paused and the listeners heard him draw his breath as though even the thought of his war heroics caused him pain.

"What I do want to talk about is the kind of politicians who would take a man like Happy Bolliver and use him for their political ends. Where have we gone, Americans? What happened to decency? I can't say how I'd vote. The FCC won't allow that. But I will tell you I am going to vote for change. I'm one American who's had it up to his gills with crooked politicians.

"I have with us today the man who produced the television spot for Hugh Conklin. His name is Christian Ahab Simmons and I think we'll be hearing a lot from him in the future. He is obviously a genius with a heart as big as New Orleans. Mr. Simmons, we were witness to one of the most unusual events of our time. I think I can safely say that Hugh Conklin was framed by some unnamed politicians in a desperate move.''

"Yes, I think this proves that integrity, honesty, and decency will win if the voter has a chance to know the truth.''

"It's only five days until election. Can you get your message out in time to save the campaign? I think the newspapers—I say *newspapers* of this state, not radio, poisoned the voters for three days.''

"Well, Dave, this is a time for the decent people in this state to pull together. We don't have the money for a television or radio message, but if every right-thinking person would call all of their friends tonight, I think we have a wonderful chance to win.''

"You heard that, listeners. I can't tell you what to do, with the FCC and all, but don't try to call me at home tonight. I'll be busy.'' Dave had a date with ace saleswoman, Betsy Lavell. It was her husband's bowling night.

**26** Christian walked out of the radio station and into the streets of the French Quarter. His interview with Ravin' Dave had gone well. He was sober and euphoric. The confession by Happy could move Hugh back into the money. And Christian needed money. Hugh had bought their bus tickets to New Orleans and had given him ten dollars in ones and quarters for cab fare. He didn't know where Hugh got the money, but he was even going to buy lunch at Mother's Restaurant. With a little time to kill, Christian walked by some of the places that would be his in a week, if his plan worked, if Happy's confession was publicized, if the gods of the voting booth had not lost their senses of humor.

He paused at Brennan's front door and gazed down the tile entrance hall to the bar. He had already begun to walk away when his mind registered what his eyes had seen. Standing at the bar, drinking champagne, was Darleen. She raised her glass to the man on her left and leaned over to kiss him on the cheek. She was laughing. Christian felt a surge of warmth toward his wife. He reached for the door to join her and stopped. He didn't have money to pick up her tab. The man put his arm around her waist and rested his hand on the swell of her hip. As always, she looked good. Money had always separated Christian from things. Now it was separating him from his wife. "You have to pay to play, son," he said aloud, and laughed. A tourist smiled and nodded agreement but picked up his pace.

Maybe Darleen was doing something for the campaign, Christian thought. He wished he were standing at the elegant bar with Flora, touching glasses, drinking champagne. Maybe Darleen has a boyfriend! The thought staggered him because he found that he cared. He cared a lot. A weight settled in his chest. Something else was being lost. Maybe he had even lost Flora. For the past week she had found excuses not to meet. He glanced into the hall again and found that Darleen and her friend had left the bar. He assumed they had taken a table in the beautiful but out-of-reach restaurant.

He walked around the corner and stood across the street from Antoine's, watching people shake hands with the maître d' and disappear into the old restaurant. Next door to Antoine's was a cigar store, where Christian bought one moderately priced cigar. He now had nine dollars. To save money, he had walked from the bus station to the radio studio. He leaned against the outside wall and smoked.

Strangers moved past him. Smells and noises assaulted him. The elation of the radio show turned to sadness. Christian rocked gently against the wall as though he were in the branches of the cottonwood and began to mutter to himself.

"Oh, you young man of electricity and ice . . .
Oh, you programmer and forger . . .
Oh, you tap dancer and clown . . .
Oh, you almost redeemed . . .
Oh, you!"

A tear rolled down his cheek. The new life had started out swell but threatened to end like his boyhood. How many times can one start again? How many mistakes are allotted? A sob escaped his throat, perhaps the first since he was a child trapped in the top of the cottonwood. He hadn't cried at his father's funeral. It was too late for tears. Now it was too late for Darleen. Too late for Flora. Too late. He never seemed to know the value of a thing until it was gone. Tourists moved nervously to the edge of the sidewalk, away from the weeping man. Christian stepped on his cigar and stumbled through the French Quarter streets toward Mother's Restaurant.

Mother's isn't an elegant restaurant. In fact it leans against the corner of Poydras and Tchoupitoulas. Only the quality of its food keeps it from being called a dive. From the napkin holders to the tabletops, everything inside is chipped or bent. The diners inhale air beautifully polluted with the heavy, greasy aroma of hundreds of hams and beef roasts baked every morning. All pretension is stripped bare and the simple New Orleans food is served beautifully cooked and sold inexpensively. Rich builders and lawyers share tables with professional drunks and whores. Insults come with the food. And though the insults are delivered in America's second-ugliest accent, they are good-natured and don't sting. One has to line up cafeteria-style and scream food orders at people behind a steam table. "Give me a plate of red beans and a couple of dem sausages, 'bout a half a loaf ah French bread, and a double scoop of potato salad. When did ya make it? Last mont?'' "Yeah, we made yours last month. I was gonna trow it out but Thelma says save the rotten stuff for that roach Mario. *Next.* What you want?'' And root beer is recommended with every dish.

Christian got a po-boy that was half fried speckled trout and half fried oysters and joined Hugh at a tiny table against the wall. People were stopping to shake Hugh's hand. He had already eaten.

"You're late, College Boy.''

"I'm sorry, Hugh. I walked and it took longer than I thought.''

"What did you do with the money I gave you?''

"I still have nine dollars.''

"You know how many times you said my name on Ravin' Dave's show?" Hugh was angry.

"No."

"Two. That's how many. Two damned times. I bought you a bus ticket and came all the way down here with you to keep you sober and you mentioned my goddamned name two times."

"I'm sorry, Hugh, I was just answering his questions."

"I don't want you talking to the press no more. From now on I'm the only one who's gonna talk to the press. You understand?" Hugh shook his finger in Christian's face.

Christian had no energy to fight. The scene of Darleen and the man, the hurt and wanting for Flora had drained him. New emotions were filtering into his body. And now this wino he had saved from the capitol steps was treating him like a servant.

Christian tried to eat by pulling the oysters out of the bread and putting them untasted into his mouth. His world was spinning again.

Three more people came by to shake Hugh's hand and promise their support. He was all smiles and backslaps and handshakes . . . until he turned back to Christian.

"The committee is some pissed at you. If it wasn't for me, you would have been fired a month ago."

"Why are they mad at me?"

"Fer one thing, the mess you made out of that TV show. They had some good ideas and you didn't pay them no mind at all. You just went off and did your own thing. And about the music . . ."

Hugh had to pause while a man in a hand-cut suit stopped with congratulations and an offer to buy lunch. Hugh accepted both.

"The music. You could have used their music. Them boys is smart. They're real people. They understand the common folk. But you treat 'em like a piece of shit. Remember this, son, you work for them boys. They the bosses. You the nigger. You understand? They the ones who raised the money. They the ones who work every day while you out fucking the preacher's wife.''

Christian put his head almost in his sandwich as though he were looking at the molecular structure of the lettuce. His thoughts didn't march through with military precision. They were pumped through his head at high pressure. He grew dizzy from the attack of things he always tried to hide from himself. ''And what does it profit a man to gain the whole world and lose his own soul?'' The Bible verse bumped through his skull. Rage boiled. He was only a second away from throwing the food in Hugh's face. Lose his own soul? Darleen, Flora, the committee, Cottonwood, white black girls, ass kissing, Uncle Reily, Calab Hudson, all-night grocery stores, funeral shoes, paper routes, bill collectors, the fights, the bullet, the governor. The fucking futility of it all . . .

If

I look up

and throw this food

in this

selfish,

ingrate's

fucking face!

I have come so far . . . so far that I have trouble looking into mirrors . . . so far there are no bridges back . . . when I climbed to the top of the cottonwood, the small limbs held me . . . but I didn't let go . . . I had to save myself . . . save myself . . . I am. I am. I am. Lose his own soul? What kind of question is that?

Christian gripped the plate and paused. "Ah shit," he said to the lettuce. He painted on his Pagliacci smile and looked up at Hugh.

"I'm sorry, Hugh. I am truly sorry. I've been arrogant and insensitive. If you will forgive me, I'll try much harder. I'll go back and tell the boys what a jerk I've been."

Hugh liked the apology but he didn't accept it. He only nodded.

Christian didn't weep again for a long time. Another scar had formed.

And Hugh didn't speak during the bus ride to Baton Rouge.

# 27

Windy's skirt was pulled to the tops of her thighs, her stockings around her ankles and blouse unbuttoned. Her left hand held open her blouse and her right hand deflected air from outside the car onto her skin. Christian drove the Blue Monster slowly, forcing logging trucks to line up behind him. When one managed to pass, the drivers cursed and made obscene gestures. Christian held the wheel tightly. One cooked tire had already blown and there was no spare. A smudge of grease was on his cheek and collar.

"It sure is hot. When we get to Washington, I'm gonna get one of them big black limos with air-conditioning so cold we can hang meat." Hugh had taken off the coat to his white suit and put his straw hat on the ledge behind the seat. Unlike the bedraggled Christian, his tie was still tight. "Pull over to that store and let's drink an RC. Might be a voter or two in there."

Christian guided the car off the road and onto the gravel in front of the old clapboard plantation store and stopped beside two old-fashioned gas pumps. He watched as Windy pulled up her stockings, fastened the stays, and buttoned her blouse. Hugh collected a handful of bumper stickers from the trunk.

The screen door slammed behind Hugh and Windy and an

old man in coveralls ambled over to where Christian slumped against the fender. "Fill her up?"

Christian only nodded.

"We get lots of famous people in here. Congressman Speedy Long's been here four times. The lieutenant governor came in once. The superintendent of education sat right on that step and drank a Coke. Earl Long once pissed right under that tree over yonder. He said, 'Son, you got a men's room?' I said no, so he just went over there and pissed on that tree. It was littler then. That was a long time ago. Me and the wife talked about putting a sign on the tree, but my wife never could agree to what it would say. She didn't want to say that the governor had done his business right there. And she's never let me say that Earl Long was drunk. That's back before they sent him away to the institution.

"And now we got Hugh Conklin sitting in there on the Coke box drinking an RC. When he gets to be senator, I'm damn sure gonna put a sign on that box."

"Do you support Hugh?"

"Sure. We ain't had a Baptist in the Senate in a long time. We had them Cat'liks—them Frenchmen from South Louisiana. Now, don't get me wrong. I take a little drink. I keep a bottle out in the garage. But them folks live to drink. And look what that LeBlanc did in the Tidal Basin up north. The church people are mad."

Windy and Hugh came back out and got into the car. The old man shyly watched his feet while Christian paid him. He had no reservations about talking to Christian but didn't have the courage to engage a "famous" person like Hugh.

They ate lunch in Natchitoches and stopped in Zwolle to shake hands. Just before noon they rolled into Many. Christian thought of Many, Louisiana, as a mistake. It is one of the sawmill towns that the land barons forgot to dismantle when they had finished raping the land and turning hundreds of miles of hills into black pine stumps. They dismantled

Hornbeck. They dismantled Glenmora. All they left were some churches, rusty rails, and signs on the road at both ends of the spots where there had once been busy if not thriving towns.

The punished red-hill towns of North Louisiana like Many in no way resemble the marshy, lowland, Cajun towns of the south. There is a line through the state almost as pronounced as those in *Rand McNally* that divide geographic area by color. The north is gray, tight-lipped Baptists and Pentecostals who hide their liquor in paper bags under front seats. The south is fiery tabasco orange and drinking is celebrated. The Catholic Church is tolerant. The mood is hedonistic.

The two regions are as different as Maine and Florida except they both share a dependence on state government. And it's Huey's fault. He shook the tree of corporate looters so hard, the fruit fell at the feet of malnourished people who were trapped in hunger and ignorance. Children went to school to get free hot lunches. Men drove to jobs over new highways and bridges. Standard Oil and Texaco and the land barons paid and paid and paid. State government became the protector of the little people with charity hospitals and old-age pensions.

Oddly, there was something about Hugh that appealed to both groups. In the north he had the look of a redneck with his bunched collars and Bible-toting wife. His speeches had Huey's fire and he reflected much of his audience's distant shyness. In the south men hugged. In the north they talked while looking at their feet.

In the south, Hugh danced the Cajun dances and was, of course, comfortable campaigning in the barrooms along the bayou. There, Windy turned from "Bible-toting wife" to "red-hot woman."

Christian thought the stump speaking tours of the state a terrible waste of time. But tradition dictated and Hugh followed. Old Senator LeBlanc campaigned in the time-accepted manner and the committee demanded that Hugh follow his footsteps.

"It's a waste of time," Christian argued.

"How many elections you won, cocksucker," Sonny answered.

"One."

"Well, old Senator LeBlanc has been in politics for forty years. You think he'd be going from town to town if it was a waste of time?"

So they were in Many on a hot August day. Hugh was seated on a flatbed truck converted into a red, white, and blue speaker's platform. Next to him in folding church chairs were Senator LeBlanc, all of the other candidates for the Senate, and twenty other candidates for school board, Many City Council, and justice of the peace. A gospel group had sung "Give Me That Old-Time Religion."

Christian sat across the street on the courthouse steps. Next to him was a young man in jeans, boots, straw hat, and a paper bag concealing a bottle of bourbon. The speakers had droned on for about an hour and still Hugh was two slots away from his turn. Christian watched wistfully as the stranger took a hard hit from the bag, grimaced, and wiped his mouth on his sleeve. In North Louisiana liquor has to hurt and drinkers are reluctant to take away the sting with water or soda.

The young man turned to Christian. "Hoss, you look hot. Why don't you sample a little of this here and throw away that damned necktie." Christian thought the bourbon for the necktie was a fair trade. He wiped the neck of the bottle off on his sleeve, which is the fashion, and took a long pull. It burned and made the dull, hot Saturday a little easier.

"Thank you."

"Sure, drink up. I got me another bottle in the truck."

Christian offered his hand. "Christian Simmons."

"J. W. Skags. I grow cotton over in Red River Parish."

The two men sat on the steps in the shade of an old oak

tree. Windy walked up the steps and into the courthouse. Both men watched. She was in a tight white dress that glowed in the fierce sun.

"Hoss, did you see that? I'd give my left nut just to kiss her tits. I never saw nothing that looked like that."

"She's something, all right."

"Something. You gotta be kidding. She's a movie star. I'd be proud to fuck her in bed right next to my wife. I think my wife would understand. I wonder if she wants ten acres of my cotton patch. Shit, I wonder if she wants a hundred acres of my cotton. I think even my preacher, Brother Emory, would forgive me for getting a little of that poontang."

Christian laughed to himself. The farmer didn't know that Windy would grant his fondest desire for a couple of hundred campaign dollars. Or for maybe nothing at all.

"J.W., she's a soon-to-be-married. She's engaged to the next speaker."

"You mean to tell me that darlin' is gonna marry Little Huey?"

"Little Huey?"

"That's what we call him around here. Now, you listen to him talk. He sounds like Huey. He waves his arms like Huey. And he ain't no Catholic Cajun. I came all the way over here from Coushatta to hear him, and damn if I didn't almost try to fuck his wife. I ain't worth the bullet it would take to shoot me. Wait till I tell the boys at the beer joint."

Christian turned back to the stand to make sure they were talking about the same Hugh Conklin. "Little Huey? I understand he had a drinking problem," he probed.

"Son, there's been only one perfect man and they nailed him to a cross. I want you to listen to him. He's for the farmers, the workingmen, and the poor people. They tell me at church he don't drink no more. But I'd be for him if he did. Here. Have another snort."

Christian took the bottle and took a long swallow and then

another. His invention, Hugh, had begun to speak. He used the same words, the same pauses, the same gestures that had been rehearsed in the shack—the same words that tumbled from the top of the cottonwood tree. Little Huey?

"You think he'll get many votes around here?"

"He'll get all the votes. Folks around here are some pissed about old LeBlanc fucking that foreign-looking girl in that pond."

Christian studied the oak tree for answers. There was obviously much he didn't yet understand.

The Blue Monster bounced toward Leesville, all its windows open so the oven-hot outside air could cool the even hotter steamy interior. Windy Dawn had again removed her stockings and pulled her skirt to the top of her thighs. "Lord, it's hot. When we get to the hotel tonight, darling, I want you to get me a big bucket of ice to pour in my bathwater." Windy pulled her skirt higher and opened her blouse. She had a fine line of sweat on her forehead and upper lip. Christian glanced across the front seat and wondered what the cotton farmer would offer just to have this view.

After the speech, Hugh had gone through the courthouse in a parade of candidates, shaking every hand. Christian stayed on the front steps with the farmer.

"College Boy, you should have gone with me. Those people really liked me. I think we're gonna carry Sabine Parish." Hugh was in the backseat and leaned forward to talk to Christian.

"Hugh, you won't like me to say this, but you spoke to and shook the hands of about two hundred people today. If every person who shook your hand every day voted for you, it would take about twenty-five years for you to see enough people to get elected. This is a waste of time."

"Senator LeBlanc doesn't think it's a waste of time and he's been in Washington for forty years."

"It's changed, Hugh. We aren't doing any harm with this

tour. But all we're doing is following Senator LeBlanc like a dog in heat. He shakes a hand and you shake the same hand. Except for the heat, I enjoy the outing, but it's a waste of time. After Happy's arrest, we hit the bottom in the polls. Now we've come back up to fifth place and are improving. But we only have seven days left. I think we could more profitably spend our time visiting our rural phone banks to encourage the workers.''

"Why spend time with them? They for me. We need those folks in the courthouse. That's who wins elections.''

"Who told you that?''

"Everybody knows that. Don't need nobody to tell me.''

"Hugh, don't be mad at me. It's just that the clock is ticking. Time is running out. When the polls open next Saturday, it's all over. Happy's arrest was a setback. We were in good position till then. Now I don't know. We have so much to do and so little time to do it. And now we're driving around North Louisiana in the heat. I'm just worried.''

"I wanted to start campaigning a long time ago, but it seems like you wanted to keep the campaign a secret. You almost kept it a secret so long we could lose.''

There was no reason to argue. Christian couldn't win. He bit his lip and concentrated on Windy's legs and the boiling strip of asphalt winding through the pine trees. Hugh sulked silently in the backseat.

"Well, Mr. College Boy. You got all the answers. Why don't you get out and go do those important things you think you do, and Windy and me will go on wasting our time. And Windy, pull down your skirt. Don't even let him look no more.'' Hugh leaned over the front seat and screamed in Christian's ear, "Damn it. I said pull the car over.''

"Hugh, there's nothing out here but pine trees.''

"Well, you're a smart college boy. You find yourself a way home.''

The car stopped and Christian stepped down. "Hugh, I'm

sorry. You're just on edge. Let's just . . .'' Christian didn't finish. Windy had moved behind the wheel and the old blue car jumped back onto the asphalt and disappeared over the next hill. Christian rode his thumb back to Baton Rouge.

**28** "Give me grace to . . . Give me grace to . . ."
Christian couldn't remember the rest of the prayer. He closed
his eyes and tried to build a link to his only religious experience, a Sunday school of innocence and short pants when
one shuddered at the fear of a menacing and spiteful Baptist
God who blessed with rewards and struck lame and blind in
punishment. "The Lord made you burn your hand for skip-
ping Sunday school," his mother told him as an angry red
blister rose on his palm.

Christian took another long swallow from the quart of hot
gin. It made a fine gurgle and then a splash in the bottle. He
studied the ridiculous Englishman on the label and then again
watched the line of people waiting to enter the school to vote.
He sat with his back against an oak tree in the middle of the
boulevard. In South Louisiana the middle of the boulevard is
called "neutral ground." Christian liked the idea of sitting
in neutral ground. It had a good feel. "I have come through
the wars and now sit in the neutral ground," he said to himself again and again in stilted drunk talk.

People entered and departed. Which of them pulled the
Christian Ahab Simmons lever in the Shoop voting machine?
Christian forgot that it was Hugh's name on the ballot. He
studied each face as they emerged into blinding sunlight. A
black guy for LeBlanc, bought and paid for? A stern old

woman with rolled-down hose for Conklin? A well-dressed lawyer for another candidate? Christian was seldom wrong in his understanding of voting patterns according to social standing and education.

Christian could hear the bell ring that signaled the curtain's automatic opening. He had voted early. A lever closed the booth with a ripping sound as the curtain sped around the track. Then *kerpluck,* the lever was pulled, followed by a bell and the ripping sound again as the curtain opened. Christian's future was being determined by *kerplucks* and bells.

The neutral ground was a sea of red, blue, yellow, and green signs on stakes. Eleven-by-fourteen-inch candidates smiled at Christian. His tree was surrounded by a picket fence of stakes and smiles. He made a lens of the gin bottle and saw millions of white teeth. He thought of the teeth and the absurd signs so that he did not think of the meeting with Flora.

Louisiana political tradition demanded a vicious sign war. Christian could not understand the logic of a campaign spending money and time attempting to erect more signs than opponents.

It was a feeble protest by Christian, but Hugh had no signs. Not only could the Conklin campaign not afford them, Christian knew that they were a waste of time. But his surrender in the sign war had triggered his most violent confrontation with the committee.

*"What do you mean that we don't got no fucking signs?"* Sonny screamed.

*"Signs don't matter."*

*"That's what you said about bumper stickers,"* Edmund reminded him.

*"People gonna be walking to the polls and they won't see Hugh's name one time."* Even Happy was angry.

*"I'll tell you one thing, cocksucker. We get into a runoff and you ain't hired. We gonna get us a professional."* Sonny

*stood close to Christian, pounding his right fist into his left palm. "And if we lose, I'm coming after you."*

*"Christian, how could you have let this happen to us?" Hugh whined. "We trusted you."*

*"We come all this way and we gonna lose it on the last day 'cause we don't got no signs." Sonny was shouting as he grabbed Christian's shoulders and began shaking him.*

*"Let me explain why you don't need—" Christian never finished his sentence. He was in flight through the open door, gaining altitude across the porch and then crashing into the cottonwood's roots. The old boxer had thrown him at the tree and his aim was only off by two hits from the white port. Blood ran down his cheek from scrapping along the rough bark. He turned over and stared at the stars, his pillow a large root. The huge bulk of Sonny appeared on the porch, blocking the light from the room.*

*"Get the fuck outta this yard. We don't want you no place 'round here."*

*Christian struggled to his feet, slightly crippled by becoming a surface-to-air missile and slightly crippled by a bottle of Four Roses he had found under Hugh's bed. He limped through the fence and into the night. There was no place left for him to sleep. Then he remembered the church key in his pocket. He and Flora had met there several more times while her husband attended to church phone banks in the state's north. Christian never again had the courage to use the preacher's bedroom.*

Christian continued watching people march into and out of the school. Each of them cast a vote on his future. *Kerpluck.* He sipped the gin and put his head on his knees.

*He let himself into the church and, after removing his shoes and pants, lay on the couch, covering himself with a shag rug from the floor. Jesus smiled at him from a far wall. Most of Christian was swollen and bruised. Sleep hung a few feet above his head, never allowing his escape into blackness. The movie projector was once again splattering his mind with images. Most of them were ugly. Christian had not lived a pretty life.*

*Footsteps! No time to run. No place to run. He felt the same resignation as he did flying from Hugh's house to the cottonwood. There was nothing he could do but go limp and accept the blow. The dark room flashed with light.*

*"Mr. Simmons? So it's you. I came back early tonight to see who has been using my counseling room. I have known for several weeks that somebody was . . . er . . . using my couch."*

*"I had no other place to go, preacher."*

*"Well, son, that's what churches are for. They're the last refuge for the hopeless."*

*"I'm sorry about your couch. Maybe next week I'll be able to buy you a new one." Christian knew that its silk had been stained by the salty sweat of passion.*

*"You'll come home with me and I'll get Flora to fix you some eggs and then you'll stay in my spare bedroom until after the election."*

*Kerpluck.* Two white-clad men with tennis rackets emerged from the polling place. They were not Conklin voters. But they were followed by a man in a baseball cap and faded coveralls. Christian retotaled the imaginary vote in his head and wet his tongue with the warm gin.

*The sun was high when Christian woke. There was a gentle tapping on his door and Flora came in with his suit in a clear plastic bag. His blue shirt was clean and stiff with starch. Next to his bed were socks and Jockey underwear, still bearing tags. Next to the underwear was a glass of orange juice. Flora smiled and remained in the door.*

*"Dick took your suit to the one-hour cleaners. He even stopped and bought you socks and underwear. I washed and*

*ironed your shirt. You had blood on the collar, but I got most of it out.''*

The curtain of sadness that had surrounded Christian for two weeks was pulled open a crack by the beautiful woman with the warm but distant smile. This was no I Pagliacci or Hank Williams-induced melancholy in the back of his head. This was not the romantic sadness of a young man riding in the back of stretch limos. This sadness was numbing and tugged his body into slow motion.

It was a sadness of reality fueled by a shattered marriage, the puke of overindulgence, the deceit of pride, the despair of sleeping under cottonwood trees, the shame of body odor and soiled suits. It was a sadness of falling in desperate love and then watching it slip away. It was the pain of metamorphosis as the boy finally shed the last of his illusions and became a man . . . a man he did not like.

"I've missed you," he whispered.

"You don't need to whisper. Dick has gone to his office. We need to talk."

"It's been two weeks."

"Yes."

"Come to bed with me." Christian pulled back the sheets.

"No." Flora sat in a chair across the room, both her knees and lips tightly compressed.

"Will you kiss me?"

"No."

There was a long silence. Christian felt naked and pulled the sheet around his bare chest.

"I'm pregnant."

The air around Christian turned different shades. The room hummed. The curtain of sadness pushed open.

"We'll make a break. I'll marry you and we'll go to Washington and start fresh. This can be the beginning of a great life. I'll make you happy. . . ."

"Christian, it's not your child."

"How do you know?"

*"I know."*

*"It has to be. You've been married for years without children. It has to be me."*

*"No, it's my husband's."*

*"You can't know that."*

*"Yes, I know all I need to know. I know my husband is a good man who has always wanted children. This child is important to him. It's his."*

The curtain locked shut. A buzzing in his head accompanied the lights flashing in his eyes.

*"You are a fine man, Christian, and I think one day you'll discover it. We had something beautiful. You gave me a kind of love I never had. It was exciting. I told you that once I smoked to see what it was like. Then one time I drank wine out of curiosity. Well, I wondered how unrestrained passion and fantasy would feel. And it was nice. You gave me so much. I hope I gave you something. I wanted to help you. Sex was the only way I knew I could get close to you. It's not the way my husband would have chosen for me to help a person, but it seemed a good and decent thing to do. I still think I did the right thing."*

*"Did you use me?"*

*"I tried to give something in return. We used each other, Christian."*

*"Then the baby's mine?"*

*"No, it's Dick's."*

*"Will you hold me?"*

*"No. I'll always think kindly of you but I will never be unfaithful to my husband."*

*"But you were unfaithful to him dozens of times."*

*"No. I was never unfaithful to him."*

*Kerpluck.*

"College Boy." Christian looked up from his knees. Hugh stood over him.

"I'm sorry Sonny chunked you so hard last night."

"I'm fine."

"Oh, you'll always be fine. You some kinda cast iron. I just came to tell you that Windy still wants you to come to our wedding."

"I wouldn't miss it."

"How you think we gonna do . . . er . . . in the election?"

"You're going to do well. I visited the phone bank and talked to the preacher. The response to our get-out-the-vote phone calls is wonderful. It all depends on how well we recovered from the dope arrest. We could run second or we could run sixth."

"Second?" Hugh was startled at Christian's slip.

"I mean first. I don't know why I said second."

"Oh." Hugh looked into Christian's eyes and did not like what he saw.

"Well, we coulda run a lot better if you'd remembered to get them signs."

"Hugh, I didn't forget. They aren't necessary. Message. Message. Message. That's what's necessary."

"I'll see you at the wedding." Hugh turned angrily and walked away. Christian put his head back on his knees. It was early afternoon but he had lost his watch and didn't know exactly the hour. He was careful to sit on some of the political signs to protect his freshly pressed suit. Senator LeBlanc smiled at him from between his legs.

*Kerpluck.*

# 29

Happy's wheelchair was rolling at full charge, forcing Windy to almost jog down the aisle to keep pace. Red, white, and blue balloons tugged at the chair. Christian, even though he had only just begun coming out from under the day's gin, thought the chair close to lighter-than-air flight. Happy's long white hair had been tied tastefully into a ponytail with red and blue ribbon.

The bride wore white.

Darleen and Flora did not look kindly at each other. In fact, even from the back of the church, Christian could feel the icy coolness. Despite their apparent lack of friendship, they stood together as Windy's attendants. Besides hate, they radiated self-confidence and wanton sex. Christian imagined that pregnancy gave Flora a special glow. Even the women's cold stares were sensual. The dresses selected by Windy were backless and clung to every turn and bulge. The three women together formed an erotic peep show of fantasy. And, as far as he knew, only Christian had sampled all three.

The groom was sober and proud, perfect in every detail except for his "Every Man a King" button on the tux lapel. He had made an early-morning pilgrimage to the big bronze statue of Huey to introduce Windy. He told Huey that if he would put in a word for him with the "big campaign manager,'' he would continue the fight to make "Every Man a King.''

Edmund and Matsu wore tails with American flags sewn on the shoulder like they were accustomed to seeing on policemen's uniforms. They wore red, white, and blue bow ties.

Sonny was splendid as Hugh's best man. If one looked for flaws and were excessively concerned with detail, the old fighter's dirty white sneakers would have been a target. But one would also concede that this flaw was not terribly important because his trousers were so long they covered the shoes except when he took a step. In fact, they wrapped around under the heels. He had marched around Happy's chair at campaign headquarters and had been given special dispensation to do away with the stiff patent-leather shoes that came with the rented tux and hurt his feet.

"Nobody will ever see the shoes" was Happy's verdict. "Besides, you pants is so long nobody is gonna notice." And he was generally correct.

The organist played "Happy Days Are Here Again" after the audience stood and pledged allegiance to the flag. Both Hugh and Windy wanted it to be a "grand political wedding."

Both CBS and NBC crews strolled and clattered in the aisles. Leslie Stahl whispered last-minute directions to cameramen who panned from Edmund's flag patch to Happy's chair to Christian. Ken Bode sat on a back pew and composed a piece about populist politics in the Bayou State.

Hugh's campaign attracted national attention after Happy's confession. The derelicts attempting to take over the state's Democratic Party had become a bright feature in an otherwise dull political year. The news crews had shot scenes at Hugh's old house and even an interview with Christian standing under the oak tree on the neutral ground.

"Louisiana always has some of the most colorful campaigns in America." Leslie Stahl stood close to Christian in the sea of signs. "Elections here always mean big money, big consultants and big surprises. We have Christian Ahab Simmons, a man many say is responsible for the phenomenon of Hugh Conklin. Yet no one has ever heard of Simmons. The financial records show that he has received payment of only twelve thousand dollars. One of the Washington consultants, Richard Gentry, was reportedly paid more than three hundred thousand to represent Senator LeBlanc.

"Mr. Simmons, how did you do it? We are told that Hugh Conklin was some sort of local joke until you joined his campaign. Now some say he may even be threatening Senator LeBlanc by taking away some of his rural votes."

"We simply took our message of change and morality in government to the people."

Christian glanced away from the camera and down to assure that his Beefeater's bottle was hidden by the signs. The glance made him appear modest. He looked back into the camera.

"Government was never meant for the privileged few. They are well represented. The poor, the disadvantaged, the down-and-out, all need representation. I was merely a communicator. Hugh Conklin was a man with a message on his heart."

"Well, you may have been 'merely a communicator,' but after this campaign, you may be 'merely' communicating for a lot of other candidates."

"I want to work in campaigns where I might be of service."

Christian smiled his meek and helpless smile and looked back down at his gin.

After the Stahl crew had packed up and left, Christian slumped back onto the signs. The gin rumbled in his stomach and tried to force its way out of his throat. He swallowed several times and put his head against the tree.

*Kerpluck.*

"And do you Windy Dawn take this man in both winning elections and losing elections, for better or worse?" Hugh and the committee wrote the wedding vows. "Let's keep that fucking hotshot out of this" was their sentiment. "He'll just come in and take all the credit."

"I do."

Christian felt a strange detachment. The wedding was a movie on a distant screen with a cast of well-known actors. His former wife, Darleen, stood next to his former sex partner, Windy, who was attended by his former lover, Flora, who stood across from a former derelict, Hugh, whose best man was a former fighter, Sonny. Even standing next to Hugh, Sonny lightly slapped his right fist into his left hand.

Former sex.

Former love.

Former wife.

Former life.

He twisted the words to make a little rhyme that bounced around in the gin sadness to the tune of "I'm So Lonesome I Could Cry." Hank was an inspiration to so many southern boys.

"Former lay, former day, former wife, former life." And so on.

Win or lose, a part of Christian had died. He was adrift in a new life, still in sight of the dangling tethers of the old. He tried to sort out his emotions. He was the balloons tied to Happy's wheelchair. He was weightless but couldn't rise above his surroundings.

He had wanted better cigars and champagne, his picture on the wall at Antoine's. But he had won only bandages on his head, odor under his arms, gin on his breath, whores in his bed, and more holes in his shoes. The young man of pathos from the backseat of limousines was dying.

The polls closed at eight and the first results were not broadcast until nine. Hugh and Windy disappeared for three hours, as tradition dictates, and then joined the cleaned-up professional drinkers and church people in the Capitol House Hotel ballroom to watch the returns on television.

Christian studied turnout and discovered it had been light. He took smug satisfaction in knowing that his control vote would become an even larger percentage of the total.

Darleen showed up in the ballroom and kissed Christian on the cheek. She was a little drunk and filled with cheer, still in her sexy, blue wedding dress. Her kiss was light, her touch on his shoulder as light as insect steps, almost accidental. And she backed away when he tried to run his hand down her naked spine.

"We need to talk," Christian pleaded.

Darleen paused and looked at him almost lovingly. "Yes, we do, Christian. We need to talk. Let me talk to a few of our county leaders and I'll meet you in the bar a little later."

Admiring women in the room watched her as she moved from group to group. Though Darleen had been rather distant, her presence encouraged Christian. She could smell blood, and Christian could see victory in the way she walked and talked.

Even though it was not time to meet Darleen, Christian's ravaged body needed a drink, so he meandered through the crowded room to the bar.

The bar was lonely, dark, and empty. Christian took a high-backed booth at the rear and ordered a double Glenlivet. Though his pockets were empty, he took satisfaction in ordering the expensive scotch. It burned going down, and he chased it with a dark Tartan Ale. The gum-chewing barmaid wiped at nonexistent spots on the bar. The manager had obviously told her to look busy.

Christian had another and another. He kept a bar tab, hoping a sponsor might drift in later. He tried to think of what Kipling had said about the toss of a coin or something, but was too drunk to remember the poem. He had actually risked it all on the toss of a coin. The room outside was filled with people who were unknowingly part of his life's gamble. A screw had been turned and all of their lives had changed track. There was much drunk philosophy in the new Christian of cottonwood wisdom and sadness.

Later, in another life, Christian would learn there is always depression on election night. You do all you can do. You are acutely aware of your failures and of the things you might have done differently. And your fate is always in the hands of some people who vote only because some illiterate tells them to, or because they are afraid of something, or because they are mad about something, or because they happen to be passing the polling place on the way to the grocery store.

Christian was making little rings with the bottom of his glass that looked like the Olympic symbol when Darleen finally came into the bar. She sat down in the tall booth next to Christian. She didn't say anything, so he asked for her favorite, gin and tonic. Gin made Darleen either mean or sexy. Christian didn't need mean, but it was worth the gamble. She drank two more and reached out to cover his hand. Obviously, the gin had taken the proper turn. Christian felt himself getting ready.

"Christian, I need to have a serious talk with you. Are you too drunk?"

"No. I've been wanting to talk. I'm sorry about so much. I had this big-screen vision of myself, Bogart standing alone as the plane left Casablanca, John Wayne taking on the town. I thought I was the puppeteer who could make people dance. But then I looked down and there were strings all over me and I was the one dancing. My strings went to an old tree in Port Arthur and quixotic fights against ghosts who turned to vapor when I swung. I was controlled by my hungers. A lot of my mistakes were because I was an alien in a foreign country. When I wake up tomorrow, I'm going to change. I've done it before. I can do it again. I think I have a better understanding of the rules. Tomorrow I'll—''

''Christian, tomorrow is what I want to talk to you about. You must know—''

A roar filled the big ballroom and flooded into the bar. A band struck up ''Happy Days Are Here Again.'' The noise made it impossible to talk. Darleen just squeezed Christian's hand.

The barmaid left and returned, smiling and shaking her head in wonder. She had to shout to make herself heard. ''Can you believe it? That old drunk was just elected to the United States Senate.''

Christian tried to stand but was pushed back into his seat by the strong arm of Glenlivet. ''Did you say 'elected'?''

''Damn straight. Hugh Conklin. He's sort of our local drunk. He beat Senator LeBlanc. Mister, I could tell you some stories about Crazy Hugh that would have you rolling on the floor.'' She waved and left the bar to join the festivities. One of her own had been elected.

Christian leaned back in the booth and screamed sounds that sounded somewhere between ''yahoo'' and ''greeeeeeeat.'' He was a rich man. He began to pound the table mildly with his whiskey glass until it shattered and cut his thumb.

''You really are a genius, aren't you?''

''I won. I won. It happened.''

Christian could hear Hugh speaking in the other room. The words were indistinct but he recognized some of them. He wrote them. Christian began to calm down. Before the interruption, Darleen had troubled him with something she was going to say. He gathered control and waited for her to finish.

They sat without saying anything for about five minutes. Christian shivered. It was over. He didn't know exactly how rich he was, it depended on how many bets Big Jim had placed. A tear rolled down Darleen's cheek. She rubbed his arm. She looked good sitting there. He moved his hand to her thigh and she didn't move it.

"Ahum."

Christian looked up. The new junior senator from Louisiana stood by his booth with his hand out. Reluctantly, Christian released Darleen's thigh to shake his hand. He left his blood on Hugh's cuff.

"College Boy, I just wanted to thank you for your help in the campaign. Without your television, it would have been more difficult to win. Now I know the committee is still a little mad about you not using the right words and music and all but I think, all and all, it came out fine.

"You know, I've spent a lot of years getting ready for this. My other two elections gave me a fine base, and as you can tell, it expanded to a majority. I want to go back out and thank those people who have been with me for so long. The steering committee should have a brass plaque put up right next to Huey's. I'm going to write each of those boys the damnedest letter you ever saw for them to frame and put on their walls."

Hugh motioned toward the door where Windy stood, refusing to actually enter because of the alcohol. "Windy says to tell y'all good-bye. She and me is gonna drive the campaign car to Washington tomorrow. I'm gonna turn on that mass-media speaker and drive circles around the Capitol to let 'em know I'm there. 'Course, by now, the whole world knows I won. But we gonna take our seats on the front rows of Congress. If the president wants something done, he's gonna have to come by me and I won't put up with no shit.

"I just want you to know that if you ever need a recommendation for a campaign, you just have them call me and I'll put in a good word for you." He slapped Christian on the shoulder and walked away with Windy.

They had to step around Sonny, who was weaving a determined course toward Christian and Darleen. He was slamming his right fist into his left palm. He shook his fist at Christian. "Cocksucker, I hope you learned your lesson. We almost lost. We won by only five thousand votes. The last poll I took we had more than eighty percent. Your stupid fucking television almost wrecked us." He picked up Christian's drink and poured it over the stunned consultant's head.

Christian didn't react. He had been shot and bounced off trees. He had slept on the ground and lost all of the sea anchors of his drifting life. A drink on his head had the importance of an insect bite. As Sonny walked out, Christian simply signaled for two more drinks.

"He really doesn't know, does he?" Darleen asked, and wiped Christian's head with a napkin.

"It doesn't matter."

"What does all of this mean, this victory of yours? I know it will make your business better for the next election, but what are you going to do now?"

Christian looked at her and felt sorry. She had been wounded. The war had marked them both.

Christian liked the cut of her jaw and the swell of her chest. He liked her fingers and her square shoulders. Maybe, he thought, I truly love this woman. She is as good a woman as I could have married. She was just uneasy about little things like the next meal and the doctor bills. She had been brought up to think security was the main goal of marriage. She couldn't help what we've both become. That had been decided generations ago.

Perhaps, he decided, their situation was a bit more complicated, but he didn't want to deal with complexities. He wanted to take his newly discovered wife to home and bed.

"You are a rich woman," he told her. "You now have more money than your father made in his entire life. It will be in twenties and hundreds. You can have a mink and a trip around the world. Go to your closet and throw away everything and start again."

"Don't say those things, Christian. I have to say some things to you and you're making it difficult."

She put her head in her arms and wept. They sat in silence except for her sobs and the barmaid humming to herself. Christian was sure that the barmaid had been a Hugh Conklin supporter.

The familiar sound of Happy's electric wheelchair filled the room and stopped where Hugh had stood only minutes before.

"College Boy, I just want to thank you for what you did for Hugh. You know, a bullet moves in a direct line from Point A to Point B. Not us. We meandered and ricocheted and climbed and dove. God shot us from A to B but he had a couple of laughs along the way. Just think. First he had to cut off my legs. Then he had to make Hugh a drunk and Sonny brain-damaged.

"I used to watch you out on that front porch and feel sad for you. I had Hugh and my chair and the newsstand and the house. But you was trying to do something we didn't understand. You was all alone. You'd make a few steps and we'd yank you back. Sonny'd hide the soap so you couldn't wash and we'd eat while you was asleep so we didn't have to share. I know you didn't make any money, so I hope this win brings you some more business.

"I'm real sorry about the way you got treated. I been wanting to tell you that. I want you to know that Hugh says I can live in his house. I just got to pay him a little rent. I just want to say you always got a room there . . . inside. No charge. You don't know it but you is a good man. Tell me one thing, though. Why'd you do it?"

"My white plume, Happy, my white plume."

"Huh?"

"Sometimes man does not fight merely to win."

"You're drunk. I'm a man who can spot it every time. Let me help you and the little lady get home. There's all kind of people around here wanting to give me a ride."

"No, Happy, my wife and I have a journey to make together." Christian pronounced each word as carefully as the scotch allowed. "Thank you, though." Happy rolled away.

"Christian, I just came in to tell you I won't be going anyplace with you. I've filed for divorce. I was wrong to make you marry me. You don't fit in marriage."

"Is there another man?"

"Yes."

"Oh."

"Is that all you have to say? After all these years. The iceman says, 'Oh!' "

"If I begged, would I change your mind?"

"No."

"I'm willing to beg."

"No, Christian. It wouldn't change my mind."

"Then *Oh.* Fucking *Oh. Oh! Oh! Oh!* Former sex. Former love. Former wife. Former life. *Oh! Oh! Oh!*"

Christian was madly hammering out the rhythm of his little song on the table when Big Jim burst through the door. "You did it, College Boy." He leaned across the table to hug Christian. He almost crushed Darleen. Susie and another girl in yellow sequins and no bra jumped around and squealed. Susie dragged herself across Darleen to kiss Christian and danced around the bar.

"Here's your first cut, College Boy." Jim dumped a paper sack of bundles of hundred-dollar bills onto the tabletop. "There's a hundred grand here and that's not ten percent of what's coming." He dropped the empty bag and began to wobble in time to the jukebox, his arms driving like pistons, as Susie danced around him. "We gonna get us some champagne and take these two women upstairs. We brought the white black girl you like so much. We gonna get us some poontang and get drunk. We gonna celebrate."

Darleen kissed Christian on the cheek and dashed from the bar. She had put five of the ten bundles into her purse. Christian watched her. He thought she deserved half.

Christian rose from the table and grabbed the yellow-sequined white black girl's behind with both hands, crushed her against him, and began a grinding dance to a rhythm only he could hear.

"Jim, this is a wonderful night. Let's get a bunch of champagne and go upstairs and celebrate. Tomorrow I start a new life."